Sci-Fi Streetz

Printed in the United States of America

First Edition

ISBN-13: 978-0-9820087-4-4

Cover Design: Maurice Scriber at Modern Day Hippie
Editing: Various editors
Typesetting:

Published by: Hip Hop Comix N Flix

Jeff Carroll
PO Box 24-5382
Pembroke Pines, FL 33024
Email: coachyojeff@gmail.com

Sci-Fi Streetz

The Book of Hip Hop Scifi stories.

Table contents

Introduction to Hip Hop Science Fiction

This is purely a labor of love. I didn't these stories to make a million dollars although that would be nice. Hip Hop Science Fiction is simple science fiction which comes out of the mind of a hip hopper. It's not stories about hip hop or the music. It can be anything a hip hop person thinks of.

Just as with Hip hop's five elements (MCing, DJing, Dance, Drawing and beatboxing) hip hop's science fiction manifestation serves a medicinal purpose. Hip hop's primary elements were not the tools of some governmental social worker they were the organic creations that the youth who were suffering from poverty, crime and poor schools. They used the arts of poetry, dance, drawing and music to ease their frustrations in these harsh conditions. Hip hop sci-fi comes out of that same energy. Born from the dreams, nightmares and fantasies of the unsettled minds of the oppressed people hip hop sci-fi is raw and unapologetic.

Hip hop sci-fi is as necessary as mainstream science fiction. Science fiction guides society. It test drives the undiscovered. It fuels technological development. It cautions our leaders. Science fiction is the most important genre of literature and it wouldn't complete without a hip hop expression.

Sci-fi Streetz includes stories from a variety of the subgenres of that are lumped into the Sci-fi section of the bookstore. The book features horror, robots, demons, time travel, alternate history, space travel, zombies, werewolves and pirates.

Nightmare at Halloween Camp.

Chapter One

"Eni you got to see this," Lasheeka said as she held her tablet sized cell phone out. "I bet this will scare you. It's a video on the internet about a man who takes kids off of the street."

Eni took the large cell phone from her friend. "My question is how do you still have internet reception all the way up here in the mountains. My phone has no bars."

"I have everywhereness," Lasheeka smiled proudly as she cracked her joke.

Eni tapped her finger on the screen large of cell phone and the video started playing. The video showed a dark street full of shadows and flickering lights. A small child walked down the dark street and out from the shadows steps a tall man. The man is wearing a white suit and without warning grabs the child before the boy can say a word. The man carries the boy up the street and out of the view of the camera.

Eni smiled and said "This is what everyone is talking about. Please." She handed the phone back to Lasheeka.

"Oh I forgot Eni ain't scared of anything," Lasheeka joked.

"No," said Eni. "Its just that once you've seen a real monster fake monsters don't do anything. I'm not trying to hate. Snatcherman is a good concept."

"Yeah Eni ain't scared because got a big father," said a boy walking down the aisle as the bus turned off the paved road.

The yellow school was full of kids. All of them were ready for the madness of a scary theme park. It was just after sunset around 7pm and in the mountains of upstate New York it was dark like midnight. There were lights on the highway but on this dirt road there were none. It was like the bus was driving into a tunnel.

For the group of city kids this was like a prelude to terror. New York City was a place where the lights never went off. There were people always walking around in the city but in the mountains there was just a wall of trees on both sides squeezed together all claustrophobic like.

"Yo what the hell is this place closed?" a kid screamed out from somewhere in the bus causing all of the kids to laugh.

"For real," another kid yelled.

The bus drove for another ten minutes into the forest before it passed under the welcome gates of the theme camp. Children pushed their faces against the windows trying to get peeks to glanced of all of the things the horror camp promised.

"We're here Eni," Lasheeka said with all the excitement of a kid opening up their Christmas gifts. She leaned over Eni to take a look for herself.

Eni sat still unimpressed by the potential of the change to get scared. She carefully sat up making sure she didn't get bumped by an excited kid.

"Lasheeka you know I'm just here for you. Don't expect me to get all excited," Eni said she looked at all of the crazed of the bus. It was bananas. She laughed to herself as she thought about how these kids would act if they saw a real werewolf. Being the daughter of a vampire and werewolf hunting gargoyle it would be damn near impossible for something made in a special effects shop to scare her.

In fact she was more amazed with how easy her father had let her come to this place. She was happy that her father believed her when she said she wasn't scared to leave his protect despite her having been kidnapped by vampires. It was a helleva wake up call for her. One day she was dreaming about flying off with a her immortal blood drinking superman and the next day she was about to be eaten by real life vampires. That would have been enough to traumatize an adult let only a teenager. Eni was tough and recovered from her experience in no time. The only thing was she didn't have to believe in demons she knew they were real.

Lasheeka was not phased by Eni's lackadaisical attitude her excitement came through all of her actions. "I want to go to the 13th street Haunted House first. No,no, the Slayer Lake hay ride. What about the Vampire Cemetery and the Werewolf Miners Tunnel."

"Well, you can leave me when you go on the Zombie Chase," Eni said.

The kids screamed when they heard the driver opened the door. "Everyone needs to be in their seats. Remember this is bus number 666 and we are leaving at 2am."

The driver stood up and turned around fast. The kids screamed in surprise because instead of his nice smiley face he was wearing a rubber ghost mask.

"Welcome to Halloween camp," screamed the driver. He turned on the bus sound system and the music from the Halloween Camp television commercial played.

"Oh my god," Eni said mistakenly loud enough for other kids to hear her. Lasheeka screamed and fell on Eni's leg. "Come on Lasheeka we're not even off the bus and your jumping like a little girl watching her first horror movie."

As the driver exited the bus Eni noticed the other bus in front of them was empty. Plus the theme park looked deserted. Maybe they had to walk up to the entrance but it didn't look like they were in a parking lot. Who knew what a parking lot in the mountains looked like. She watch as the driver to one bus and then to another bus. He looked more scared than lost. He kept looking over his shoulder as he ran.

The kids on the bus cheered his performance.

All of the kids were now looking at the bus driver run. The lights made it difficult to see but the moon rose above the trees its light picked up the slack for the dark. They could now see their bus was in the center of the park. There were still areas they could not see big shadows like black holes in space.

The driver ran back to the bus screaming with the music playing his words could not be heard. He ran past the side of the bus and disappeared into a shadow. Then from the front side of the bus where a large dark spot moved into the shadow the driver ran in. The moving shadow was barely noticeable.

The kids cheers died down as moments passed and there was no movement in the shadow. The driver had been gone for almost five minutes. The kids began to get restless.

"Yo what's going on?" one of the kids yelled over the music.

"I'm ready to get off of this bus," another kid said.

"Did anybody hear what the driver was saying?" Lasheeka asked.

Before anyone could answer her a large object flew from out of the shadow and into the window of the bus. The object left a big smear of blood on the window. Kids jumped back in fear. Eni didn't move not impressed with fake blood and simple theme park theatrics. The object laid on the grass beside the bus. One of the kids only able to lean their head out of window because school bus windows only opened half way for safety purposes. The kid saw that it was the driver's arm and screamed in horror.

As the kid pulled his head back into the bus another object hit the bus's window. This time it wedged into the half opened window. Kids fell back as the blood object splashed blood all over the seats. After the kids stopped moving away they could tell the object stuck in the window was the driver's head.

The driver's mouth moved and to word "Run" came out.

The kids screamed out of controllable. One kid walked over to the driver's head to inspect it and an arrow crashed through another window and into the kids head.

Kids moved away from the window to the other side of the bus as fast as they could. They climbed over seats in fear. These were all charter school kids who were scared of their own shadows and rubber masks so the sight of real blood was terrifying to them. Kids climbed over the bus seats trying to get away from the window.

Eni and Lasheeka where sitting in the back of the bus and could not what was going on outside. So, Eni pushed kids out of her way as she slide over to the window. She looked out of the window and couldn't believe what she saw. Out from the shadows walked a giant sized man. The man looked like he had come back from the dead. He was dirty and had blood smeared all over him. He was dressed in denim camouflage hunter's overalls. And what was only Eni was able to notice was that the man had no aura, just a white blur. This confused her because she didn't remember vampires having white auras. She tired to remember even though she had only came into contact with real vampires not too long ago.

The man carried a large crossbow which he held up at the bus and fired. Eni's mouth dropped as another kid fell dead with an arrow in his head. Eni backed away from the window as another arrow flew in the direction of where her head had just been. Eni fell back into Lasheeka's lap.

"Oh my god we going to die," Lasheeka said.

Eni sat up and looked Lasheeka in the eyes and said "no we're not." Then Eni turned toward the front of the bus and yelled "Somebody drive the bus and get us out of here."

As the angry Huntsman shot arrows few through the windows more kids fell. The theme music paused a little when the bus was started. A tall kid backed the bus up and pulled it around the bus in front of it. The Huntsman ran over to the bus and grabbed on to its window as the bus sped up trying to turn around.

Kids punched and hit the big Huntsman but their blows failed to deter his slaughter. The Huntsman snatched kids out of the window only to be crushed by the bus. The Huntsman was finally torn from the bus side as the bus collided with the side of another bus as it turned. The kids cheered as they were finally free of the murderous Huntsman.

The Huntsman laid lifeless on the ground. The pressure of being squeezed between the two buses would have been enough kill any man but the Huntsman only laid for a few seconds. He was back on his feet and out of his side pulled an axe. As the bus completed its turn the Huntsman's axe was hurling toward the bus. The tall kid driving had not time to move out of the way. The axe broke through the side window of the bus and plunged into the kid's neck. The kid slumped forward onto the stirring wheel. The bus swerved and plowed into the vampire cemetery.

The kid righted himself in the driver's seat and brought the bus around. The Huntsman stood directly in his path. He mashed the gas pedal and rammed the Huntsman with the fourteen ton bus. The Huntsman dragged underneath the front of the bus but pulled himself up just over the hood of the bus. The kid's vision was blurry as blood spurted out if his neck but he wanted to kill the Huntsman more than anything. Ahead of the bus was the side of the mountain. The sign read Werewolf mine tunnel.

"Let's see if you can survive this," the tall boy said as he drove the bus straight into the side of the mountain.

The bus crashed into the entrance to the mine and the weight of the heavy bus continued to drive bus down into the mountain. The mine attraction was made of plaster and wood so the bus fell straight down. By the time it came to a stop the entire bus was in the mountain. Even the end of the bus was inside the mountain mine.

Kids piled on top of each other inside of the bus. Eni and Lasheeka were now at the top of the pile. The theme music still played over the bus sound system. Kids moaned and cried in pain from their bruises. "Is everybody okay?" a girl asked. "We got to get out of here. There were other buses that we can _____." The girl's voice cut out and a gurgling sound came next. The gurgling was followed by a scream.

"Its him the Huntsman is still alive," another boy screamed.

"What the hell Eni we got to get out of here," Lasheeka said.

Eni moved quickly as she opened the back door and climbed out. "Come on Lasheeka we got to call my dad."

A bunch of other kids followed Lasheeka after she climbed out. Eni pulled her on leading her to the Haunted Mansion attraction. Only two kids followed Eni and Lasheeka. The other kids ran to another bus. As they ran across the parking lot they could see blood on the wooden sign markers. The bus that was in the lot was covered in blood. The place looked like a battlefield or the aftermath of a mafia shoot out.

"Let me get your phone," Eni said as they entered the Haunted Mansion. Lasheeka gave Eni her phone and Eni dialed her father's number. He answered right away.

"Hello," Eni's father Maurice said.

"Daddy, some type of monster is trying to kill us," Eni screamed. "Everybody! He's killing everybody. He killed the bus driver. He can't be a vampire unless it is a super vampire."

"Calm down," Maurice said. "What happened?"

Eni told her father everything.

"His aura was white. And then when he was on the front of the bus, the bus crashed into the mountain and he got back up."

"That doesn't sound like a human or vampire," Maurice said. "Find a place to hide. I'll be there in a few minutes."

Eni, Lasheeka and the two other kids looked for places to hide inside the Haunted Mansion attraction. There was a swiveling for and room of all mirrors. Eni motioned for Lasheeka to follow her up the stairs. They ran up the stairs to the second floor. There were torcher themed rooms and they found a room with a window overlooking the entrance of the mine.

Eni and Lasheeka peaked out of the bottom of the window and watched as the Huntsman walked out of the mine. He didn't look injured at all. He walked steadfast and strong out into the parking lot. As few kids were still making it to the bus. One kid carried another kid who's legs looked broken. The Huntsman shot an arrow in the back of the child's head who was carrying the injured kid. The kid with the broken leg hopped on his good leg until he tripped and fell. The Huntsman walked over him and pulled out a large knife and cut his head off.

Eni and Lasheeka covered their mouths in pain. Even though they didn't know the kid personally it was hard for them to watch a child their age get killed like that. Lasheeka fell back against the wall next to the window and covered her eyes as tears started to roll down her cheeks.

"Why did you call your father instead of the police?" Lasheeka sobbed. "You should have called the army."

"Quiet," Eni said. "He doesn't see us."

The Huntsman walked over to the bus and pulled the bus doors off like they were made of cardboard. He stepped in the bus with his big knife in his hand. Eni watched as blood splattered the already blood stained windows of the bus. The bus shook like an elephant was in it. Eni hoped one of the kids would kill the Huntsman but she remembered the Huntsman was on the front of the bus when the bus crashed into the mine and he still alive. He couldn't be a real man. Maybe he was a robot or something.

The back door of the bus flew off and the Huntsman jumped out. He wasn't injured at all. A sound came from first floor of the Haunted House and the Huntsman turned toward the house.

"We got to get out of here," Eni said. "He's coming this way." The two of them moved as fast as they could.

Screams and sounds of furniture being tossed around came from the floor beneath them. They ran across the hall to a room with a guillotine in it. It was a dead end the window was bolted shut. The next room had a witch tied to a stake with fire around her. As they searched the windows in the room for an open one to exit through the stirs squeaked with as the Huntsman made his way to the second floor.

Eni looked out of one of the windows and saw there was a hay filled wagon just below. She turned to Lasheeka "We gotta jump."

They could hear the Huntsman's footsteps down the hallway and they were getting closer. Eni one of the fake torches under the witch burning figure and swung it at the window. The torch flew the window but the whole window didn't break. As Eni reached to grab another piece of wood the Huntsman walked in the room but didn't see them. Eni had to make a bold decision. She jumped on the top of the witch statue knocking on top of the Huntsman. Then she grabbed Lasheeka and the two of them jumped through the half shattered window.

They landed on the hay, rolled over and hit the ground running. They ran across the vampire cemetery and through a large mausoleum. They stopped just long enough to catch their breath.

"We got to find somewhere else to hide," Lasheeks said.

"My father should be here any minute," Eni said. She turned to look back out of the thick door. The Huntsman was marching directly toward them. The sky was clear not a cloud in sight and the moon light illuminated the entire cemetery. The forest trees surrounded the cemetery like an outdoor stadium.

Eni looked up as what appeared to be a plane approached. As figure got closer what first looked like a plane started to look more like a large bird. Then as the Huntsman walked through the center of the tombstones and vampire decorations the large bird like figure swoop over the tree tops and knocked the Huntsman across the cemetery.

Eni looked on as the Huntsman slid on his back with the large bird on top of him. Eni now recognized the large bird as her father in his gargoyle form. Her father did a forward summersault as the two strong figures slid. The two goliaths crashed over stone tombstones and wooden fences making a spiral of dirt smoke. Eni's father Maurice ended on top of the Huntsman when they came to a rest.

Maurice clawed and pounded the large man in green and brown camouflage clothes until his head was buried in the dirt. He sat on top of the Huntsman for a few moments as the Huntsman's chest stopped moving.

The huntsman laid motionless as Maurice flew over to Eni. Eni stood outside the mausoleum and her father still in his gargoyle form spoke to her.

"Are you alright?," Maurice said. "Is there any other kids?"

Maurice barely finished his greeting when an arrow flew his wing and into the wooden door behind Eni. If he hadn't been there the arrow have hit his daughter in her head. He had just killed this murderer of children. He had watched his heart stop beating. One thing he hated more than slaying a demon was having to slay the same demon twice.

Another arrow shot through Maurice's wing causing him to fall forward into the side of the mausoleum door. He had to brace himself in order to not fall on Eni. That was it this demon was getting on his nerves.

Maurice said "Find another place to hide." Then he turned and flew toward the Huntsman.

The Huntsman shot two more arrows at Maurice catching him in the same wing. The additional damage to his wing made it impossible for Maurice to fly and he zip zagged to the ground. The Huntsman jumped on Maurice stabbing him with his big knife.

Eni grabbed Lasheeka and they ran out of the mausoleum. Eni looked for a place for them to hide. She thought about the Huntsman and what he was.

"Let's find the office," Eni said.

"I remember seeing a sign for the office when we first arrived," Lasheeka said as she ran ahead of Eni. "Its this way."

Once inside the Halloween camp office Eni and Lasheeka couldn't believe their eyes. The Halloween camp office was destroyed. First there was blood everywhere. Then dead bodies in every corner.

"They must not have known the killer was here," Lasheeka said.

"They also must have done something to unlease his wrath," Eni said. She pushed a desk out of her way. "If the released him then we can send him back."

Eni searched for something with a hunter on it. She remembered when her father had explained the world of supernatural beings to her he had told her about demons. Finding clues to this Huntsman's origin and connection to this camp was paramount to vanquishing him.

"What was that fighting that killer hunter?" Lasheeka asked.

Eni was busy looking through the office drawers and opening up cabinets. "What? I didn't see anything but that big man shooting arrows at us."

"There was something fighting him in the cemetery. It looked like a big bird or somebody in a batman costume."

"Lasheeka if there is something trying to kill that big monster man then, I'm it's best friend," Eni moved a body out of the way and dumped files on the floor. "Why don't you call the police or something? Or better help me find something on this hunter killer guy."

Lasheeka walked over to the front entrance and in the lobby there was a big poster size map of the full Halloween camp. Next to the poster was a variety of brochures. Brochures titled *What is Halloween?* Another one that said *Halloween camp fun for everyone*. Lasheeka grabbed one and ran to Eni.

"Here's a brochure that says *The Huntsman and Lake Friday*," Lasheeka said.

"That's it," Eni said as she took the brochure and quickly opened it.

The cemetery was a cloud of dust as the two figures fought. Maurice's wing was of no use but he didn't need it to throw the big Huntsman around. The Huntsman was big and burley but he was no fighter. His blows laid heavy on Maurice. He pounded on Maurice with uncontrollable. A blow to the head and then another to the ribs. Maurice could not figure out to counter. The Huntsman delivered two straight punches to Maurice's head which made Maurice stagger back. Maurice's eyes went black and he lost focus.

Maurice a knife slice his leg and the pain brought him back to fighter concentration. Maurice saw the Huntsman's big knife swing towards him. He leaned back to avoid the wild slash. Maurice let the Huntsman finish the motion of his swing and gave the Huntsman a powerful blow to the back of his head. The Huntsman stumbled forward and that was enough for Maurice to grab the Huntsman by his lower leg.

Maurice pulled back on the Huntsman legs dragging him on the ground. Maurice dragged the Huntsman all over the vampire cemetery. The Huntsman reached for anything he could but every time he touched a tombstone or a bush the force of Maurice's tug ripped his hands away. Maurice pulled slamming the Huntsman head and body into the thick stone grave markers.

The Huntsman would not die. He kept reached for something grab. Maurice grew move frustrated with this undying monster. He channeled all of his strength to spin the Huntsman into a windmill. Maurice spun whipping the Huntsman around crashing him into tree after tree. The Huntsman bounced back and forth like a pinball in an old arcade game. The Huntsman's finally fell limp. Maurice's fury was peaked and his rage would not let him stop. He spun so hard he flung the Huntsman so hard the Huntsman crashed through three mausoleums until he stopped.

Maurice flew over to the mausoleum and found his batter body under a pile of concrete. He gave the Huntsman stab with his claws in his neck for good measure.

Eni was still reading the brochure when Maurice flew over to the office. He was still in his gargoyle form when he landed in front of the office. When Lasheeka saw the massive green figure outside the office door her nerves got the best of and she immediately collapsed.

Maurice made his transformation back into his human form and he lifted Lasheeka to a seat in the lobby.

"Eni," Maurice said and he looked around the bloody office. Blood was splashed everywhere and slashed bodies lay all around the place. It was like someone shot a Quentin Tarantino grindhouse movie in the office.

Maurice found Eni reading about the Huntsman.

"He's a demon daddy," Eni said. "I don't think he is a poltergeist and he can't be a succubus."

"Well whatever he is dead. I just killed him," Maurice said braggingly.

"You can't beat him to the afterlife," Eni said.

"My daughter schooling me," Maurice said as he took a peep out of the window and sure enough Eni was correct. The Huntsman was up and walking toward the office building. "I'm glad I had Margery teach you about the supernatural world." Maurice remembered when he first met Margery and she told him she sister of Wiccan and how happy he was to have a witch on his team. Having someone to go to made things a lot easier. Remember spells to remove demons was a pain in the ass. Slaying vampires and werewolves was simple even though they fought better.

"Can you hold him off a little longer while I try to figure what we need to do to vanquish him?" Eni said.

Maurice looked out at the Huntsman who was steadily approaching and said "Why don't you just call Margery. Tell her its some sort of Sakarabru or Sonneillon but it's a revenge demon for sure." Maurice took a deep breath and changed back into his gargoyle expression. Weak wing and all he flew out the out the front door with ease.

This time there was no unexpected blows from the Huntsman. Maurice made quick work of the sluggish demon. He flew over Huntsman latching onto his head with his feet claws. He flipped forward and threw the Huntsman into a car parked in front of the office building. He jumped on the Huntsman before he could recover and hurled him across the lot into another car.

"This will be your last beating Huntsman," Maurice said as he pounced on the Huntsman.

The Huntsman's camouflage was now covered with as much blood as his victims. He staggered and he had bruises over his face and arms. Maurice did not let up he continued his relentless he ass whipping.

Eni dug into Lasheeka's pockets to find Lasheeka's cellphone. Lasheeka slowly opened her eyes when she felt Eni going through her purse. Eni motioned to Lasheeka to hold up a second. She dialed Margery's number and quickly explained the demon to her.

"Well your father is right," Margery said. "Bear mountain. Humm. It sure isn't an African Sakarabru maybe a Sonneillon. Try a basic German cast away spell."

Eni took a pen off a desk and wrote down the incantation. She thanked her god mother and hung up the phone.

"Lasheeka my god mother told me what we have to do," Eni said.

"What about that big bat?" Lasheeka said.

"I told you don't worry about that," Eni said as she ran into the office kitchen. "Help me find some salt."

Lasheeka opened up every cabinet. There was no salt, all that was in there was junk food potato chips and popcorn. One the counter was a coffee maker and a microwave. Next to it was a sugar dispenser and a salt and pepper shaker.

Eni grabbed the small salt shaker and ran into the lobby. She hoped she had enough salt for what she had to do. They pushed the furniture against the wall.

Eni poured a circle with the salt. Then she poured a five pointed star inside the circle but before she could complete the star the salt ran out.

"Oh my god Lasheeka I need more salt to finish the Pentacle," Eni said. "If we don't finish this the Huntsman will keep killing."

"I know what we can use," Lasheeka said and then ran off to the kitchen. Seconds later she came back with three bags of potato chips.

"Let's see," Eni said as she took the bags and crunched the chips into fine crumbs. She quickly finished the star. "Only one way to find out now."

Eni was now ready to meet the Huntsman face to face. She walked out of the office building and looked for her father. The fight was not hard to find. Maurice was still throwing the Huntsman into things even thought he was tired. As hard as Maurice beat him the Huntsman was still getting up and asking for more. Maurice was convinced that the Huntsman would not stop until he killed everyone at the lake.

Eni yelled over to her father. Maurice could not be happier. He gave the Hunts a devastation round house kick which he knew would knock the Huntsman out long enough for him to drag him over to the office.

As soon as Maurice entered the office Lasheeka took one look at him in gargoyle form and fainted again. Lasheeka had fallen on one of the chairs. Eni positioned Lasheeka in a more comfortable position and grab the paper she had written the incantation on.

As soon as Maurice dropped the Huntsman in the Pentacle Eni read the German words.

"Ben zi bena, bluot si blouda. Lid zi geliden, sose gelimida sin!" Eni said and looked as her father. Maurice remained in his gargoyle form to make sure if the spell didn't work he would have to cut the Huntsman up in pieces.

The Huntsman opened his eyes and stood up. He reached for his knife but he couldn't pull it out of its holster. He grunted and snarled at Maurice. The floor beneath him started to glow. The Huntsman lunged at Maurice but collided with an invisible barrier. He fell back and turned toward Eni and lunged at her. The same thing happened. The entire Pentacle glowed bright gold and then a black dot formed in the center.

The black dot traced the five pointed star and then the star turned black. The outer rim of the circle remained gold. Maurice just smiled as he turned back into his human form. The smell of rotten eggs filled the room causing Eni to cover her noise. The Huntsman started to fade and then turned completely white. He banged on the invisible barrier and he dropped through into the black star. He tried to fight by hanging on the edge of the star. The Huntsman held a look of rage on his face until the black star sucked him up. Once the Huntsman had disappeared completely the entire Pentacle disappeared into the floor and the floor's original surface returned.

Eni gave her father a tight hug. "We did it."

"No baby girl you did it," Maurice said. He changed back into his gargoyle form then picked up Eni and Lasheeka. "Let's get out of here before the police get here."

"What do I tell Lasheeka if she wakes up?" Eni said.

"Nothing cause all she'll do is faint again when she sees me," Maurice said as he carried them back to New York City.

THE END

The Screaming

Chapter 1

A crowd of students mixed with kids from the neighborhood gathered around the intersection of 5th and MLK Ave to watch another group of kids approach members of Pimp Psi Phi fraternity. One of the kids approaching the fraternity was holding a pitbull. The fraternity members were talking to some other students sitting on concrete benches lining the walkway running from the center of the dormitory buildings to the intersection of 5th and MLK.

"Yo who the fuck is Senior Dogg?" said the loud raspy voice of Gripp the leader of the group. Gripp proceeded to look around until his eyes found the Pimp brothers.

"What's the problem?" said a tall Pimp brother who was dressed in a jeans, black shoes, a long purple trench coat and holding a cane with a glass ball on the end. Each of the four Pimp brothers standing behind him had on trench coats and canes as well.

"Look here are you Senior Dogg muthafucca?," Gripp said. He walked up to the Pimps with his gang close behind him and continued "cause he is going to have to catch a grip." The kids with him all repeated "catch a grip."

Another one of the Pimp brothers walked up to the kids from behind the tall Pimp brother and said "whatever you got to say to one of our brothers you can say it to us."

The five Pimp bothers were all well-built and they walked up to faces the younger kids with confidence. The kids who numbered about 15 were smaller than the Pimp brothers and all had tight looks on their faces.

A girl sitting on the other side of the benches saw one of the kids from the gang slip a knife into his hand from under his sleeve and screamed. "His got a knife." Her scream broke the momentary silence of the guys sizing each other up.

Before the she could finish her scream the kids all threw punches at the Pimp brothers. The Pimp brothers blocked the punches and countered with punches of their own. The tall Pimp brother was knocked to the ground by a wild hooking right hand punch from Gripp. Gripp jumped on top of him. Two other Pimp brothers were back to back catching kids punches and swinging their canes.

In the middle of the chaos another girl screamed "please stop." She ran over to Gripp and jumped on him, which pulled him off of the tall Pimp brother. She sobbed in Gripps ear "wait a minute. Please wait." That gave the tall Pimp brother the chance to get back on his feet.

Gripp who was now being distracted by the girl and another one of her friends said "M-Squad for life." While Gripp had everyone's attention another kid holding the pit bull released the dog letting it run free to attack people. The pit bull started biting one of the Pimp brothers and redirected everyone's attention to their his struggle. The girls let Gripp loose and

Gripp lowered a large steal dagger from inside his sleeve and griped it tight. Gripp then sneaked up behind the tall Pimp brother and stick the sharp dagger in the Pimp brother's lower back. The tall Pimp brother let out a loud sigh.

*****

Unaware of his tall Pimp Psi Phi roommate getting stabbed outside Rafael was sitting at his desk studying hard, his sound proof headphones kept him from being disturbed by the noise outside of his dorm room. The corner of Fifth Street and Martin Luther King Avenue was where the Ben York College campus met the outside neighborhood. It was also where every conflict took place between kids who attended Ben York college and kids who did not. For as long as anyone could remember there has been competition between the kids from Monument City and the students of Ben York College. With the increase in gang violence in the city no student was surprised that it would reach fifth and MLK. All semester the number of students getting harassed by kids from the neighborhood had been increasing. Most of the students were assaulted at night. After some kids from the city got thrown out of the homecoming after party the tension has boiled over.

The homecoming party conflict was four months prior and it was over a girl from Monument City who was also a student at Ben York. The way the story circulated around the campus was her high school boyfriend a tough kids name Gripp came to talk to her about why she had broke up with him. By the time he got into the party she was already dancing with a guy who is in Pimp Psi Phi. The word had gotten around that Gripp her X-boyfriend had gotten locked up after the homecoming incident and now he had just been released. Since Gripp was a member of a gang called the M-Squad everyone new something would happen soon.

Rafael sat in his room, which had a view of the intersection other students would cherish. Not only could he see all of the fights he could hear them and there lied the problem. Rafael hated loud talking and noises. His mother was what he calls a loud Dominican. In his apartment in Jersey City, New Jersey he could hear noise all day and night. If it wasn't his mother and two sisters in the day time it was Fire trucks and police car sirens at night. He blames his mother who he says is also an old Trujillo follower. He says she ruled their family with a loud voice like Trujillo did when he would blast big speakers mounted on trucks, and drove them down the streets of DR.

"I named you Rafael after Rafael Leonidas Trujillo Molina who ruled the Dominican Republic from 1930 until he was assassination in 1961." She said. "He was our only officially elected president from 1930 to 1938 and again from 1942 to 1952."

What she didn't like to talk about was he ruled the other time as an unelected military Dictator. She said "he was an angel dispite the fact that he was a dictator because the country was beautful."

After Trujillo was assinated and the country went crazy she immigrated to America in the late 60's Now, his mother is a disciple of the American dream. She always said "American is the best place on earth."

Rafael hated her unconditional love for governments. He would refer to her as a Government Groupie. When President Reagan said ketchup was a vegetable she believed it. It's so bad that because Trujillo control the radios and Television that when McDonalds has a commercial saying it's burgers are healthy no one could convince her that weren't. She would say "the government would not let companies lie on TV." She would yell at him "you question everything and believe nothing."

She would justify her love for Trujillo by talking about how clean and crime free her birthplace was during his rule. When people would mention Trujillo murdering thousands of Haitians and the fact that outspoken Dominicans would go missing she would stay quiet. "She is a peace lover" Rafael would say. "Arguing is not fighting, it's how we learn. We have to debate mommy if we are going to advance the human race" he would say to her. To avoid her screaming debates he shut himself in his room, which was the most quiet, room in his the house.

If it weren't for the police and ambulance lights Rafael wouldn't have noticed the fight at all. "Ah boy now the campus has become as stupid as the city" he said as he looked out of the window at the crowd of students standing around. Unconcerned as to what happen he lowered the shade and turned on his desk light as he sat back down to finish studying.

Chapter 2

In his Chemistry of Nature class the next morning Rafael was sitting next to Aubrey a young white girl from New York. They met the first day of class. She wasn't a skinny white girl like the ones he saw on TV, Aubrey had meat on her bones. She had a pretty face and a round butt, which got her mistaken for a Black girl from time to time. Aubrey was studying to be a Psychiatric chemist and took the class only because it was rumored to be easy. She wanted to learn how to develop drugs to help in the fight against mental disease.

Rafael was excited to take the class because the instructor Dr. J. was considered a pioneer of a new school of thought. Dr. J was a leading advocate of natural medicine. The instructor Dr. Clark John's known affectionately as Dr. J. was the only professor teaching The Chemistry of Nature class a class he created to promote his medical philosophy. The class was held on Friday mornings and had only a few students in took it and lot of people from the community.

"The University can say who gets a degree but they can't control who I teach. This information I want teach you is too important for our people to have a price tag attached to it." Dr. J said as he looked toward the back section of the lecture hall where just a few older people were sitting "That's why I'm the only teacher who will let people who are not students sit in on their classes." Dr. J was now a community activist and respected African historian. "When I was a biochemist in the military I traveled to over 75 countries where he studied medicine but it was a Black American George Washington Carver who said Reading about nature is fine, but if a person walks in the woods and listens carefully, he can learn more than what is in books, for they speak with the voice of God. So, don't expect to do all your learning in this room or the text books I suggest." The people in the class applauded enthusiastically.

Dr. J turned back to his desk. "Last night was an embarrassment to this institution. We are people who seek education. We should not be taking on the behavior plaguing the city" said Dr. J as he walked behind the podium.

The ascending configuration of the chairs of lecture hall usually made him look small but not today. Dressed in what could be considered his uniform a kente cloth dashiki his arm extended toward a picture of a hyena on the projection screen. "Now don't think I am digressing from the syllabus just to make a social comment because it is true. If you eat what these animals eat you will behave like them." He clicked to a picture of a high school cafeteria with piles of hamburgers, hot dogs and other meats with no vegetables. Then he clicked to a picture of two wolves fighting. "Then you will act like them." He switched to a picture of a Chinese calendar followed by a picture of the solar system. When he put a picture of a group of people and he faced the students. "We are divine beings. We are connected to the universe. The cycle of the sun affects us. While this is something I teach about in my advanced class The Astrology of Medicine I felt it was appropriate to share with you now. Do you think it is just a coincidence that violent crimes increase during the Lunar moon. Remember a full moon is when the Sun is on the opposite side of the Earth from the moon. Not only is it important for us to understand the natural elements of this planet we call food, we also have to learn our body's relationship to the cosmos. This is the energy, which can make a good man go bad. Its what makes a child behave in contradiction to what their parents have taught them. America's medical world knows nothing about this connection. We have to understand that the knowledge of the doctors of our time do not know all of the answers."

Aubrey looked at Rafael in surprise. "So, what is he saying?" she whispered to Rafael.

"I think he is telling us the truth" replied a person from the community sitting behind them.

"Ben York who this school is named after was an explorer. You were taught how he lead Lewis and Clark across this country. He wasn't just their slave. He knew how to talk to the natives with respect so they let them pass. He willingly joined the exploration because he too was an explorer. Together they searched for new land and opportunities. Ben York's life guides the mission and teachings of this school. While you think you are just like other medical students you are not. Ben York students are to be explores of new lands of medicine."

A few people from the community start to cheer Dr. J's rhetoric. Rafael said "This class feels more like a rally then a class."

Aubrey nodded.

Rafael straightened his body and kept his eyes glued to Dr. J. His palms moistened as the fear of Dr. J saying something, which would get him kicked out of the school.

"One of the Pimp Psi Phi brothers was stabbed last night and he is in the hospital. That's why he's going off like this" Aubrey said in a low voice. "I'm surprised you didn't hear it. It happened on 5th and King."

"Wow. I bet my roommate was right in the middle" replied Rafael.

"Who's your roommate?"

"Reggie Mitchell from Charlotte, North Carolina. He's a six feet three black guy and they call him boss dawg or something."

"Senior Dog?"

"Yeah that's it" Rafael screamed.

"Excuse me I like to know who the students are who feel they have more important things to talk about?" said Dr. J steering directly at Aubrey and Rafael.

"Ah Aubrey Winberg and excuse us."

"And who is that with you?"

"Rafael Medoza and I think you're making an excellent point. I just found out that it might be my roommate who got stabbed last night."

"Well in that case excuse me." Dr. J looked back at the whole class. "Rafael this is information you really need to have. Wait for me after class I would like to talk you so I can you tell about this Bum rushing activity."

After Dr. J finished up his lecture Rafael and Aubrey closed their notebooks. The stage quickly filled with students and community people.

"I can't wait with you I have to catch my next class," Aubrey said as she threw her book bag over her shoulder.

"It's cool I don't think I can tell him any more than he seems to already know about the fight" Rafael smiles almost laughing as he lifts his backpack on to his back.

"See you tomorrow for lunch then," Aurbrey as she gives Rafael a kiss.

Rafael walks over to the group of people around Dr. J. He is taken by the love that Dr. J is receiving from the people. He has never seen such a variety of people in a class before. For it to be a Friday afternoon class it had the energy of a Monday class. There was an old lady who was using a cane who looked to be about 70 years old. Another man wearing a Native America poncho and long beads. There were even two guys in suits who looked like they were from the Nation of Islam standing by the door handing out flyers. As Dr. J finished talking to group he came over to Rafael.

"Now, young man you seem like a nice child. I know your parents would be upset for you to be involved in fighting."

With his voice full of surprise Rafael said "No way Dr. J I am not a member of Pimp Psi Phi my roommate is. You don't have to worry about me I know how to behave. Plus I'm not stupid or on drugs."

"Do you think drugs are responsible for the violence or is it as simple as stupidity?"

"Oh me I'm not anything like those kids. I don't fight. I got too many dreams and aspirations to let myself get involved in fighting."

"So you think these kids fighting don't have aspirations and because you are in college you are somehow better than them?"

"No I don…."

"One thing you must learn is how connected we all are. These kids running the streets getting into fights with students like your roommate are no different than you or I. Where are you from and I don't mean what state?"

"My parents are from The Dominican Republic."

"Just what I thought Caribbean. So, your folks just got off on an earlier stop then the Africans brought here. You've seen poverty up close so you should understand what I'm saying."

Rafael thought about his mother and how she would pray to God for poverty to be eliminated and believed her son would save the world by healing the poor people.

"Too many times students coming to Ben York think they are better or different than the people in the community. We are not. The Universe controls our destiny. Our people in the community are crying out to us for help. We who are privileged enough to go to college. If you quiet your mind you can hear their screams of pain. I would like you to join me at this community forum." Dr. J waves one of the guys in the suits over to him and takes a flyer. He hands the flyer to Rafael.

"Do yourself a favor and come to this it will help you better understand why you are here and the impact you can have on this world" he patted Rafael on the shoulder and walked away.

Rafael stood there looking at the flyer. He was shocked at how Dr. J had taken time to talk to him. "Okay, thank you. I must tell you, you sound like my mother. She would always tell my sisters and I that we were just people who spoke Spanish. And we were no different than any other people." He folded the flyer and stuck it into his pocket.

Chapter 3

Rafael and Aubrey walked down the serving lane of the crowded cafeteria. Aubrey took a large piece of steak, mashed potatoes with gravy and a piece of bread. Rafael took a salad, a piece of baked chicken, rice with a scoop of black beans, which he poured over his rice. It was lunch hour and the cafeteria was filled with students. Rafael and Audrey sat next to a group of regular undergraduate students. One of the students had a bowl of fruity flakes cereal and instead of having them in milk he had them in red fruit punch.

"I thought you had a bad diet Aubrey" Rafael turned to the student and said "what are you eating? A sugar bowl!"

Aubrey said "It's called a Breakfast boost. This is what all the kids in Monument city eat. One of the children in my mentoring program showed me. It tastes pretty good. Leave it to one of our kids to replace milk with fruit punch."

Rafael's mouth dropped open and nothing came out.

Aubrey put a fork full of steak in her mouth. She grabbed a copy of the City Message the local newspaper she saw laying on the other side of the table. She flipped through the pages and when she found a large headline she looked up at Rafael.

"Wow, do you see this Aubrey? I really thought Dr. J was reaching when he blamed food for being the cause of violence. If all of the kids are eating so much sugar it's no surprise they are behaving like wild animals."

Aubrey nodded her head and saw a picture of Reggie Mitchell. She slid the paper over to Rafael before he could get his next comment out. "Is this your roommate?"

"Yeah. He's lucky they bullet went straight through his body. He will be out of the hospital later today. Not that I will notice anyway, he only comes to the room like once a week." Rafael looked over to the kid eating the fruity cereal. "Yo how can you eat that? That's like the most unhealthy meal I ever seen. That's wild the kids are bum rushing" Rafael said.

"Man these kids need love. That's why I volunteer. I eat the same food as they do and I'm not out bumrushing anybody. What do ya'll do? Ya'll just sit up here judging people. You should be out in the community working with these kids if you really care. And who eats salads anyway" said another student sitting behind them.

"Well I'm doing an internship at the Future in Medicine Center. Dr. Norris Bryant is working on a vaccine to give to these violent kids" said Aubrey.

"Vaccine you're crazy. Why not examine their diets? Everything is always a vaccine. Like there's no way to prevent this behavior. I feel like we go from one drug to another" said Rafael.

Another student across the table leans over "I think y'all are all wrong. These kids are scared of punishment. The police have gotten soft. All of these video camera lawsuits. The police are scared to use even a taser on someone. We need tougher police and more jails. Face it, some people are born violent and no vaccine, or love diet is going to change how people are."

****

Later that night Rafael took Dr. J. up on his invitation to his community presentation. Rafael came solo because Aubrey had a lab session with Dr. Norris Bryan. The community center was packed and Dr. J was on stage being introduced. Rafael got there just in time.

A lady in a big Angela Davis Afro was speaking "Dr. Clark Johns is a more than a professor at Ben York Medical College and Biochemist, he is an activist. He loves our people. We are lucky to have him helping us deal with our youth. If you never heard him before I urge you to listen to his information. I'm sure you will find out just like I have that he is right on point."

The lady's hand shook nervously as she handed the mic over to Dr. J. The audience applauded before Dr. J was able to say his first words. He sat his briefcase, which was full of books on a chair on the stage.

"Peace be with you all. I am here just like you are because I am concerned with the actions of our children. If it were up to the police they would have precincts in every high school and lock our children up as they left school. If it were up to the Medical world they would give them all drugs. They would call it immunization to prevent violence or something. Thank God it is not up to them. What is done to our children is up to us."

Dr. J's smiled and walked with more spunk. The people clapped and threw up their fists. Rafael found himself saying yeah a couple of times. After Dr. J talked about the history of violence, which took about half an hour he pulled out a book.

"This is my latest book The Screaming of Earth. It was scheduled to come out next month after the semester ended. But I felt it was appropriate to mention tonight. If you haven't noticed the Mayor is here and the President of the Board of Education." Dr. J pointed his arm over to the gentlemen.

The mayor and president waved their hands reluctantly at the audience.

"Our children are being poisoned. Now it's not the intention of the mayor or the board of Ed to do this. This poisoning is nationwide and has been going on since before these people took office. Matter of fact their children are being poisoned also. The poison is legal and it's everywhere. I am talking about processed sugar. This hyper activity, this violence we're seeing is caused by the food our children have been eating all their lives. It is everywhere and in everything. It's hard to eat something without it having sugar in it."

Rafael immediately thought of the student in the cafeteria with the fruit punch cereal. Even what the student said "This is what the kids in Monument city eat." He couldn't believe something as simple as eating could be responsible for the violent behavior. He thought of the comment the other student made "Face it some people are violent and no love diet is going to change how people are." While Rafael felt the energy of the people in the room he just felt in his heart that most people wouldn't go for the solutions Dr. J offered. As powerful and as loved as Dr. J was it wouldn't make any difference. Rafael thought about the white bread Aubrey had for lunch and the food he ate white rice. It was a processed food and even it had sugar. Dr. J outlined so many things that had sugar in them. Rafael started to think there wasn't anything he could eat which didn't have sugar in it.

Dr. J held pictures of things from toothpaste to cough medicine had sugar in them. He proposed modifying the school meals and the food people ate at home.

After Dr. J finished speaking Rafael waiting for the crowd of people to leave but before he noticed Dr. J was gone. He ran out of the door and saw

Dr. J walking to his car. He ran up to catch him. His car was parked on a dark street in the back of the community center.

"Dr. J thanks for inviting me. It was very informative. I wanted to ask you a question."

"Yes Rafael, what is it?"

"So, you say that our bodies are all polluted. I don't want to be one of these people who say one thing and do something else. How can I get myself on a healthy path?" Rafael asked.

"You may think you eat better because your mother is from the Caribbean but Rafael the vegetables we are cooking our meals with don't have the nutrients. You have to practically change everything you eat. You're not ready for that" said Dr. J.

"Please I just want to know so I can at least try."

"Do a cleansing and then let me know how you feel" Dr. J unlocked his car and started putting his bags in.

Rafael stood back and watched Dr. J drive away in his car. He was impressed at how a little old man was so cavalier. After Dr. J's car turned the corner Rafael observed a rat crawl from a crack in the side of a building to the garbage dumpster. Then suddenly Rafael realized where he was. He was standing in the back of a building at night on the dangerous side of town. Dr. J walked around like he had nothing to worry about and Rafael forgot he was not on campus. Rafael was so scared of violence never left the campus. All of those stories his mother told him about the violence in DR had spooked him. Growing up she never let him play outside without his sisters to protect him. He hadn't even had a fight growing up. Now, alone on a dark street in this violent city no one would even notice if he got bumrushed.

The streets light weren't really lighting up the street beneath it. Even the moonlight was brighter than the streetlights. There was garbage on the street and the air smelled like rotted food. Crumbled papers blew against the walls, which made a scratching sound. Rafael looked toward the front of the building and saw a couple of people walk by and it looked like a group of kids. He stepped behind the garbage dumpster to avoid being noticed. Knowing that the college shuttle bus would be leaving soon he nervously sneaked a peak around the side of the dumpster. If the bus left him he would be stranded in this hell. As soon as the people passed he took a deep breath and ran back to the front of the community center. Once there he realized the people he thought were kids were some of the people from the meeting.

Chapter 4

The mall was packed. Friday nights were the time when everyone mixed together. The sounds of people walking and talking to each other filled the air with a constant noise. Kids from both the private and public high schools intermingled together just fine.

A kids body breaks through the front window of the movie theater and shattered glass flies everywhere. Panicked people start to run. The blooded boy slowly gets up. When he reaches his feet Gripp runs over to him and kicks him in the face.

"Argh" screamed the boy.

Other kids rushed over to the boy's aid. As they got close to Gripp kids in sweat jackets with the letters MS on the back cut them off. The kids in the jackets stood in the way preventing the other kids from helping the boy who was now being punched in the back of the head.

"Somebody call the police" yells a lady from the running crowd.

Kids run out of the movie theater lobby knocking over the velvet ropes separating the people holding the tickets from those buying them. Kids run through the scattering crowds of people while popcorn flies in the air. Theater ushers run up against the walls. Some kids hop the concession counter and start pouring themselves sodas. The security, sells people and ushers were confused and overwhelmed by the raid.

A total bumrush was in effect. The M Squad was successful in starting the chaos. They had done it so many times before that the other kids waited for them to start so they could partake in the madness.

Gripp grabbed the kid by the shirt collar and put his face close to his. "Yo, don't you ever try to diss my boys again you hear me!" his spit flew out of his mouth. As soon as he looked around to partake in the mayhem behind the concession stand he heard police sirens in the parking lot. He turned to his other gang members who were now fighting the boy's friends and yelled "Five-O."

With Gripp's call all of the M Squad members stopped fighting and ran into the mall to avoid the police in the parking lot. As they ran they were met by police who were coming from inside to mall. The police were able to arrest almost all of the M-Squad members but there are so many kids running around the movie theater they couldn't get all of them. Gripp is able to avoid the police by running into a dark costume store.

The Next morning Rafael was sitting at his desk in his dorm room reading about cleansings. He had a big pitcher of orange water. He had a bottle of maple syrup next to a container of cayenne pepper and green bottle of lemon juice extract on his desk. He flipped to a section in the book with the heading Raw Food Fasts. He wrote down Raw food. Behind him his roommate's bed was nicely made up. With the window shade up he has the sunlight shinning on his book he put his hand out to shade the light off the page so he could read it. Just as he reaches to get a sip of his orange water he heard a knock on his door. He took quick sip and said "come in Aubrey."

Aubrey walked in and sat on his bed. Looking over at the other bed she said "So your roommate is still in the hospital?"

"Yep."

"So how are you doing and what is in that water?"

Rafael grabs the pitcher and takes a sip. "It's the Lemonade cleanse. Wanna try?" He holds the pitcher over toward Aubrey's face.

"Ah no ill. That doesn't look like lemonade, it looks disgusting." She wrinkled her eyebrows and pushed her lips together.

"It's incredible how are bodies don't need food. All we need is the nourishments," Rafael said.

"Well I like food. And food hasn't killed anybody that I know of. It's people who I'm worried about. This mental illness these kids have is what is killing people." She reached over to his desk and picked up his juicing book. "So, how long are you supposed to drink that stuff?"

"It's not stuff. It's a cleanse. I'm going to do a 10 day cleanse and then after school lets out I'm going to do a raw food fast."

"Man you really believe that guy Dr. J huh?"

"Sure what's wrong with Dr. J? Everything doesn't have to been in a pill."

"I'm just taking his class to get an easy A. Dr. J is out there. He's a dinosaur. Somebody from the past. The world is better now than it was in those primitive days before we had test tubes and microscopes."

"It was also before we had side effects. Look Aubrey I understand you don't believe in natural medicine but, my mother grew up without all of these new world things and raised me fine. So, what Dr. J says makes sense to me. That's why I changed my major to Holistic Medicine."

"What? Are you crazy? How much do alternative Doctors make? Nothing. You might as well become a teacher."

"I'm not trying to make money and you know you aren't either. But, when I take that Hippocratic oath I want to believe in my heart that I will help people, not doing what everyone else is doing just because I'm scared to be different or paid less." Rafael takes another sip of his orange water.

"Well I think you're wasting your time. Natural medicine had its chance and it failed. I can't wait till Monday I heard some of kids who were arrested last night at the mall are being transferred to Dr. Norris's Medical center."

"I can't believe you're hating. I didn't say anything about your new human lab rats!"

"You just did. Let's stop arguing and come over here and give me a kiss. How long did you say your roommate was going to be away?" Aubrey pulls Rafael to her by his arm.

Allowing himself to be pulled to his bed Rafael lays Aubrey down on her back and gives her a big kiss. She reaches down to lift his shirt up.

Rafael pulls away from Aubrey's mouth and says "You know since my body is fasting I'm not suppose to exert myself."

"Well I'll just take it easy on the little cleanser" Aubrey says as she pulls his shirt over his face and pulls him down to her then starts kissing him again.

Rafael closes his eyes and starts to take deep breaths. He pushes her off of him and shakes his head. "Aubrey please. I'm trying to clean out my body."

Aubrey straddled Rafael and took off her shirt. "Listen baby I understand all of the power you believe the mind has over the body but we all have a primal urge in us that cannot be controlled. So, lay back and let me do all of the work." She unhooked her bra and started kissing a path from his chest to his belly button.

When Aubrey's kisses past Rafael's naval he shrugged his shoulders and lifted her head up. "Please baby. I promise when these tense days are over I will break your back."

Aubrey frowned.

"Okay I'll do a chippendales dance for you and then give you a full body massage. I know you'll like that."

Aubrey picked up her bra, snapped it back on and got off of him. "Okay Rafael whatever." She turned and walked to the door. She opened the door and turned back to him "You know how many guys would love to have their girlfriend excited for them?" She walked out of his dorm room.

"I love you to Aubrey."

Chapter 5

Monday morning Aubrey was at the Future Medicine Center observing Dr. Norris Bryan interview one of the young kids arrested for bumrushing at the mall. The Center was located on the water front section of the city just across the Mississippi river from downtown Monument City. Only the Lenox Street bridge connected the two. Inside the center Dr. Bryan was sitting across a table from a teenager writing notes on a clipboard. The kid was sitting sideways at the table facing away from Dr. Bryan. The room was the size of a classroom with plain light green walls, an observation window and only one door. Outside the door stood Doris a very friendly nurse who stood about six foot three inches tall and well over 200 pounds. Aubrey was watching Dr. Bryan through the window.

"So, what is your name young man?" asked Dr. Bryan.

"I told you Ice".

"That can't possibly be your real name. What is the name on your birth certificate or better yet what does your teacher call you?"

"I don't go to no school."

"Look, I am not a police officer. I am a Doctor. So, you don't have to…"

"So, if you ain't the police then why am I here?"

"Well you're here because the police in this city have asked me to figure out a way to make people like you less violent."

The kid stands up and leans over the table. As he stands the chair he was sitting on falls back against the wall and it made a loud noise. Dr. Bryan slid back from the table as Doris ran in and grabbed the boy. She sat him back in the chair and strapped his arms to the table.

"You will sit here and talk to this man he's trying to help you. So stop acting like a stupid tough guy" Doris said.

"So, Ice. It says here your 13 years old. Do you really want to hurt people?"

The young thug twisted and turned in his chair he gave Doris a look before he uttered calmly.

"I don't know why. But who cares. Gripp says nobody cares about anybody but themselves. And the only reason why you got me up in here like some lab rat testing me is because you don't want your little rich children to get hurt. Ya'll are scared of city people just like Gripp says."

Although Aubrey was from New York where there was plenty of violent young kids but this was the first time she had ever been this close to one. Ice seemed to have programmed logic, which justified his violence maybe from this guy Gripp. She thought for a 13 year old kid there was no way he could develop his opinions on his own.

"Do you want to hurt innocent people? Because young mothers with small children got hurt at the mall" said Dr. Bryan.

Ice seemed like he hadn't even heard Dr. Bryan's question. "I told you ain't nobody care about us. You don't care about me. You ain't trying to help me you just trying to control me. You punkass doctor just like Gripp says." Ice stood up as straight as he could with the arm straps holding him down. Leaning in toward Dr. Bryan knocking the table over. Doris grabbed Ice holding him tightly as she called for assistance. "I'm not like one of your crazy people in here. And when I get out I'm going to bring Gripp and the rest of M Squad back here so you can see what a bumrush is really like ya heard" screamed Ice.

Dr. Bryan grabbed his paper work off the floor and scrambled to the door. "This interview is over. Calm him down before I talk to him again. He's too hyper." Two assistants wearing white lab coats listened to Dr. Bryan as they walked into the room to help Doris. One of the men had a needle and the other men grabbed Ice in a tight bear hug. Doris pulled up the shirtsleeve of Ice as one of the assistants injected him with a strong sedative. Aubrey was glued to the window she had never heard comments like Ice's before.

Rafael stepped off of the bus at the corner of Lenox Street. He could see the words Future Medicine Center mounted on the top of a large gray building at the end of the block. When he stepped through the door the receptionist asked him if he had an appointment. When he mentioned Aubrey Winberg she pressed a buzzer. She guided him through two sets of heavy double doors. The reception counter was behind a large glass window. She told him to have a seat in a waiting room on the other side of the reception counter. Inside the waiting room there was no glass so the inside the center could be seen and heard. He looked around in the waiting room. It had connected chairs along the walls and a coffee table with medical books. There were pictures and posters mounted on the walls with a saying he'd seen in the professor's offices on campus. One poster had a picture of a war torn city street with garbage laying around and across the top the words "No Healthcare". Then the poster next to it had a picture of a bright clean suburban street with two little girls sitting in a wooden lemonade stand. The words across the top that poster were "Free Meds". Rafael reached over to the table and picked up a copy of a magazine titled The American Druggist. In the background the receptionist voice was all he heard.

"Hello The Future Medicine Center, where medicine is our future" said the receptionist holding the phone to her head.

A young girl wearing a gown with long sleeves walked in from inside of the center. She was holding a little doll and sat down next to Rafael.

"Are you hungry? Mommy will get you something to eat as soon as lunch comes out," the young girl said.

Rafael noticed the nice young girl from the corner of his eye. She looked to be about twelve or thirteen years old. Too old to still have a doll but he assumed it maybe something related to the work of the center.

"You know my sister used to have a doll when she was little."

"This is not a doll this is my daughter Mister. Why would you call my baby a doll" screamed the young girl. "That's a very mean thing to say Sir."

"Assistance in the waiting room" said the receptionist as she got up and ran around the counter into the waiting room. She put her arm around the young girl who is now crying profusely. The two assistants in the white lab coats walked in the lobby and escorted the girl out of the lobby. As they left Rafael noticed them roll up the sleeves of the girl before the door closed. He hopped over to the receptionists counter so he could see what the assistants were doing to the girl.

Rafael said the receptionist "I'm sorry I didn't want to hurt her. I just told her my sister had a doll when she was little."

"Don't worry she thinks the doll is real. These people in here are crazy."

Rafael watches as the assistant gives the girl an injection from a needle. "What are they doing to her?"

The receptionist lowers the curtain blocking his view of the inside hallway. "Just have a seat sir Aubrey is on her way."

Moments later Aubrey walks into the lobby. She is smiling and perky. She walks over to Rafael who stands up when he sees her. They hug and she sits him back down.

"I know I said I get a hour lunch break at 1pm but, I only want to take 30 minutes." Aubrey said.

"Oh okay that's fine. This place is wild there was this little girl out here with a doll she thought it was a real baby" Rafael said.

"I saw her in the hallway. Her name is Jessica. She lives here."

Rafael now had to quench his curiosity "so what drug did they give her in the needle Prozac or Risperdal no umh Haldol?"

"I can't tell you that because of the privacy act but Dr. Bryan is the leading researcher in Methylphenidate."

"Ritalin!"

"Dr. Bryan doesn't like to call it that. He says it carries too much prejudice."

"I can't believe you guys are giving that little girl drugs."

"She's violent Rafael and very dangerous. All of the kids in here are. You should be happy that they are not on the streets. Most of the kids in here would be in jail or would do something that would send them to jail. Medicine research is the only way to save our world."

Rafael looked up to the ceiling "Okay I get it. So, you don't think kids eating those Breakfast boosts and fast food has anything to do with it?"

"Rafael I don't want to argue with you. We've talked about this a thousand times. Sugar may have something to do with it. Dr. Bryan says it could be a trigger. But people have the right to sell fast food and you can't stop people from eating it. That's why we're using modern technology to find a solution to the violence in our children."

"Aubrey there are schools where they have changed what the children eat in the cafeteria and their grades went up and the fighting decreased," Rafael said.

"Rafael that is an isolated school. The answer isn't in the grocery store or the cycle of the moon. Look baby we are treating people not animals. Dr

J. acts like its fantasy and we're dealing werewolves or something. The reality is the soil the food is grown in has changed and it doesn't have the nutrients it had before back in the day. Our children are chemically different now. These poor neighborhoods are violence breeding grounds because they don't have the money to eat everything organic. That's the reality. You have to fight chemicals with chemicals."

"Maybe that's what Dr. Bryan tells you" Rafael said.

"Dr. Bryan is trying to develop a vaccine every school can afford to use. But, my lunch is almost over so let me go inside we got some of the kids who were fighting at the mall this weekend. I'll let you know what he finds" Aubrey said as she stood up and open her arms.

"Okay baby I don't like fighting about fighting. Especially with someone I love." Rafael stands up to give her a kiss on lips.

"Woow, that cleanse has your breath on fire baby."

"Don't worry it will be over soon. And don't forget my massage promise." Rafael said as he walked through the double glass doors he waved goodbye to Aubrey. Aubrey dropped her mouth open and pushed her hands over face.

Walking back to the bus Rafael wondered why intelligent people like Dr. Norris Bryan could be so opposed to nature and so easily pursue drugs that created other problems. He wondered why people were so violent? Was it something the government was doing like in the Dominican Republic or was it because of poverty or quality of food? Maybe it was the universe like Dr. J said. He got so caught up thinking about it he got on the wrong bus. Before he realized it he was already downtown and had to pay full fare to get back to the campus. Before he snapped at the bus driver who knew he got on the wrong bus he closed his eyes and prayed for the man. This was the way his mother had taught him who to deal with his frustrations.

Chapter 6

Rafael is at another community forum at a church where Dr. J is sitting on a panel. The audience is even more excited than before. On the panel with Dr. J are two men. One man was wearing a black shirt and a tam hat just like the Black Panthers. The other man was wearing a tie and a collar shirt.

The man in the black shirt and hat said "I'm not going to sit up here and let this man tell us we raised our children to be violent. There's only one group of people who have proven how violent they are and it ain't us. In the 60s we ran after school programs and breakfasts for the kids. If anything we need to get back to doing things like that. Maybe we should march in front of some of these grocery stores so they'll get the point. Now I like what Dr. J is saying. He's not saying poverty makes people violent like this drug pusher Dr. Bryan is." He sits back down still looking at Dr. Bryan.

Dr. Bryan looks over at the pastor who is sitting on the side of the stage. He starts to take off his lapel microphone. "I don't have to sit here and be insulted like this." He gets up and walks off the stage. "These people are closed minded."

The pastor walks over to Dr. Bryan and puts his arm around him. He says "Don't leave we need everyone. I'm sorry."

Dr. Bryan says "I thought we were going to have a civil conversation not a damn sixties freedom rally!"

"You don't have to apologize he's showing his true colors" yells the man in the black shirt.

Dr. J starts to put his books back into his bag. The audience is in starting to talk to each other. People are getting up and leaving. Rafael tires to squeeze through the wooden pews of the church past the people to reach Dr. J but it is impossible to move around them. By the time he gets to the front, Dr. J is shaking the pastors hand outside the front door.

Rafael runs out after Dr. J. Even though there is light coming from the streetlights the street is still pretty dark. He can barely see which way Dr. J walked. There is a group of kids with a large dog between him and the corner where he thinks Dr J turned. He instantly thought of the reports on the news of the kids who were bumrushing. Now they are not on TV they are standing between him and the corner. His palms start to moisten and he looks back at the church. However when a cloud passes allowing the light from the full moon to add to the streetlight he takes a deep breath and runs through the kids to get to the corner. When he reaches the corner Dr. J is just opening the door to his car.

"Dr. J I wanted to ask you a question back in the church."

"Sure son. I was just leaving because I don't like to drive home in this darkness if I don't have to." He closed the car door and looked at Rafael. "Now, what would you like to ask me?"

"When I was little some boys stole my friends bike and when his father went to talk to the boy's father, the boy's father pulled a gun out and killed my friend's father."

"That is a horrible story but what is your question?" Dr. J said as the kids dog at corner barking in the background.

"Well do you think people are naturally violent? My friend never tried to get back at the man that killed his father. I would have done the same thing. Are we weird?" Rafael pleaded.

"No you're not weird. There is an animal in every man and woman. Humans are nothing but animals with the mental ability to think intelligently and control their behavior. Something has caused our children to lose that ability."

"What's up Doc" said a voice coming from the end of the block. The voice seemed to stop the dog's barking.

As Rafael and Dr. J looked toward the voice the group of kids from the corner were now walking toward them. Rafael looked down the street to see if he could get away but it looked more dangerous because the streetlights are out.

"Dr. J get in your car" Rafael said.

"Calm down. They mean us no harm" Dr. J told Rafael who is now starting to sweat.

"Ain't you one of those doctors trying to study us kids?" said Gripp whose face was barely visible.

Gripp walked over to Dr. J followed about 4 other boys and a large pit bull. He had his eyebrow arched as he pushed Dr. J back up against his car. The other boys grab Rafael and the dog started growling at him.

The small five foot five inch tall old man looked up to the six foot thug. "Young man I am the one who's trying to help you." Then Dr. J pushed Gripp away from him. "I don't think it's smart for you to behave like this."

Before Dr. J could finish his words Gripp grabbed him on his shoulders and pushes him back against the car. "Where are our boys? You took them somewhere so you can cut them up and study them." He smacked Dr. J knocking him over on the hood of his car.

"Leave him alone he is an old man" cried Rafael trying to shake free from the other boys.

"Shut up college boy. I don't even like yall mutha fuckers anyway" He looked at his boys and says "Let's teach smart people some of our own lessons."

The boys took turns punching Rafael in the stomach Dr. J slide to the ground between the car and the brick wall of a building. Gripp says "Yo doc you can open a rat but you can't take a punch."

Gripp turned to walk around the car but got knocked across the street as the car was pushed away from the wall. The boys let Rafael go and ran over to the side of the car. The pit bull jumped over the car ahead of the boys. Rafael ran around the other side of the car and a large object hit him in his chest knocking him high in the air over another car into a wall.

"Run" is all that was heard by Rafael before his body crashed into the roof of a car and his eyes closed.

Gripp wondered what the old doctor used to push the car so hard. He wiped his face and stood up. He looked over at his boys who punching in a wild frenzy. Gripp ran over and as soon as he got close a blood body of the pit bull hit him in his head knocking him back to the ground.

"What the fuck!" Gripp said.

As he looked up he saw the rest of his boys being ripped apart. The moon was shining brightly in the cloudless sky and he was able see the pain on his friend's faces. Blood is everywhere on the car and on the wall. Gripp stood in shock as he let go of his dog's torso letting it fall to ground. Gripp lowered his sharp steal dagger from inside his sleeve and gripped it tightly. Emerging from the pile of body parts was a six foot figure covered in long black hair with long human like hands and large claws. It shimmered in the moonlight. The hairy monster had look of fury and rage as it tossed the kids body parts around.

Gripp turned to run away and the beast jumped on him with an agility of a giant monkey. Gripp screamed as his gusts were ripped out of his body. Still screaming he watched, as his stomach was breeched and he's intestines were held in the claws of the monster.

Chapter 7

Startled by the sound of loud talking voices Rafael squints when he tried to open his eyes. The bright sunlight shined on his face. A light breeze blew across his body. He shock his head as he looked around to gather his bearings. He grabbed his head and let out a loud moan. He heard one of the voices say "We got a live one over here."

The police officer looked Rafael over while he is lied in the street in the North side of monument city wedged between a building and a car. After they helped him to his feet he saw remnants of what looked like a human blender. He saw lots of blood and piles of mangled body parts. Suddenly the air became fowl and the smell of dead flesh made his stomach tighten. He covered his nose and noticed his arm was covered with blood as well. He immediately looked down at the rest of his body and it looked fine. His shirt was torn and when he lifted it up he had a long gash on his chest.

He walked over and looked for Dr. J's body parts but he was unable to make out any parts from the mound of flesh that was there.

"Seems like you were bumrushed" says one of the officers.

A EMS person put a bandage over his wound then took his name and address. Rafael was asked a few simple questions and then they dropped him off at the campus. When he got back to his room he felt a piece of paper and a set of keys in his pocket. The note read take my keys and go to my apartment and was signed Dr. J. Below the signature was an address. He called Aubrey and got her voice mail, which meant she was either in class or at the Future Medicine Center or sleep.

When Rafael arrived at the address he heard a soft ringing in his head. He thought it was a result of the impact of hitting the wall. He walked down the stairs leading to the door of a basement apartment in downtown Monument City. It looked like no one had been there in years. He said "Dr. J couldn't possible live here." When Rafael walked in the apartment door the scent of fresh fruit hit him like an organic grocery store. He took a deep breath and enjoyed the smell of the fruit. The furniture was a mixture of antique log cabin and a modern science laboratory. On a wooden kitchen counter there is a new Jack LeLanne power juicer, a commercial blender and Cuisinart food processor. The appliances looked so clean they seemed out of place. The counter looked like a fruit stand.

There were bananas, oranges, apples, mangos and plantains. Rafael thought *what did Dr. J know about plantains*.

In his main room there is a three-foot high bookshelf running the length of the room. There are a few books he could recognize on astrology and natural foods. The walls had different kinds of moons drawn on them. On the ceiling is the formula $D = 20.362954 + 29.305888531 \times N + 102.19 \times 1012 \times N2$. There was an Orrery of the Solar system on one shelf and another Orrery of the moon and the earth on another shelf.

Rafael walked into the back to what he thought was a bedroom but instead of finding a wooden door he found a barred metal door. When he walked in the room he saw that the bars ran across the ceiling and down the walls. He slid back the rug and all that was there was a solid concrete floor. There was a metal frame bed with a note on top of it. Rafael sat down in the large metal chair and read the letter.

Hello Rafael I am sorry I had to leave without saying goodbye. Our attack last night disturbed my aura. Due to my actions I had to leave Monument city. I have left to regain my nirvana if it is possible. Needless to say I cannot do that in the city.

Now, what I'm about to tell you is of the utmost importance. I have an infectious disease and judging by the scratch on your chest I may have infected you. In order for you not to hurt other people you need to do exactly what I tell you.

I have the ancient disease of Lycanthrophy and up until last night I had it under control. I have left my journal for you to read so you can have a better understanding of the curse I have. I have been researching the effects of diet and the rotation of the moon to learn how to control its rage. You will find all you need to protect yourself from others so you won't pass on the infection.

It is important for you to lock yourself in my cage tonight. To make sure you have the disease. If you do have Lycanthrophy you will need to cage yourself for this last day of the New Moon. Do not tell anyone about your illness. The barbarians at the Center for Disease Control would not know how to deal with this disease. The CDC would only try to create another vaccine.

You maybe already be hearing what I call the screaming. As the night grows closer the screams get louder and that is all the warning you'll get and it is not much. When the screams become one constant tone your transformation will begin. I have video of the compete process in my cabinet.

Please listen to my instructions your life isn't over. You can survive without becoming a monster if you heed the screams of the earth.

Sincerely, Dr. J.

Rafael now recognized the ringing in his head to be the screams Dr. J said was part of Lycanthrophy. Different from the screaming his mother did these screams were sounds of pain and torment. Now he was scared by the note Dr. J left, he found the journal and took the bowl of fruit into the bedroom cage. He saw a time lock device on the outside of the cage's metal door and set it for 12 hours. He lied down on the bed to read the journal. As the screaming started to be unbearable his muscles started to contract. Out of the ceiling high windows the full moon was visible.

Rafael's skin hardened and his hair started to grow all over his body. His back stiffened throwing him to the floor. His bottom jaw widened and his canine teeth grew larger and sharper. His hands and feet swelled and large sharp nails pushed out. The pain was unbearable but in less than a minute Rafael transformation was complete. As hunger filled his stomach and his recently cleansed body craved flesh. He ran to the barred door of the of the cage and shook in an uncontrollable rage. He looked up to the window and jumped up to it. Hanging from the ceiling bars he swung trying kick the windows out with he's feet. Only able to kick out the windows he fell back on to the concrete floor. His eyes shined piercing red he arched his back and then let out deep bellowing roar. The roar was more of pain and sorrow than the anger and rage of a beastly werewolf.

THE END.

The

Adventures of the

Black Star

The Black Pirates of the Caribbean.

Chapter One: Born for the Water

"Ijeoma why must we go so far from the shore? The Niger is not a fan of our fishing," Aneesa observed. Both sisters had rich, dark-brown skin. Ijeoma, the oldest, was also the larger of the two girls.

"Never mind the rough waves. This boat is carved from the boba tree." Ijeoma replied.

"It is not the boat that I fear will not survive these waters big sister. It is us."

Their boat rocked from side to side in the muddy waters, as the craft passed through a bend in the river. Ijeoma steadied it with her oar, and Aneesa rowed. It was just past dawn and the animals were awake. Birds flew over the river looking for fish, and large fish hunted the smaller ones.

"Why do you fear the water Aneesa?" asked Ijeoma. "You have been my fishing partner for over a year, yet you do not trust me."

"I am not here because I enjoy the water like you," Aneesa retorted. "I enjoy eating fish, and if I wait for mother to fish I will go crazy."

Ijeoma smiled at her sister. "When father started taking me out on the water, he calmed my nerves by telling me the story of 'The water and the lad to me.'"

"Well, tell me the tale so that my nerves may be calm."

"If you quiet your running mouth, I will."

"Just tell me the story."

"Father explained to me that we are always on water," Ijeoma said. "In fact, it is water which we are made of. Water loves the land. And water surrounds all land."

Annesa looked interested. "Really? But all I see to the East is land."

"Well beyond our forest are hills, and past the hills is water. You can take this river, the Niger, to that great water. Father said: 'Land rests in the palms of Yemayaa. She is the Goddess who creates and loves us.'"

Aneesa laughed. "Well I don't want to drown in the hands of this river. Maybe the story was more effective when father told it."

"You need to worry less about drowning," her sister scoffed, "and start gathering the net as we are almost near our fishing spot."

"I am only worried about falling into the water, because you are as big a man with arms and legs like a ayyu."

"Oh, so you feel my legs are as fat as a manatee?"

"Yes, a big fat ayyu."

"Well, it's not my size and strength that threaten the capsizing of our boat. It is your melon head. At least I am balanced, as your head is as big as a manwawi. When you were little, mother said you might need a crutch for your head if you were ever to walk straight."

"You always talk about my head. You're just jealous because the boys like it better than yours. Wait until we get back to the village. I bet Musu helps carry my fish basket. I can wait for us to get back," Aneesa teased. "He's going to try to kiss me again

. . . Why we must travel so far from our village anyway? We have passed our land."

"Hush, Aneesa! Father said land is of no one tribe's possession."

As Ijeoma and Aneesa's boat came around the bend, they saw another craft with two boys throwing their nets into the water. One youth was the size of Ijeoma. The other one was much larger and had longer hair.

Both boys seemed strong. Their skin was as dark as midnight, and their muscles shined bronze in the sunlight. The young men's teeth were so white and shiny, they could be seen across the river. The larger boy was throwing a sharp stick into the water; with a rope tied to the end of it.

"Meeng-gah-bou!" said the larger boy as he looked down at his fishing partner. "The women are here early, too! Don't let them see that we haven't caught any fish yet."

The sisters steered their boat up beside the men. "Ga Kojo, I see you came early to see if you can out fish us!" Ijeoma called out. "I'm sorry, but you and Kwame will not be winning today. We have a hungry village to feed."

"You will loose this time!" Ga Kojo said. "I have a new fishing tool. And we have already caught a few fish." Kojo said.

"Is that why Kwmae's net is dry?" the young woman taunted. "Do not lie to me Kojo! You are no better a fisher, than Kwame is a fighter. Let us get on our way then, and see who will be the better team."

Aneesa stood and almost fell, as she threw her fishing net over the side of the boat. Kwame quickly stood and threw his net into the water as well.

"We cannot loose to these girls again Kojo! Enough with your silly fishing pole! Fishing has not changed since the time before our fathers. Now sit down and help me win this contest."

*   *   *

The two groups fished until sun set. As the river began to darken, they made their ways to the shore. They quickly pulled their boats out of the water, and unloaded their baskets of fish.

"Those are very big fish that you have caught, Aneesa," Kwame said. He smiled slyly. "Let me see one of them. . ." He reached toward her basket.

She balled up her fist, and shook it in front of Kwame's face. "Touch one of my fish, and I will toss you in the water!"

The young man laughed. "Look at this small fist." He cupped Aneesa's hand. "It looks like a decoration. What, may I ask, do you plan to do with a little fist like this?"

"I bet this little fist caught more fish than you did."

"Just be glad we let you fish here, in our tribe's water." Kojo retorted.

"What do you mean?" Aneesa bristled. "The river is not the possession of any single tribe. It is here for us all."

"You are as wise as you are beautiful. You will make quite the wife one day. Maybe I will come rescue you away from you poor tribe, and bring you to live with the kings and queens of my tribe." Kojo grabbed his fishing pole, and placed it next to their pile of baskets.

"You can't even out fish me how will you be able to afford me." Aneesa said, while smiling. She dropped her last basket, making her and her sister's total of four baskets—one more than Kwame and Kojo's three.

Ijeoma grinned. "We won again. It is always nice to fish with you."

As the four sat down, a twig snapped loudly behind them. Kojo grabbed his fishing pole.

"That sounds like a monkey or something," Kwame scoffed. "Put that fishing sick down," Kwame said.

The brush behind them was pushed aside and ten, heavy-set white men stepped through. Two of them were holding long rifles. The men wore clothes which fitted around their legs, chest and arms loosely. Their bodies were hairy, and they looked dirty and smelled of body waste.

"Look what we've got here!" the fattest one of the white men said, in a language the four barely understood.

"Yes, Cortland," his blond friend replied. "It seems they have also brought us lunch."

"What do you want from us sicklings?" Ijeoma demanded. She spoke the language of whites, once helped by her tribe.

"Dirk, this one knows English!" the fat one exclaimed. "And we're not sick!"

He grabbed Kwame, and the youth flipped him over his back. Another white man punched Aneesa knocking her to the ground. Kojo grabbed his fishing pole, and threw it into the chest of a white man. Ijeoma was punched in the stomach and returned with a blow to the face of her attacker.

Kojo rose to throw another of his fish spears, but was shot in the chest before it could leave his hand. His body was blown across his boat — landing the water. Ijeoma and Aneesa froze, as the other whites pointed guns at them.

Kwame turned toward his brother's motionless body, floating on its back in the Niger's water. "KOJO!"

Rifles were pointed at each of the three friends' heads. They were shackled, and led to the brush to a group of other shackled Africans; then they were dragged through the woods. They walked the whole night. The other African captives were so battered they could not utter any words.

Just before dawn, they reached a large stone building surrounded by water. Kwame was separated from the women, who were pushed into a dark room with only a small opening in the top. The dark room smelled of human waste and rotten flesh. They could hardly see each other, and not make out any of the other women.

"Aneesa are you okay?" Ijeoma said. By now both sisters were tired and scared.

"Yes. . . What happened? Is our tribe at war?" Aneesa asked.

"I don't think so. They told us this building was a castle, but it's a dungeon of some sort. This is no war! War is fair, this is a sneaky capture!"

"I wish Kojo had killed all of them!"

"We must calm ourselves so we can think of a way out," Ijeoma said.

The other women in the room moaned and cried. The sun beaming through the small window, was the only light they had. Ijeoma held her sister close. They closed their eyes, and the smells and sounds of the other captors faded.

*   *   *

"Bring him four women and one boy for me," said a white red-haired man pointing a rifle as the wooden door opened. Two other pudgy men strained, as they pulled the door open.

Ijeoma and Aneesa fell back, covering their eyes from the glaring sun light. One of the men walked through and grabbed Ijeoma, Aneesa and two other women.

"Let me see them first." The red-haired man said.

The captives were pulled to their feet, and spun around before the man. Two of the women were thin, and coughed when their clothes were opened.

"I will take these three," the man with the rifle said; as he pointed to all but Ijeoma. "Take this large one back to the hole. She will fetch a high price at the market— that is if she, or any of these withered animals can make it."

Ijeoma jerked Aneesa back as they pulled her away. "Get off of my sister!"

One of the pudgy men hit Ijeoma in the back. She turned to block the next blow; and blocked two more, before the butt of a another white man's rifle crashed under her jaw knocking her to the ground.

"Gentlemen," the red-haired man ordered. "You must stop playing with these savages!" He was obviously in charge. "As you can see they get quiet aggressive, when they are from the same tribe or family."

"That is why you must separate them all. They must not be able to even communicate with each other. We will ready the ship and leave before night fall. Notify the crew that they have two hours to finish up their fornication."

Ijeoma was dragged into another dark room and thrown inside. Before her blurry vision fully dissipated, she saw Aneesa taken upstairs.

Chapter Two: In the Palm of Yemayaa

Ijeoma rocked from side to side. Her eyes opened and closed. Images of her captors, Kojo being shot and Aneesa being snatched away, flashed before her. The screams of Kwame and Aneesa grew in volume, growing louder and louder—so loud her head began to throb.

The screams merged with the moans outside of the realms of her mind. She opened her eyes, to find she was shackled to the other female slaves. The smell of salt and the rocking of the room, told her she was in the palm of Yemayaa. . . in the endless water only the big men of her village could fish or swim in.

"Wha, wha!" the lady next to her screamed. Ijeoma jumped and nudged another women in her side. The woman's only response was a soft moan.

"What is this place? Where is my sister? Aneesa! Kwame! Somebody tell me what is going on!" Ijeoma cried. A chorus of voices answered her.

"We are captives of the devil, being punished for something we have done wrong!" a man's voice said.

"They are white traders!" another voice exclaimed. "Maybe they are going to sell us to the Arabs or Moors!"

"They can't be Arabs, they did not mention Islam," another voice from the far end of the room said.

"I was taken with my sister Aneesa, and another boy named Kwame!" Ijeoma said. "We were just fishing!"

"The Arabs don't have boats this big!" the male voice answered. "My village was raided by them two seasons ago. We were converted to Islam and I was given the name Kalif.""

"My name is Maremba I was given to them with my uncle. We were supposed to be representatives from our tribe to their tribe. As soon as we got out of the village, we were beaten and shackled."

"My best friend Kojo and I were taken in by the Mali tribe, after our parents were killed by Arab and Moor raiders," a young male voice said.

"Kwame the fisherman is that you?" Ijeoma said.

"Yes, Ijeoma! Where is your sister, Aneesa?" Kwame said.

Ijeoma bowed her head. "I don't know. . ." she began to sob.

*   *   *

The door of the ship's hull squeaked open and moonlight shined through. Three heavyset, white men walked into the center of the room. A thin, white man with a long beard followed. He was holding a scroll tablet.

"Amazing," the thin man said, while looking around the hull. "You have taken a three-mask, galley warship and simply boarded up the cannons ports. This ship designed for the British Royal Navy. It carries eighteen six-pound cannons. It was not designed for human cargo."

"Take the dead blacks, and pile them over here," The largest of the men said; pointing to the right. "We'll wait until morning, and throw them into the water. I like to watch the sharks tear apart their flesh."

The thin man looked shocked. "Commander Millroy you mean to tell me, you're just going to throw them overboard?"

"Mr. Clarkson, you may have been given permission from the Lloyds market to work with us," Commander Millroy sneered. "but those prissy businessmen from London, know nothing of the trade of these savages. . . I must remind you that this is a Dutch Trading vessel, and you could find yourself fighting off sharks in the morning if you do not mind yourself."

Clarkson turned red. "Captain Alonso, my employer, is far from being a byproduct of Holland! I am well aware of your countries pride and involvement in this Atlantic trade. But mind you this," Clarkson went on, "I am not only an inspector for the Lloyds council. My trip is partly funded by the Brotherhood of Abolitionists."   "Therefore my dear, Dutch trader if you want to continue to brave these seas, and make a living in trade; you'd be wise to make my return to England a safe one! Or you will find yourself in a British jail!"

The white men inspected the various African captives, and separated the ones who were dead from the living. The woman shackled to Ijeoma was still moaning when they unchained her. She let out another soft moan when her heavy chains were unlocked.

"What are you doing? This woman is still alive!" Mr. Clarkson said.

"Mr. Clarkson this is not the work for the squeamish," Millroy drawled. "This is a dirty job. You enjoy your tea from the East, and sugar from the Caribbean. But you are having a hard time accepting where they come from."

"What does the treatment of this woman have to do with my love of tea?" Clarkson shot back.

"She is rotten and will be jettisoned with the dead. She will die before morning. And if she hasn't already infected these others God has blessed us. A rotten one like her could destroy entire booty. We are very lucky if she hasn't already past her disease on." Commander Millroy grabbed Ijeoma by the arm. "Look! She is next to this strong female! This young one could balance our books, and yield a lot of your beloved sugar barrels when we make it to Hispanola."

Clarkson shook his head in disgust. "I'm surprised any of these people make it anywhere, being treated like this. No wonder the Lloyds only insure one third of your cargo. These people need food and water."

"I have heard enough from you! If you continue to be of nuisance to me, I will have the captain lock you in your quarters for the remainder of the trip. That is something, my good fellow, well within our agreement with the Lloyds."

"Very well commander Millroy. I will document my observations and you will hear no more from me."

The men continued to examine the African captives in the room, and pull dead slaves out. Then they passed out cups of water, and tossed bread for them to eat.

*   *   *

"Ijeoma I do not know what is happening to us!" Kwame seethed. "But as soon as I get my hands free, I will knock one of those rock shooters out of their hands and seek Kojo's revenge!"

"Kwame I think I have an idea," said Ijeome, "Do you remember why you have to club a Tiger fish, when you take them out of the water?"

*   *   *

The next morning, all of the captives were dragged on deck and allowed to exercise. Ijeoma gazed into the waters of Yemaya. She looked on as the sick woman next to her, was pushed over the side of the ship.

Ijeoma closed her eyes in horror, when she saw large fish devouring their flesh. She also observed the size of the ship. . . and each of

72

the men working on it. Just when she heard the command to bring them back down to the dark room, the young woman fell to the floor and began moaning.

"What is wrong with this big one?" a pudgy white asked.

"She is too big to have her thrown in the water," another slaver replied. "Give her a second ration of water and bread. Maybe it will strengthen her by morning."

"Very well then."

*   *   *

That night in the captive's quarters, Ijeoma moaned and made herself vomit. She lay in the vomit and smeared it over her body. When the men came down to pass the drinking cups and inspect for dead, Ijeoma closed her eyes and lay still.

"Well it seems Mr. Clarkson has brought us bad luck!" a slaver exclaimed. "This big one has caught the dead disease, from the old one we threw over this morning." He unshackled Ijeoma, and tried to pick her up. He gestured to his pudgy friend: "Dirk grab her legs. . ."

They tossed Ijeoma into the pile of dead. Ijeoma lay motionless until the door was closed again. The she pushed through the few bodies laying over her and stuck only her head out.

Lying in the pile of dead bodies, Ijeoma was reminded of an experience with her father. She was clubbing fish in their boat, and her father asked: "Why are you so passionately killing the fish?"

Ijeoma had pointed to her father's leg, and told him she didn't want the tiger to jump out and bite her like they done him. Tiger fish would lay motionless in the boat; and, without warning, wake up and hop back in the water or bite the fisherman.

Her father had said: "Even a fish has a spirit. It is still a life you are ending. We are fishermen not killers. Killers take lives for no reason. We take lives for food. We honor the spirit of the animal by eating its body, and not giving it a gruesome death."

He'd looked into her eyes. "Be mindful of the taking of life and ending spirits. Even ending the spirit of an animal, has an effect on the hunter. If you fail to respect that you can become a killer. A hunter— even a fish hunter— is a dangerous person. Because they are used to the feeling of a spirit's transition."

"Ijeoma, the spirit of a man is no different."

After think about what her father said, she asked: "Father why didn't you tell me this, before I clubbed my first fish?"

Her father's face was solemn. "I am telling you this now, so you will only club fish."

The smell of dead flesh was nauseating. But not enough to wipe out Ijeoma's fear; that she would become the very thing her father warned her of. A killer.

As Dirk and two other men, walked down the stairs to the holding room. "We are going to have call in a claim for this entire booty," Dirk complained, "if we continue to loose slaves at this rate."

"I think the captain enjoys fornicating with the savage women too much; and we stayed at the fort longer than we should have," another man said.

Dirk joined in their laughter. "Well you can't blame him for that. I find myself lost in the flesh of these primitives."

The third slaver held a long rifle pointed to the ground, as the two others walked among the Africans. "Just make this fast because I do not enjoy the smell of dead flesh. We only have two weeks left. I won't make it, doing this every day. I'll to climb the mast or something."

A body slammed against the third man, knocking him into a group of waiting Africans. Ijeoma legs swung into Dirk, and the second white. Kwame caught Dirk and twisted his head. . . he squeezed, gritting his bright white teeth until he heard the snap of Dirk's neck.

Ijeoma jumped on the other mate and delivered a blow to his groin. The white man was only able to open his mouth, before her fist connected with his jaw knocking him to the hard wood floor. Kwame found the keys to the shackles in Dirk's pants.

Free of his shackles, he joined the other Africans; and found another named Kalif, struggling with the slaver holding the rifle. In the next instant, the gun was pulled from the white man's hand, and the rifle barrel came crashing through his skull.

"I say we kill them all!" Ijeoma said, pulling the long rifle out of the fat white man's head. "There is at least 75 of us and 50 are strong enough to fight! Twenty, of these white remain on the other side of this door! I am going to kill as many of them as my strength allows me too! I ask that you do the same!"

Kwame unlocked Kalif, and the rest of the captives. They rushed to the deck catching the ship's crew of guard. The raging Africans tossed as many slavers as they could into the waiting waters.

"Send them to Yemayaa, and let the fish feast on their white flesh today!" Ijeoma cried.

Three white men armed with rifles, rose up from the port side of the ship. Ijeoma dove to deck as shots fire flew over her head. Kwame charged and was hit in the shoulder knocking him to the ground. Ijeoma squeezed behind a barrel, trying to figure out how to fire a rifle she took out of a white man's hands.

Kalif jumped up to confront the men. He grabbed one of the guns and engaged the man in struggle. Another man aimed his rifle at Kalif, and shot him off the side if the ship. As he aimed at another African, he was overtaken by five skinny weakened Africans.

Captain Alonso stood on the quarterdeck shooting Africans with his pistol. Ijeoma and Kwame watched: trying to figure how to get to him without being killed. Kwame held his bleeding shoulder, and shook his head at Ijeoma. She pointed motioned to a long piece of wood.

"Go fishing Kwame!" Ijeoma yelled.

The wood was long and sharp just like his brother's fishing pole. Kwame grabbed the wooden pole, stood up and hurled it through Captain Alonso's chest. As Alonzo fell into the ship's steering wheel, the remaining Africans stood up and cheered.

Chapter Three: Did we win or lose?

"Search the ship! Find my sister! Make sure we have killed all the Europeans!" Ijeoma said, as she finished wrapping Kwame's shoulder. "This should hold you. . ."

"I can't believe something like this has happened!" Kwame exclaimed. He stood up and looked out into the open water. "Where are we, and where were they taking us?"

"I don't know. We are so far out in this water, I cannot see land. We need to get back to our villages and warn others," she choked back a sob. "And where is Aneesa. . .?"

Two Africans dragged William Clarkson out to main deck. He was dropped in front of Ijeoma and Kwame.

"He says he can help us," one of the Africans said. "He had no weapon. We found him hiding in a room under the captain's room."

Ijeoma looked into Clarkson's sky-colored eyes. It reminded her of her first meeting with a white person— and of how her mother cured their disease. She remembered too, the blue-eyed man who taught all of the children English.

"You are not like the other sicklings are you?"

"No I am not. My name is William Clarkson. I was on this ship to document the treatment of Caribbean labor transfer."

Kwame stood and walked over to him. He grabbed William by the shoulder and lifted him up. "I heard you talking to the men who guarded us. I believe you. Do you know where they were taking us?"

"You were being transported to a trading port on the island of Hispanola?"

"Do you know how to get us back to our villages?" Ijeoma said.

"I am not a sailor. Or a navy officer. But if we can decipher the captain's charts, we should be able to figure out how to get back to Africa."

"Where will they be? These charts of the captain," Ijeoma asked.

William pointed behind the wheel. "Please follow me. I'm sure captain Alonzo kept them in his quarters."

Ijeoma and Kwame went with William to the captain's quarters. She asked another African to count how many survivors there were, and get an overall report on the ship while they were gone.

The Captain's room was fitted with a desk and a cushioned chair; embroidered with Adinkra symbols, and precious gems. There was also a large rug from Persia, copper pots, Arabian clothes and other European items.

"May I ask how is it that you know how to speak English so well?" William asked.

"There are white people who were given land near our village. They taught us," Ijeoma said. "They were very sick when they came to us; and that's why we call them sicklings."

"I know how to speak English, because many of the traders who came to our village spoke it," Kwame added. "Can you speak Ga or Yoruba?"

"No I am not familiar with your native tongue. However, I am aware that in the colonies the laborers have created a patwa, of both the Spanish and English languages."

Ijeoma finished her search of the room. "I see no charts. There are valuables from everywhere, but no charts. What would these water directions look like?"

"They should be large, rolled papers," William said.

"What if we don't find these papers?" asked Kwame.

William whipped his head around toward them and shook nervously. He was clearly afraid of telling them his answer. "It is quite possible that Captain Alonzo was so experienced, that he no longer required charts. And if that is true then we must set our sails, say a prayer, and hope we drift to land and not another slave ship."

*   *   *

Just before dawn, across the ocean, a dark skinned crewman climbed the mainmast of another ship. He hooked his legs around the thick pole and looked over the water through long copper telescope. Something sparkling on the horizon. Another dark-skinned crewman stood below him on the deck; holding a back-staff and looking out in the same direction.

"Oh, oh! I see a ship! Tell Captain this morning brings us English booty," the hanging man exclaimed.

The crewman ran across the deck to the captain's cabin. It was an elaborate room with flashy cups and huge gold picture frames on the walls. A large chaise lounge lined the wall; giving the room the feel of a mini castle.

"Caesar, Caesar! There be booty at sea!" the crewman announced.

"Why, why, why you address me as such? And who is this Caesar you asking for?" shouted a voice from the behind the shadow, cast by the morning sun.

"Excuse me captain! That be Black Caesar, sir. The one and only free man of the high seas. Feared by all who dare to sail the seas."

Out stepped a block-shaped man almost as wide as he was tall, with skin as black as the night sea. Though Black Caesar stood a little over six feet, he was without doubt a monster of a man. He flashed bright, white teeth with a wide grin; that in contrast to his dark skin, would strike as much fear as it would signify his pleasure in conquest.

"Where is this booty you speak of?" Black Caesar demanded.

The crewman led Black Caesar to the quarterdeck, where they were both were able to see the ship using the telescope.

Black Caesar's face broadened to a smile of excitement and eagerness. He threw back his arm holding the telescope, into the chest of the crewman. "Well make haste and ready the crew for it's booty we be getting today!"

The crewman smiled, and quickly walked down to the ship's lower levels to rally the other men.

Adams Brown was playing a game of chess with another crewmen, as Black Caesar approached him.

"Why do you teach my crew these games of conquest, rather than enjoy the real conquest we pursue?" Black Caesar asked.

Adams was clothed in a wore-out sweater vest, made in his birth place of Virginia. He looked up directly into Black Caesar's eyes. "I play these games with my fellow crewmen, so it will sharpen their strategic minds. This game is a game of moves. You cannot simply win it with one move. You must plan three and four moves ahead in order to trap your opponent. You learn to use your pawns to—"

Black Caesar took in a deep breath and, let out a laugh full of bass. "You are no different than the day you joined our crew! The time you endured as a war captive on that slave plantation has served you well! But listen up: on my ship we have no room for pawns!"

"Now take your mind away from the artificial and ready yourself for reality. We are preparing to take a ship which seems to be adrift. "

"Captain we are going to seize a ship in the day?" the crewmen playing with Adams asked.

"Why not? Do you think we need the cover of darkness to pirate these waters? We cannot limit our actions to the cover of night—whatever we encounter!" Black Caesar bellowed. "We must be able to handle it if we are truly the source of fear of these waters."

"Adams I see you still wear the ragged vest of yours. Why don't you put on something more battle-ready; like this black leather coat we took from that last royal ship we sank?"

"This is what my father was wearing; the night we ran away from that prison the Europeans call a plantation," Adams replied. "It is all the armor I need in any battle with people traders."

The crewmen all stood ready as Caesar's ship cruised up alongside the ship. The ship was empty. No life was visible on it. There was rope tied to the wheel. And all of the sails were drawn leaving the ship drifting.

"Caesar. The ship looks to be empty. I see no life aboard," Adams said as he held the wheel of Black Caesar's ship.

"Maybe a case of scurvy?" another crewman cried.

"Just bring us up close and everyone stay ready," Black Caesar ordered. "No crew suffering from scurvy would tie rope to their wheel. Something is wrong. They wanted the rudder steady."

The black ship of Caesar bumped the side of the ship. Caesar's men threw anchor ropes pulling the two ships together. The captain was the first to board the main-deck of the barren ship. He held a flintlock pistol in each hand. Following him were several crewmen holding a variety of daggers, knives and muskets. The deck was stained with blood. As they continued to explore the ship, they walked with heightened caution.

Adams was a wiry figure, not as burly as Black Caesar; but he stood a little taller than the mincing Captain. He was dark, but not as dark as the rest of the crew. Having to hunch down, he cautiously approached the door to the barren ship's captain's quarters.

Adams motioned with his knife, to a crewman holding a short barrel musket. He thought the ship may have been in a conflict with their human captives, injured and out of ammo. They thought playing possum was their best strategy.

Although Adams was thin he had what he called "a country boy strength," which all of Caesar's crew learned to respect. Caesar often relied on it himself when he needed it. This was one of those times. So, Adams leaned back and kicked with the heel of his foot to break the door.

The door flung open, revealing an empty captain's room. He stepped in looking around as he entered. The cabinets were opened and a variety of charts lay scattered on the floor. He saw a desk with a large gold chair and no sign of life.

Adams turned back to announce his findings, when an arm wrapped around his neck and a knife's blade pressed against his groin.

"Drop the knife and put the gun down," said a female voice, Adams found surprisingly sexy.

Chapter Four: We Be Black Pirates

Ijeoma walked Adams out onto the quarterdeck, and faced Black Caesar and the rest of his crew. "All of you put down your weapons! Or else I will cut this man so he will never have descendants!"

The ship decks filled with Kwame, Williams and the Africans who'd overthrown their European kidnappers. They surrounded Black Caesar and his crewmen, many were shaking nervously.

Adams's tall, lanky body was twisted down, and sideways in order to be held in Ijeoma's grip. Even twisted he managed to smile at Black Caesar. He turned a little and Ijeoma tightened her grip.

"Hay, sister ease up!" Adams said. "We're not here to hurt you!"

"You want not to be pointing your weapons at my men," Black Caesar growled. "See, we be pirates. . . and the threat of a conflict is only a turn on for us. You'd be a smart girl to release my first mate Adams, and let us go about serving you some food."   Black Caesar gave one of his broad smiles. "It's obvious you liberated yourselves from your captives. And it is also obvious you are lost and rationing your food. So, my dear, put down your gun so no one gets hurt."

Kwame threw his machete down, and walked toward Ijeoma. "Let's see what they have to offer. If we slay them we will be in no better position."

"Well. . ." Ijeome hesitated, "let's all put down our weapons."

"Exactly what I was thinking," Adams added. "You can start by pulling your knife away from my baby maker."

Black Caesar looked around at his men. "Very well then on three. One, two, three. . ." They all dropped their weapons on the floor of the ship.

Ijeoma released Adams. He grabbed his groin, and stretched out his shoulders, as he stood upright. Then shook his head, and let out a laugh.

Ijeoma looked at him. "What are you laughing at?"

"I haven't been touched by a woman in so long, I was enjoying your grasp," Adams replied. "But you have nothing to fear from us, even though your prejudice was wise. Allow me to introduce myself. I am Adams Brown, a free man of the sea."

"And who is that?" Ijeoma pointed her gun toward Black Caesar.

"I be the one and only Caesar of the sea," Black Casear growled. "I be known as Black Caesar— terror of all who trade in my waters. My crew here are liberated booty. They are all men, like myself, who were taken from their own families; to be used to work as slaves. Just as you here freed yourselves, so did these men."

"Where did you come from and where are we?" Kwame asked.

"By the look at your ship you were being taken to Santiago; a port on the Island of Haiti." Adams replied.

"Excuse me but wouldn't that be in Hispanola and port-o-prince be in Haiti?" William said, as he stepped into visibility of Black Caesar.

Two of Black Caesar's men immediately grabbed Williams. "Who is this?" one of Black Caesar's men said.

"My name is Williams Clarkston, I am a journalist from London. I am of no threat to you —please believe me!"

"Let him go! He's telling the truth!" Ijeomo said. "If he were with these kidnappers, we would have already fed him to the sharks!" The men released Williams.

Adams put his arm around Ijeoma's shoulder. "Dear lady, the more you speak the more I want to know about you."

Ijeoma shook out of Adams embrace. "So, Caesar—"

"Ah, ah that be Black Caesar to all," Black Caesar corrected.

"Black Caesar we want to get back to Ghana to our families. We just need you to show us how to steer this ship in the right direction."

"That be no problem but first let us feed your crew, and I will have my men ready your vessel." Black Caesar motioned for his men to do his wishes; then he walked up onto the quarterdeck and took in the full view of the ship. "This is a fine vessel! You need come and join me in the captain's quarters, and I will tell you what you need to know."

Ijeoma, Kwame and Williams joined Black Caesar and Adams Brown in the cabin, while the crew got to work.

*   *   *

Black Caesar stood looking out the window into the sunlight. It was a clear day and the ocean was calm. " You are days from the African coast. The current has taken you to the Caribbean Sea. In fact, you are lucky we found you first; or else your revolt would have been in vain. It is best you come with me to The Black Island. There, we can stock your ship and find you a navigator for your journey home."

"Caesar you would do this for us?" Ijeoma asked.

"Black Caesar it is. And yes Black Caesar would be happy to aid you. We will arrive in the morning. This will give you enough time to learn about what's going on in these waters."

"Black Caesar what is this war we are involved in?" Kwame asked passionately. "My village fought no war with Europeans. We've only encountered Arabs and Moors from across the sands, seeking conquest. How did these Europeans come to go to war with us?"

"I am also curious to know who it is that you are war with." Williams added. "It is not a war we know of in London."

Black Caesar cleared his throat to begin his story "It is a shame that the details of this war are not known in Africa. But the explanation is simple. There is no war in Africa. The war is in the Caribbean. That is where the crimes are being committed."

"I think perhaps the investors in Europe," the captain went on, "like these Lloyds of London, turn a blind eye; that is to say if they care at all. What I do know, is that ships have been transporting our Black people for as long as I can remember."

"They are working us in these death camps, which they call plantations, from America down to Brazil," Adams chimed in. "And every European country is involved— Dutch, Portuguese, English, Spanish and French. They are all involved in this war." "Ijeoma and Kwame my ancestors were brought to Virginia from Africa. And I would love to go back and visit—just to see what it's like. But I could not stay, because I have left friends on the plantations who are still being tortured."

"Mr. William I have met several men like you. Men, white like you, who could not understand the actions of their own kind. If you are true to your heart, you will join us and help end this war. There are many pirates who fought in your country's Royal Navy," Adams continued, his eyes flashing. "But once they see what their government is doing, they can no longer participate."

"On Black Island you will meet some of these men. You may know of them as pirates or deserters or even criminals. But to me they are allies, because they would sooner cut off the head of a British ship captain than I."

"Well, if righting this wrong will have me called a pirate," Williams said, "then a pirate I'll be."

One of Black Caesar's crewmen brought in a bottle of rum and mugs, and passed them out. "Here, here then! Let it be resolved!" Black

Caesar bellowed. "Adams we have ourselves a new army. Let's drink, with full cups, of some of Jamaica's finest rum to this new ship of soldiers."

Ijeoma raised her glass and drank the rum. She thought about all that had happen to her and Kwame. She pictured Kwame laughing with Kojo while fishing on waters of the Niger river. She felt the warm and love they had for each other.

Then she pictured Aneesa running and laughing, and began to daydream. . . Aneesa smiled and ran toward her. But before Aneesa reached her, the old white man who traded goods out of the fort near her village, grabbed Aneesa around the neck. The old man was not strong enough to hold her. But somehow she could not get loose.

Ijeoma watched as the old white man threw Aneesa to ground. Ijeoma watched without the power to do anything. The old white man took out a knife, while pinning Aneesa to the ground with his knee.

He looked at Ijeoma and laughed. Imoja tried to move, but for some strange reason she could not move. The old white man said "What are you going to do?" Ijeoma felt a cold strike of lightning shoot through her body. The old white man raised the knife high in the air and plunged it into the chest of her sister. . .

Ijeoma spit out a mouth full of rum as Kwame threw his arm around her. "Are you alright?"

"Yes, I just think it was a little strong for me. . ."

After everyone had eaten, Ijeome, Kwame and Williams followed Black Caesar and Adams; as they showed them details of the ships.

They walked the planks over to Black Caesar's ship: a Schooner with two large masts. It was a massive ship. One main deck had three lower desks. There was another level with nothing but canons. She counted six on each side. He had canons on another level where the crew slept. There were even four canons on the quarterdeck.   Black Caesar's ship was one big canon! He had cut out canon ports on the deck below his cabin, so he could fire at ships behind him.

By the time they finished learning the operations of the ship it was dark. Black Caesar pulled Ijeoma, aside while Adams showed Kwame how to lower the anchor. Williams joined the crew for a meal of salted meat, and more dried bread. Williams was eager to hear the stories of the various crew members.

Black Caesar walked with the young woman on the deck of his ship. He leaned on the railing, looking out into the night sky. He pulled out a back-staff and held it out showing her. "This is what is used to guide ships. But a pirate must learn to read the stars. Being able to read the stars allows you to navigate your ship at night. The brighter and whiter a star is, the better it is for a night reader."

"Are there Black stars?" Ijeoma said.

"Yes there are. And just like the nights when the clouds cover the sky, they are the nights when pirates wreak their most terror on the ships. We hang black sails on these night, so we can surprise these ships. The element of surprise and fear are a pirates' greatest asset."

Ijeoma starred off into the night sky and absorbed the immense darkness. She imagined the fear of the attacked ships—giving herself goose bumps. "How does one become a pirate?"

"That is the question I have been waiting for you to ask. A pirate is not something you can want to be. A pirate is something you are made to be. I was raised with my brother and family in the sugarcane fields of Haiti. My father worked during the day for the Spanish plantation owners; and at night he worked for the rebellion."   "One night he said goodbye to us, and said he was going to build a great citadel in the hills. He said when he would return he would bring freedom. Months later the revolution started and our plantation was destroyed. The Spanish army fought our great leaders Toussaint L'Ouverture's army, in the very fields my family worked. Everyone in my family fought."

"Separated from my family, my brother and I were driven into the sea. We drifted on a raft until we landed on the shore south of the Spanish colony of Saint Augustine in the land of the Mayaimi Indians. We were taken and feed by the Mayaimi Indians. My brother was too sick and died shortly after. It was there in Florida, where I met a man trading stolen goods with the Mayaimi. I don't remember his name but I do remember he was a pirate."

"I learned from this pirate's crew members, that Toussaint drove Napoleon's army back to San Domingo. Many of his crew were younger than me. Boys and some girls just like me but, fighters nonetheless. They told me that the war spreading throughout the Caribbean." "They said they were fighters in this war."

I decided then, that I would become a pirate. I joined with these men and we took two ships in our first years. Now, I command a navy of four ships. We have found several ships like yours, which have had revolts. But, none have had as many survivors as you."

Black Caesar put his arm around Ijeoma and said: "think hard about your future. What you have experienced since your capture has changed; and what you thought your life would be. As I did when the rebellion changed mine."

Chapter Five: Welcome to the Black Island

The ships arrived on the sandy beach of Black Island. The smell of land and fresh vegetation filled the air. The clear blue water, and the swaying of the palm trees only made Ijeoma's desire to return home even stronger.

There were buildings made of stone just beyond the shoreline. She stood looking over the side of her ship . . taking in the view of this island, Black Caesar called home.

There were three other ships in addition to Black Caesar's and Ijeoma's ship lining the bay. Although it was bright and sunny, there was dark, luminous energy about the place. A hint of sulfur lingered in the air. There were children playing on the beach; but even they looked sad. Their smiles were hard— unlike the children in Ijeoma's village. They wrestled and fought, snatching toys from each other. As a child, Ijeoma would have never fought with another child from her village.

The houses all looked like fortresses. They were run down and painted in bright colors; their paint faded and splotched with dirt. The women looked tired and old. They yelled loudly at the children, and used foul language. Their clothes were ragged, and falling off their bodies.

She had thought that Black Caesar's men looked frightning, because they were at sea. Even more they were pirates; and perhaps pirates were supposed to look scary. Now she wondered.

"I see you're already up. I bet it feels good to be on land'" Adams said as he walked up behind Ijeoma. He handed her a coconut with the top sliced off, and a mango. "I brought you some coconut water and some fruit. It will make you feel better. You can drink it while I show you the place. Black Caesar is already setting up a big feast of fresh fruits for you and your crew. It's the best thing to eat after a long trip at sea."

"Let me tell Kwame. I'm sure he would like to come as well," she says. As she turned toward the door of the captain's cabin, Adams frowned.

"Alright. . . But don't you think it is best if he continues to sleep.? Maybe he is tired. I could come back for him." Ijeoma stopped before she reached the door.

"Let me show you this place, that the Good Lord blessed us with. And I can show you a hot spring where you can wash off the ocean salt."

"Okay. . ." Ijeoma said. She followed him off the ship, and into the town.

*　　　　　*　　　　　*

"Whata-gwan Adams! Welcome back, my brother!" a voice called from inside a bar, as Adams and Ijeoma approached it.

"Oh no," Adams sighed. He turned and greeted a dark-skinned man wearing a multicolored outfit. He wore a green shirt and red pants, with a yellow scarf. "Good day Brother Coconut. It's good to be back. How are you?"

"Everything is irie, man. Much better than if I were in Kingston. I see you and Black Caesar found a beautiful treasure! And what is the name of this sight, warming my eyes?" Coconut asked.

Ijeoma smiled. "My name is Ijeoma, and Adams rescued us at sea. We would have been a dead treasure, if they would not have found us when they did."

"Coconut is the best cook on the Island. He escaped from Jamaica a few years ago; and he has been blessing us with full stomachs ever since."

"Well Black Caesar has broken his chest, and has me cooking for an army today. I've got your favorite curry chicken, and the biggest red snapper you've ever seen. Come see and I'll set you up with you some conch soup."

"Get that ready and we'll be back," Adams said. "I want to finish showing her the island."

"Yeah man, do your ting!"

Adams walked Ijeoma down every dirt road in the village. She saw houses, more women with hard looks on their faces, a few older people and more rough children.

"So why do you all call him Coconut?" Ijeoma asked. "Because he is hard on the outside and soft on the inside?"

"No, because his a fierce fighter," Adams said with a smile. "He earned his name because he is dark like chocolate, and fights like a nut."

"Really? He doesn't look like a fighter."

"I am joking. I don't know, I never asked. Everyone here has taken nicknames. My mother named me after my grandfather; so that's why I haven't changed mine."

They reached a secluded lake, surrounded by large smooth rocks with a waterfall in the back.

"Here you are my African sister," Adams said, "you can bathe here. I will return in an hour."

*　　　　*　　　　*

Kwame and Williams were sitting across from each other in Coconut's bar, talking to Black Caesar. Both had plates of food in front of them. The crew members of Ijeoma's ship, and the other ships filled the rest of the bar. And there were some white pirates as well.

Ijeoma and Adams had just entered the bar, when Coconut rolled out a large barrel. Black Caesar stood and raised his glass. "As the Buccaneers say: ahoy, matey here be your rum! And listen up all you new pirates! Grab a mug and fill them full of some of this good Trinidadian rum!"

"All you scallywags raise up your drinks! I want to say a toast to our new friends. It was just a couple days ago when we found you drifting. We thought you to be lost booty, from a ship gone waste from scurvy. But when we walked onto the ship there you were—blimey!"

Black Caesar eyed his audience. "See, I've learned one thing on the seas and in this war. That is to expect the unexpected. That's what my mother told me. And she be one of the strong black women who fought in the war of Haiti. What she told me, was to also enjoy your goods times, for they are far and few between."

"So drink up Ijeoma and all you successful revolutionaries, for this be a good time. Eat all the oxtail and jerk chicken you can. I will have Coconut make some cod fish for your journey back. Maybe I get him to throw some ackee in with that cod fish for you."

It was late night when Caesar walked Ijeoma back to her ship. He handed her a cup of coconut water. They walked slowly and Ijeoma took in the night sky. She heard every word Caesar spoke but saw little of his face.

"The stars are the same as in my village," she said. "They just seem to be twisted."

"You have all the makings of a good navigator," Caesar replied. "A good Pirate captain can see the sky, as a hawk sees the earth. To the royal fleet's navy men, the sky is just darkness. It is of no use to them. It's as if the stars were black. But the moon and the stars are what guide us."

"The blackness others fear is what we must learn to use. The sky never changes, only your place underneath. If you can learn to read the blackness, you will have an advantage over those who only know how to chart their course by the sun."

"My father read the sky to tell when to plant," Ijeoma said softly, "and when to fish but never for travel. This is new to me. Will you teach me?"

"Adams my first mate has offered to lead you back to whist you came. You can learn from him. He can read both the black sky, and the navy sun charts like the ones found on your ship. He will be a great loss for us. But I send him in hopes he will influence you to return, and wage war with us here in the Caribbean."

Ijeoma turned her eyes toward the captain's voice. "I thank you for your kindness, but do not under estimate the war in my land and my usefulness there. If you like, you can follow us and take our ship back with you."

"Your wisdom and foresight continues to amaze me," the captain answered. "However, I must decline. Your ship is yours, and you must decide its destiny. And as for Africa, I will not journey there until I have won this war. Africa to me, is where we all came from. And to go there, may only boil my rage over to as where I could not control it. I allow myself only short trips here to Black Island. I fear if I stay away from the water-war, I will loose my edge. These robbers have learned to fear my black sail. And I never want them to stop."

*   *   *

Black Caesar's men carried the last of the water barrels on to Ijeoma's ship. Kwame and William pulled the plank back up on the main deck. Ijeoma stood beside Adams, who stood at the wheel.

"Weigh anchor!" Adams yelled. The former kidnapped captives, pulled the heavy anchor out of the water and the ship shook free. They were all in better shape than when the first arrived on the black pirate Island.

Ijeoma waved to Caesar and Coconut who stood among the trees lining the beach.

Chapter Six: Return of the dead

The African coast was unusually calm— almost welcoming as Adams steadied the ship for the traders port. He was wearing a shirt he had taken from another Dutch ship they robbed. The shirt made him look like a person suited for the trade across the Atlantic.

The trader's dungeon's rear gate opened wide. William stood at the edge of ship on port-side. He was dressed in the high fashions found in the captain's cabin. Ijeoma and Kwame stood out of sight inside the ship. William walked out with his shoulders arched back while leaning back on his heels as he walked to shore.

A white man met him as he stepped off the ship. "Greatness, captain! We had not expected your return so early. We have only a few slaves for you at this time."

"Is that so? Let me speak to who's in charge!" Williams replied haughtily. "Else I'll have to go out to the jungle and find my own slaves."

The man led William in to the dungeon, and had a mulatto slave fetch him a cup of water. "I will trust sitting here is okay? Captain ah—"

"The name is Captain William! And this is not acceptable! I will have my laborers teach your half-whites how to serve a drink."

"Very well then. Please wait here. I will wake the Governor, and tell him of your arrival."

*   *   *

Kwame stood facing the ship, while Ijeoma's back faced the interior of the fort. She concealed her musket, as she looked out the main gate toward her village.

She'd hoped to spot a few children playing or even a woman washing clothes along the beach but so far there was nothing. She smiled as she listened to William continue his slave trader impersonation.

"I'm sorry you had to wait," the governor stammered. "If I have known—"

"Spare me your excuses! Your aide has informed me that you have no slaves for me!"

"I have only a few, who I've kept for my personal use." He winked at William. "You know fornication!"

William regarded the governor haughtily. "Let me see them. You may satisfy your quota if I find them of interest to me."

"I assure you that with all of the goods we have stored here, your trip will not be a loss."

"Just show me these women."

The pudgy governor motioned to the men around him. Young girls in torn clothes, were pulled out of each of the rooms of the dungeon's upper area. The girls moaned and sighed as they were showcased to William.

Ijeoma peeked through the corner of her eye as she looked for Aneesa. Her anxiety grew as she did not spot her sister.

"She is not here!" Ijeoma said as she turned around. She pointed her musket at the governor. "Remember me!" she flipped the long gun around catching the chubby man under the chin.

Kwame stepped aside and pointed his gun at rest of the men. More men from the ship rushed through the port door. Adams came in and picked up the governor and held him in front of William.

William spit in his face. "You disgust me! Death is too good for you! But is a gift I will gladly to bestow upon you today!"

Ijeoma pulled William back, pulled a knife from her side and raised it to the governor's face. "Where are the rest of the girls? You took my sister!"

"I will not cooperate with you savage!" the man snarled, as he spit out blood.

"I expected you would say that! Let's lock this uncooperative barbarian up!"

Ijeoma grabbed the man up, and threw him in the same dark cell she was once held in. The rest of the white men and mulatto slaves were thrown in there as well.

Ijeoma and Kwame searched the rest of the dungeon. It was in the governor's very own room where Ijeoma found Aneesa and two other girls. They were weak and thin, lying on the floor in a corner of the room on blankets.

"Kwame!" Ijeoma yelled. "She's here!"

*   *   *

Adams, Kwame and Ijeoma crossed the road leading to the center of her village, each one carrying a young woman. Ijeoma was holding Aneesa. They saw no men when they entered the village they only saw children and women.

The women were busy crushing meal in large mortars, sweeping floors and sowing fishing nets. When they saw Ijeoma they all dropped what they are holding to greet Ijeoma and her crew.

Ijeoma's mother ran over and embraced her. "Oh momma I am so glad to be back home!"

"I thought you and your sister drowned fishing!" Ijeoma's mother fell to the ground and wrapped her arms around Aneesa's head.

They carried the young women to a house where others brought water, and herbs to nurse them back to health. They removed their clothes and cleaned them, combed their hair and brought in clothes for them. The men who had come with him, bathed and then joined the villagers.

While the girls rested, Ijeoma's mother brought them bowls of soup and ushered Ijeoma out to the central area; to have an audience with Queen mother Asantewaa and the other women of her village.

*   *   *

Aneesa faced the Queen Mother while behind the Queen, sat the people of her village. "Nana Yaa Asantewaa, we would like to inform you of the devils we have been trading within the dungeon on the shore. This man here," she pointed towards Adams. "He is from across the water from a place called Virginia. He is not from there although he was born there. His parents were from here."

"They were kidnapped and not traded as we have been made to believe." Ijeoma looked around and saw she had everyone's attention. "My sister and I were fishing with Kwame and his brother when we were kidnapped, and Kwame's brother, Kojo, was killed." Ijeoma now spoke loud enough for everyone to hear.

"We were taken to their dungeon, and Kwame and I were separated from Aneesa. We were chained and dragged to a ship, where we met other black people from different tribes. On the ship our white captors tortured us. Afraid they would kill us, we fought back and won. Captain Black Caesar, Adam's captain, helped get back here."

"Your story is familiar to one I heard as a child," the Queen Mother said. "It was of the Europeans who first came here. The Europeans said it was not true, and we believed them. They built these big trading castles. But there is so much emotion in your voice as you speak, I am compelled to believe you."

"Oh, Queen my story is true!" Aneesa cried. "When we came back, we tricked the white men at the dungeon into believing we were one of their ships! Please come with us we have the men locked away in the cells they locked us in."

Queen Mother brought a few men with her to inspect the dungeon. William opened both of the large doors. But the dungeon had been cleaned! There was a wooden sign over the cell she'd been held in, barrels of grains and crates full of Arabian treasures just—like in the captain's cabin.

Ijeoma introduced the Queen Mother to William, and he bowed. "Greetings Queen."

"I have brought my Queen here so she can see for herself the harsh treatment we endured." Ijeoma said. "Queen Mother Asantewaa this is William, a good white man. He was on the ship with us as a reporter to a group in England, trying to stop the Caribbean war."

"I am very pleased to meet you William. Now if what she has told me true, why is this happening?" Queen Asantewaa asked.

"Yes and there's much worse than what I have witnessed. I've interviewed the other Africans on the ship and some were volunteering on what they thought was a missionary trip while others were tribal war captives. But I have not met one person who deserved this inhumane treatment."

"Well William we plan to deal with these men with our justice process. Do you have a problem with that?"

"Not at all. In England, none of these men would escape the verdict of a public hanging for what they were a part of."

Ijeoma stepped into the open area of the dungeon and looked around, this time searching for evidence. She ignored the screams from inside the holding cells. Then Ijeoma walked Queen Mother around and showed her every part of the large dungeon. She opened the cell and dragged the fat, white man who had been known as the governor out. He was now an even sloppier mess.

"Oh, you can throw people end here but you can't handle it yourself!" Ijeoma sneered.

She raised the governor's head with her gun, and Queen Asantewaa walked in his line of sight. "You come to us sickly and hungry! We feed you and cure you of your plague and this is what you think you can do to us! You are a devil of a people and you will not get away with this!"

Queen mother Asantewaa threw her robe off of her shoulder, cocked back her hand and punched the governor square in the eye. The governor fell from Ijeoma's hold. As his face crashed to the ground, a gun went off.

The white men who had captured Ijeoma and Kwame, were now triple the small number of men Ijeoma and the Queen brought with them. "Listen you niggers," one of them snarled, "Now just what do you think you are doing here?"

They quickly filled the dungeon and tried to disarm Ijeoma's crew. Ijeoma reached for her musket but it wasn't there. She then reached for her knife. But by the time she had it in her hand, the barrel of her kidnaper's rifle knocked her on her back.

It took only a minute for a full out riot to break out. Even Queen Asantewaa displayed her fighting skills. She tossed a man over her shoulder, and then stabbed him in the chest with his own knife.

The governor muscled up the energy to tackle William. The men exchanged blows falling into crates. Kwame was fired at, and had to flip behind a barrel of grains to avoid getting shot again. As the slaver reloaded the rifle, Kwame raised the crate over his head and dropped it on the man.

Just then two other traders jumped him. Adams ran to Kwame's aid, but was hit in the head with a long piece of wood. Ijeoma was pinned to the ground and could not free herself.

Queen mother was finally overwhelmed by two attackers. Adams and Kwame were being subdued, William had gashes on his face making his vision blurred. And Ijeoma was now held up against the wall by two of the head captor's men.

"What was going on here?"the white slave runner sneered. "You are quite a feisty group! You all will make excellent slaves on the plantations of the Caribbean! Oh you may have a lot of fight in you now, but we have ways of breaking you! You may have figured out what we are doing, but you will not live to tell anyone!"

"Take these jungle monkeys out to the water and shoot them." Queen Asantewaa's escorts and Ijeoma's crew were taken out through the ocean side door of the dungeon.

The governor grinned. "Leave these few in here with me!" he gestured to Ijeoma, Kwame and Williams. "Lock them in the breaking room. . . I'll show you what I did to your sister tomorrow."

* * *

"Hey what is taking so long?" yelled the head captor. Hearing no response he walked out of the back door. As soon as he turned the corner, he was grabbed in a tight choke-hold. Coconut and three pirates were holding five of the captors. Coconut held a knife to the neck of the head slaver, and walked him back to the dungeon door.

The other slavers turned to run out of the front doors, and were met by Black Caesar and the rest of his pirates.

"You jungle—!" the Captor said, as he was shot in the head.

Before the body hit the ground, Black Caesar was blowing smoke out of the barrel of his pistol. "Ooowh, oh, oh! I have heard enough from these White men away from Africa! I do not wish to hear the speak when I'm in my homeland!"

Kwame grabbed the two men holding Ijeoma, and threw them to the floor as Adams did the same.

William delivered a fatal blow to the governor. He then turned to Queen Mother Asantewaa. "Shall we skip your justice process and decide their fate right here?"

Black Caesar flipped open his long coat and bowed to Ijeoma and the rest of the Africans with her. "Black Caesar is pleased to make your acquaintance. Now, let's see the beautiful land Ijeoma told me so much about."

Chapter Seven: Rise of the Black Star

The dungeon was very difficult to clean. The blood and tears of the many Africans who had been held there, had merged with the structure. The tribesmen and women scrubbed the walls and floors for hours, before they join the Enstoolment ceremony.

They rushed out of the building as the sun began to set. Others who were burning the last of the white captors' bodies, quickly finished what they were doing.

Just outside the large structure, Ijeoma and Black Caesar sat atop of two wooden carved stools. They were surrounded by Kwame, Williams, Adams and the entire village.

In the center, stood the Queen Mother Asantewaa and another woman, the spiritual leader. The spiritual leader dusted both of their heads with powder.

"Ah Shay!" the spiritual leader said.

"Ah Shay!" repeated the audience.

On the left side were drummers and dancers, and across from them were the village children. Ijeoma's mother and sister were led into the circle, by men dressed for war. They sat across from Ijeoma and Black Caesar.

"You have displayed nobility to our people," said the Queen. "From this day forward you will be appointed representatives. This Enstoolment will grant you entry into our place in the here ever after."

Queen Asantewaa stretched out her hand to Black Caesar, and he nodded respectfully. "You, Black Caesar are truly the real fighter of our distant tribe. The story of your life is that of a divine prophecy." She turned her head toward Coconut sitting next to the drummers. "And your cook, Coconut is skilled with a knife in all of its uses." Coconut offered a wide smile back and nodded his head.

"Sister Ijeoma your fearless leadership is historic. Your happenings were not an accident." Everyone cheered and the drummers played louder. The dancers danced a circle around Ijeoma and Black Caesar. And the men dressed in battle garb, lifted them in the air.

They were carried to the shore followed by a parade of villagers. The tall ship which was first where Ijeoma thought would be her tomb. . .But later became the place she would become a leader.

The spiritual leader threw dust on the ship and turned to the audience. "Ah Shay!"

"Ah Shay!" the audience repeated.

Queen Asantewaa stood between the audience and the ship. She turned facing the ship. "Let this vessel be used, to carry our sea warriors to this war in the Caribbean. Let this ship's canons blow holes in all ships who stand in its way. Let this ship's hull protect our warriors from all who seek to destroy it."

Ijeoma stepped forward and stood next to Queen Mother. Her body was tense with focus, on the importance of the ceremony. She longed to look at Kwame, but she maintained her composure. This was something she had never dreamed of! Her father had taught her to honor those people, enstooled into greater responsibility. Now she was given greater responsibility herself.

"Ijeoma what name to you give this ship?" Queen Mother asked.

"It will be called The Black Star. Night without stars strike fear in the hearts of those whom we fight. So I will use this ship to do the same."

"Who here will assist our new sister in her efforts to make war at sea?"

Kwame stepped forward. "I will, Queen mother."

"And what is it that you will make your worth?" the Queen Mother walked in front of the strong young man.

"I will protect her from harm at the cost of my life."

The spiritual leader then flicked powder over his face.

"Ah Shay!" the spiritual leader said.

"Ah Shay!" repeated the audience.

"Are there others who will aid?"

Adams and William stepped forward. The men shook nervously, and held expressionless stares on their faces.

"You need not be so tense. We are your people now. You need not fear us," the Queen Mother said as she put her hand on William's shoulder. William still held a deadpan face.

"Relax, you have both displayed your commitment." Then the Queen Mother shook him a little, and he responded with a small smile. "Good. Now, you are from the land of the people we make war with. You know the stories of pain and suffering. I expect you to make Ijeoma's efforts precise and efficient. Use what you have learned to take our ship The Black Star to the heart of these people, who use race as their battle lines."

"William Clarkson you are a master of disguise and communication. I anoint you linguist. You are to assist Ijeoma in all areas of communication." She walked in front of Adams. "Brother Adams, we are glad to have you returned to your motherland. See to it, that this is but the first of many trips here. I anoint you navigator."

"Who else?" she said.

Out stepped twenty-five other men and women. They were a mix of villagers and people who had fought for freedom with Ijeoma. They were all anointed with powder by the spiritual leader.

After being sprinkled with powder, Ijeoma's enstooled crew all shouted: "Ah Shay!" over and over. . . they danced and cheered throughout the night.

*   *   *

Ijeoma stood on the main-deck her ship, The Black Star, and waved as Kwame lead the crew in the raising of the anchor. Queen Mother Asantewaa, her mother and Aneesa looked on from the shore. The dungeon now flew a flag with a black star on it, identical to the flag on the ship.

"Everything Irie!" Coconut cried from further out to sea, on the deck of Black Caesar's ship.

"It's all good my brother!" Ijeoma yelled back. As the ship floated into the ocean Kwame joined her on the main-deck.

"We are in the hands of Yemayaa, and she will protect us now," Kwame said.

"I'm just glad she will not be protecting the traders," Ijeoma said.

William stood next to Adams, as if he was helping him steer the ship.

"You do not need to be so close to me," Adams retorted. "I think I know how to get back to the Caribbean."

"Who said we were going to the Caribbean? Have you heard about Sara Bartmann?"

THE END

The American Gangstress.

"Jeremiah please we are tired," the woman said. Her voice was cracking and her breath wheezed. "The children are dragging their feet. We must rest."

The woman was running down a dirt road pulling along two children one each arm. The children one a boy and the other a girl looked to be nine and ten years old. They were sweating and breathing heavy. It was late evening around nine pm and the August heat had even the nights hot. The road cut through a thick forest in Southern Virginia, twenty miles east of an area called South Hill.

"We are just going to have to carry them," Jeremiah said as he approached them from down the road. "I ain't seen nothing down yonder. Sally we are just going to have to carry them. We come too far to turn back. We gotta keep moving. Lady Moses mussent be too far now."

"Shush now," Sally said. "Listen I hear something coming from back there." She pointed over her shoulder.

Jeremiah stopped talking as he reached Sally and the children. He closed his eyes and the sound of horse was in the distance. He pushed the group into the brush on the side of the road.

"Hush now. Sure enough someone's coming," Jeremiah whispered.

The horse steps got louder and the grinding of a wheel could be heard under the steps. The voices of men were also behind the horse's steps.

Jeremiah and Sally squeezed their children trying to hide them behind a bush that was too small to conceal all of their bodies.

Jeremiah would gladly die if it would guaranty the safe passage of his family. Living on the Blackridge Plantation was not the life he wanted for his children. He was saving up to buy his wife and children freedom but things changed after the loss of just one crop. George Peterson took all the workers money back after his father died. He was a nasty man and would make a mean overseer. It wouldn't be long before his brutal violence would end up killing one of the field hands and that would most certainly cause a revolt. Every revolt that Jeremiah heard about ended in a death for every Black family.

"This some of the best shine I've had in years," one the men riding on the carriage said. He was wearing jean overalls which were dirty and smelly. He only had a few teeth in his mouth. He stringy hair was matted and looked like it hadn't been washed in a month.

The carriage had a bench which could fit three but only an old black man sat there holding the rains for the horse. It was moving at a slow but steady pace. There were two white men riding in the rear bed of the carriage. Both of the white men had jugs in their hands.

"You drank enough of it I guess so. If I'd had enough money I'd buy all Mr. Boyd's moonshine," The other guy said. This guy was also wearing overalls but he had on a hat was a little taller than his partner. He had a long straggly beard and he spit flew out of his mouth as he spoke.

"Hey you see that?" the matted haired guy said. He hopped out of the carriage and grabbed a hunting rifle.

"Hey boy, stop this thing," the man with the beard said.

The black man driving the carriage slapped the rains down on the horse and pulled back on them causing the horse to stop. The bearded man jumped out of the carriage and exchanged his jug for a shot gun. The moon light shined through the trees casting enough light for him to see that there were people hiding behind the bushes. He joined his partner over at the bushes.

"Well look a here. Seems like we got ourselves some run a ways," the matted hair guy said. He pointed his rifle at Jeremiah. He shoved the end of the barrel under Jeremiah's chin. "Get your ass up boy."

Jeremiah stumbled in the road. Sally squeezed and the kids as the shot gun was pointed at them.

"Hey Roscoe," the man pointing the gun at Jeremiah said. The black man sitting in the front of the carriage turned around.

"Yessir," Roscoe said.

"Bring me some of that rope and tie this here run away up. We are going collect us a finder's pay for taking these here slaves back to their owner," the matted hair man said. He pushed Jeremiah to his knees.

"He brought us a gift." The bearded man stood with his shot pointed at Sally and her kids. "Stand up and let us take a good look at ya. Seems like we are going to be able to have little fun tonight." The man licked his lips as he sized her up.

Sally shivered as the white man stuck his dirty hand in her shirt and grabbed her breast. She held back any reaction to keep her kids from noticing what the man was doing to her.

"Please don't hurt my family. I'm a good worker. I can make anything you want from wood," Jeremiah said.

"Look here nigger. We don't need you making nothing for us. Roscoe here does everything just fine. You're goin back too whoever you belong to." The bearded man stepped back and allowed his slave to fix the rope around Jeremiah's neck. Jeremiah twisted his head trying to avoid the rope. Jeremiah was a big man about six feet and strong but he was no match for the rifle the bearded man was holding. He fell over on the ground as the metal gun caught him in the back of his head.

"Fix that rope real good. Ain't nobody gonna believe this big brute didn't fight back."

Roscoe did as he was told and tied a knot which choked Jeremiah enough that it made it hard for him to breath.

"Tie that rope to the back of that carriage." He jabbed Jeremiah in the jaw with the rifle causing Jeremiah to fall back. "Now fetch me my whip. I ain't use in a while. We gotta give this field hand some behavior marks."

"We're gonna show you what you get when you try running," the man with the beard said. He pushed the kids to the side of the road.

Jeremiah was turned around to face the carriage by Roscoe. The man raised his arm holding whip. Jeremiah's family looked on. Jeremiah looked over at his wife Sally. He was helpless and she knew that if he tried to resist the white men would do worse. She was afraid for her children. She knew Jeremiah would do want ever he had to save his family. She was prepared to risk her life and so was Jeremiah.

As the man began to swing his arm a leather strap wrapped around his wrist. He fell down from the jerk caused by the leather strap.

The other white man aimed his gun in the darkness but could see anything. He then turned his shot gun toward Sally and the children. The trees started to ruffle around him. Then a knife flew into the man's neck. His beard was so thick the only end of the knife was visible. The man grabbed his neck as blood started spraying out. He dropped his shot gun and screamed in pain.

"It's a ghost," the man holding whip said.

"A Black ghost. The Black ghost is here," Roscoe said.

The white man with the messed up hair untangled his hand and grabbed his rifle.

"How the hell is there. You better get from around here. Cause if I catch ya I shot you back to the darkness you came from." His hands shook while he panned the area with his rifle.

Sally grabbed the kids and ran to Jeremiah. By the time the reach him the white man with the beard shook. His body jumped off the ground by like two feet. His head swung from side to side. Low thumps came from where he was.

"Hey man what's going on?" the messed up haired white boy said as he held his gun toward his friend. "You alright?"

The bearded man fell to his knees and then over on his side. The shadows were thick on the side of the road. None of them could see clearly. Sally, Jeremiah and the kids huddled nervously next to the carriage. Roscoe and the white man holding the gun just looked on.

The breaded man's body slid around with his legs in the darkness. He screamed as his body was dragged into the night. His hollering could still be heard even though his body had disappeared. His screams got louder and softer. The white boy stepped closer and then all of a sudden the bearded man's flies out head first into the white boy with the gun.

The white boy dropped the rifle. He struggled to get from under his friend. His friend's limp body was heavy and awkward.

As the white boy with the matted hair crawled away the sound of another body came from behind him. He turned as fast as he could and a when he did a figure in a hood stood over him.

"These be my people. You won't be catching no run-a-ways tonight," a female voice said from inside the black hood.

The hooded figure swung the pole around in the air and brought it down on the head of the white man. The pole slapped the white man a few times. The white man crawled as fast as he could trying to get away.

"You can have them. Take all the niggas you want just don't hurt," the white man screamed. He crawled away from the hooded person with the pole and slowly climbed to his feet. His head bruises made his vision blurred. He wiped blood from his face and squinted his eyes.

"The best I can do for you cracker is give you the opportunity to go out swinging. Now raise your guard because I fittin to send you to join you friend in God's glory," the dark figure in the hood said.

The white man looked around searching for his rifle. Jeremiah, Roscoe, Sally and the kids looked on. Scared they didn't move fearing the hooded fighter's wrath.

The white man raised his hands in a defensive boxing stance. His clothes were dirty and blood stained. He had sweat trickling down the side of his face. The blows from the pole had left painful marks.

The hooded fighter stepped to the side and squared up in front of the white man.   Then the fighter stuck the pole on the road and threw the hood over it. The fighter wore a tight black suit which clung to the body. The fighter was now easy to see it was a black person and from the two bumps on the chest it appeared to be a woman.

"What. That's looks like a woman," Jeremiah said.

"A colored woman," Sally said.

"Now let's get this started I don't have all night," the fighter said.

The fighter walked around the white man and the white man shuffled his feet trying to follow.

"You're a gal! Ain't no way I'm going to lose a fight to a woman. Especially a nigger," the white man said. He threw a wild punch which missed the female fighter. He threw the blow so hard he stumbled forward.

The woman pushed the back of his neck down as the white man came forward. Even though the push was soft the man was of balance and fell face first into the dirt road. The man got himself up quickly.

"You say nigger like that's what we are," the woman said. She then chopped the white man in the front of his neck and the spun a round house kick catching the white man in the center of his head.

The white man fell back on the ground. He held his neck with both his hands. He rolled over and tried to get to the edge of the road.

The woman jumped on the white man's back and put him in a headlock. The man gagged and reached with arms back trying to grab her. Her grip was tight and she squeezed.

"Who's the nigger now?" Her grip was tight and the man tried to speak.

"Ah. Who?" the white man said.

"Looks to me like you are. Tell these people who the nigger is."

The white man clawed the road. He scratched and kicked but the hold was to good.

"I am."

"What. Who is the nigger?" the woman asked.

"I am the nigger."

"Louder," she said.

"I am the nigger, I am the nigger," the white man screamed.

The woman released the white man and the grabbed his head. She held it with one hand on the white man's forehead and the other on his chin. Then she quickly twisted the man's head breaking his neck. The man flew lifelessly to the ground as a puff of dirt filled the air over his body.

The woman stood and turned toward the group. "Now what are you doing on this road? I ain't not taking people on the Underground tonight."

Jeremiah pulled the rope from around his head and said "I heard the singing of steal away. Are you the one who will take us to freedom?"

"Yeah I was just joking with you. My name is Harriet, AKA the Black ghost and some call me Lady Moses," the woman said.

"Would you be able to take me to freedom?" Roscoe said. "I didn't mean to hurt these people."

"I have no problem taking you but you must first bury these bodies and then you must follow my rules. If you don't I'll kill you myself. It's freedom or death if you come with me."

The group stood and walked over to Harriet. Sally said "we want freedom and are willing to die for it."

THE CHURCH OF

GOD

&

SPACE

Chapter One   The Mission

Reverend Abraham Miller had everyone's attention as he issued his last prophecy. The United Nationalities committee on Global Governance meeting was packed. This year's summit was held in Jerusalem.

The entire world watched, and listened to Reverend Abraham's every word. "It was no simple task to disarm the world. It was a major accomplishment. Never before in man's history has every race of man embraced each other like this."

Reverend Abraham's solar system pendant sparkled in the lights. He smiled, turning his head to everyone as he talked. "Glory be to God. This is a day our Creator has dreamed of. It was not the might of any great nation, or backhand deal from any businessman or politician. It was the clarity of the Lord which made the nations of our humble planet see the light, and lower their weapons. The years of man conquering and destroying himself are behind us. Today we celebrate a planet free of nuclear weapons."

Long applause interrupted his speech. Everyone was clapping—Even Old Lady Mullings was cheering. She used to always tell me how she liked my smile. And that is was nice to see a beautiful white girl with a beautiful black man. She said we were the future of mankind.

I had long ago learned the power of the word of God, and the need for man to follow a Higher Being. Even seeing the entire planet get along was beyond my wildest dreams. The audience was more excited than Reverend Abraham. He seemed to channel the energy from the people, and send it to the God of the Heavens like a conductor. He was by far a master preacher: A man of God. While not allowing anyone to call him a prophet, he was the closest thing to one we ever had.

He continued his address, "We have mastered our Father's lessons. We are now the stewards of the planet God the Almighty has given us. Hallelujah!"

Even in a government meeting people's spirituality could not be contained causing the audience repeated, "Hallelujah!" People say there was a time when people separated their religion from their politics. In all my twenty-eight years I could not image hiding my love of God from anybody.

"We now insure every animal and plant is cared for in a way that is best for it. We have fulfilled our purpose for creation. We have now, by this fulfillment, acquired the responsibility to share the path to glory with the universe. It is no coincidence that we find another planet with life at the same time we have brought peace and harmony to our own. Glory be to God! We have also at hand the ability to travel to it, and reach out to them. At this very time, we have selected our missionary team; and are planning their departure on The Evangelist, our state-of-the-art spaceship, in six months.

"Forty years ago, when we formed this Church of God and Space, we could only dream of this day. Our Father in the heavens above will be pleased when we bring the gospel of Christ to his people on this new planet. We know that whatever aboriginal or primitive people we find there will be placed under the loving arms of our Lord and Savior.

"Oh Lord, we ask for you to bless this diverse group of humble servants who make up all of the variations of man that you created on this planet Earth; as they bring your plan for salvation to the people on this new planet. As always, you guide us through your son Jesus; who in the Book of Mark, chapter three, verse sixteen directs us, 'Go ye into all the world, and preach the gospel to every creature.'

"It is through the guidance of your son that we charge our first space mission with the same goals as our Earthly missions. We understand the goals to be no different than they were at the time they were written. One, Exalt the Name of the One True God. Two, Exemplify the Body of Christ. Three, Evangelize Unbelievers. Four, Educate Disciples. Five, Establish and build Churches."

My husband Kem and I hung on the eighty three-year-old pastor's every word. This missionary trip, our mission, was the product of his life's work. Pastor Abraham had worked every day of the forty years, building and laboring for the Earth to have one God. It was his idea to commission a multiracial and multi-religious team to re-translate the biblical scrolls. It was this team that developed the principles of our global faith, and collectively write the new Bible, simply called: *The Life Manual.*

We don't call ourselves Christians anymore, but we still follow Jesus' teachings. We simply call ourselves "Believers." In the early years, before other religions saw the light, we were called Inclusionists and Accommodationists. They made jokes of how Pastor Abraham, and the new Nicea council, made Buddha, Muhammad, and Olodumare saints. But it was a brilliant move, one of divine insight, to accept these great men as the prophets of God that they were.

Every religion was included in the unification process. Even followers of the Jewish faith accepted the message of Jesus. In the old days, everyone imagined and predicted a globalized government bringing order to the world; but it was a unified vision of God that did it. The Church of God and Space had temples in every city and village in the world. Pastor Abraham's message was broadcasted globally each week. Instead of fighting each other for one man to be king of the world, the Church of God and Space allowed God to rule.

Now, our crew of one hundred humans, representing all races and a wide spectrum of occupations, waited upon the assignment of a lifetime. The church's focus on the heavens had helped it to become the first church with a space program. Once the world accepted the Universal God, the exploration of space then became a mission to bring the message of Christ to all corners of the universe.

The planet Dogan had only been discovered ten years ago, through satellites and long range probes that also enabled us to recognize that the planet supported humanoid life forms. One particular image really resonated with me. It was of a woman, who appeared to be very strong and respected by her people. Her skin glowed a healthy, dark green. When I first saw her, it seemed like I'd traveled back in time. There were always stories about life on other planets, but who knew when we would find it? Now we knew, and I couldn't wait to meet them. What were they like? I couldn't imagine how they would feel when they heard the message of the Lord. I wanted to bring that to them. I felt that it was the ultimate act of kindness, and my heart beat faster every time I thought about it.

No major technology was detected on the planet, which had over an estimated million human-like lifeforms, but no electricity or cities. We would usher an entire race into the modern age. By our scientists' estimations, the journey to reach Dogan would take just over a year. I couldn't wait.

"Jodee, how do you feel? Do you think you'll miss Earth?" Kem's voice was warm and loving.

"No baby, not as long as I'm with you. Plus, doing God's work is a honor," I replied.

Chapter Two   The Departure

The alarm rang throughout the quad, signaling a call to attention. Although we were regular citizens, and not military-trained, Pastor Abraham said it was best to adopt a military structure for our trip. Our group assembled in the main briefing room. The old man was still in his pajamas and robe. He walked to the front of the room with a visible reluctance. Church aides stood by each of the doors.

Something strange was going on.

"Now, it is not my goal to break rules but what I'm about to tell you … Oh, forget about it! Who am I kidding? I have always followed my inspiration. So, let me get to the point. Due to some unforeseen changes in the immediate space forecast we have been asked to delay our departure."

All of us missionaries inhaled in shock.

"Now hold on—let me finish. Many of you may not know that I was diagnosed with prostate cancer, and have been blessed with extended life from our Father above, and a few chemo treatments. I believe the Almighty has kept me around to see you all off. We called you down here, Captain Blake and I, to inform you of the change."

Captain Blake walked to the front of the room. At seventy, he was our shinning example of discipline. His body was as cut as a twenty-one year old college athlete, but his voice held fifty years of military service. "Is everyone familiar with the Space Cannon defense system we have? As most of you were taught in school, it was created for keeping peace on Earth. However, that is just one of its uses. The other purpose is planetary defense. What do I mean? Well, after hundreds of years of pollution, our planet's atmosphere is not the same. Because of the changes in the Earth's energy, or what some scientists call the torsion field, our little planet has been bombarded with meteorites.

"The space cannon defense system has been deflecting these meteorites for the past thirty years, before some of you were even born. Recently we've tracked a large meteor heading toward Earth. Now we know the space cannon can handle it, but the debris from this meteorite will prevent the launch of our mission. For how long, I don't know. The last big meteor to come our way was only one-fourth the size of this one, and there was significant space rubble for over ten years."

Pastor Abraham took over, "We thank the Lord for giving us the knowledge of science to protect the planet he has given us to live on. Now, we could wait ten to thirty years to launch; but I may or may not be here even next year. God's will be done. So, here's my plan. The meteor is two days away. The space cannon will intercept it one day away. That gives us a window of less than twelve hours to send you missionaries off, so the ship will have enough distance to escape damage from debris."

The room burst into cheers. All of the missionaries had been selected, and our scheduled departure was six months away; but we were only halfway through our space training. Still, I'd felt I was ready two months ago. I was happy that Pastor Abraham, being a man of God, had faith enough to send us on our mission.

That night, Pastor Abraham held a mass wedding for couples that wanted an Earth-side ceremony before the journey. Everyone, including myself, called family to say our goodbyes. Being away for a few years wasn't the end of the world. I figured we would be back in no time. How hard would it be to civilize some primitives? With our planet fully managed, we were perfect examples of God's will.

The last of our food pills, medications and supplies were loaded into the ship, and everyone finished boarding. Kem was smiling ear-to-ear when Pastor Abraham anointed him the mission's guidance leader.

"Young sister Jodee, please be the support our brother Kem needs to be a good leader. Go with God: He will guide you."

Our blast-off was smooth. I was only a little queasy. The simulators were pretty good, but nothing could duplicate a real lift-off. Space was not as dark as I thought it would be. The first day into our journey, we all gathered to watch the space cannon system blow up the meteor. Our ship had large observation decks, and Captain Blake had the event broadcast on all of the ship's monitors.

"You know Jodee, I am very happy about this journey. I feel the power of the Lord flowing through me. Seeing our planet from out here, it looks like a trophy—like a monument to our achievements. When we reach Dogan, I will be proud to say I'm from Earth. Can you imagine what it will feel like when we bring somebody from Dogan back to Earth? How do you feel?" Kem asked.

"I can't wait to get there, either," I said. "Maybe they'll have something better to eat than these food pills."

"Don't worry my love, the food pills are only supplements. There's a large supply of dehydrated and preserved food as well. Matter of fact, restaurants from all over the world supplied us with meals. We can dine like gourmets every day for five years if we want."

"Thank God!" I gave Kem a hug. "You know, I'm okay with the food pills. I was just checking because I heard other girls complaining." I kissed him on the cheek just as I saw a projectile shoot out of the space cannon. "Wow!"

The missile looked like a paper clip, but was half the size of the ship we were in. It was amazing how something you could see so clearly could be over a day's travel away. The closer the missile and the meteor got to each other, the faster my heart beat.

Then, just like in the movies, the two objects collided.

The collision sent a beautiful shower of colorful fragments into the space around it. The radiant cloud shower provided a perfect background for our celebration. Everyone on the ship cheered in relief—knowing that our dear planet was safe. Sounds of joy could be heard from all parts of the ship.

Kem, our newly christened leader, seized the moment to offer us some spiritual guidance. He grabbed the ship's communications mic and spoke from his heart. "Behold my beloved children of God, hailing from the great planet he created named Earth. We have just witnessed the power of God, through the science he has taught us. I ask you to use this moment to close your eyes, and take this time to thank our Father. Please join me in prayer."

The entire ship went silent as my beautiful husband said the most inspiring words. He was truly a gifted orator; maybe even as good as Pastor Abraham. While listening to his words I nodded my head, and absorbed the magnitude of what we'd just witnessed. I could not imagine Earth being destroyed. Now that this threat was past, I began to process everything that had been at stake. The Earth could have been destroyed. Crazy. I let those thoughts float through my mind, as I listened to my husband pray.

Chapter Three   The New Mission

Once the cloud dissipated, we were able to see something we'd missed in all the praying, and celebrating: Large chunks of the meteor still heading toward Earth.

I grabbed Kem, and winced as two huge rocks looked like they world narrowly miss Earth. Closing my eyes, I prayed under my breath, "God, please don't let the Earth get hit by a fragment of the meteor!"

Before I could finish, Kem jumped, and I heard him scream, "Oh my *God! No!"*

I didn't even have to open my eyes to know what had happened. I just hugged Kem, and kept my eyes closed. I couldn't bear to look.

The next few days, no one on the ship talked much about what happened; in fact, the whole ship was eerily silent. Kem said the impact of the fragment didn't destroy Earth completely, but it may have destroyed all life, like the meteor that destroyed the dinosaurs. Captain Blake couldn't tell for sure because the cloud covering the Earth prevented accurate readings.

Kem and Captain Blake called an assembly, and we gathered solemnly to hear our next steps.

Captain Blake looked like he hadn't slept since the disaster. "I know it's hard, but we need to continue on our journey. If we were to turn back now, our ship would not make it through the cloud. I know you're worried about your loved ones left behind. But by my estimates, when we return from Dogan in a year, things should be clear enough to navigate."

Kem asked everyone to focus on our journey, and our assignment. We were more than missionaries now, he reminded us, we were *survivors*.

Over the next few months, a gradual change took place. The missionaries went from stunned, emotionless robots, to an excessive, even reckless state. They threw big parties, got drunk and demonstrated godless behavior.

Not everyone partied. Others raided the preserved food stocks. They stopped taking food pills because they felt God had abandoned us, and science had let us down. They locked themselves in their cabins, and wouldn't come out. They felt we were being punished. They were mad at God. These people were more than angry. They were depressed.

I was somewhere in between. I understood what both groups were feeling. I couldn't understand why God had let the Earth be hit by the meteor. Truthfully, I tried not to think about the answer to that question. I differed to Kem. He was our spiritual leader now; so I let him guide me.

Kem tried to explain to both groups that they needed to stay focused. He shut parties down and had Captain Blake post guards outside the food storage compartments. No matter what they tried, it didn't work. The partiers just moved their parties, and the depressed people always found the food.

Kem was running around like a chicken with its head cut off, offering explanations and trying to counsel everyone. My husband was running out of things to say. He must have quoted every scripture in the Life Manual.

Six months into our trip, and Earth was no easier to see than Dogan was. Nothing had changed. The cloud still made it hard to see. On the ship, the party people were still finding ways to have their parties; and now they were wildly sexual parties. Some of the depressed people hadn't been seen in weeks.

Worry lines started to become permanent features on my husband's face. The stress of not knowing the condition of Earth put Kem in a constant state of tension. Honestly, I don't know how he was able to handle things so well without breaking down. The Lord had given him a special strength, and this mission was testing it. Even the other missionaries were no help. They, too, fell prey to the freak parties; or became anti-social, avoiding contact with anybody. All they did was eat and sleep. Kem worried about them all. I didn't know how much worrying he could handle.

One night, Kem and I were talking to Captain Blake, and First Mate Gohem Suri. Gohem was a very even-tempered young man from India. He never got excited, but even he looked strained when Dr. Richardstein's voice screamed through the com speaker, "Captain Blake and Pastor Kem, I need you to meet me in Level Three, Room 219 immediately!" Dr. Richardson was the head medical person.

I decided to accompany them to investigate the emergency. I hoped it was someone who only needed counseling, and maybe I could talk to them. I didn't want Kem to have to deal with something I could handle.

We arrived at Room 219, and Dr. Richardstein greeted us at the door. His eyes were red and it looked like he hadn't slept in a month.

"Hello Doctor, what seems to be the problem?" asked Kem.

"A woman called me down here, saying her husband suffered from severe headaches, dizziness, nausea, and he was constantly going to the bathroom."

"That sounds like sea sickness," Captain Blake said. He shook his head and squinted his eyebrows. "We have some pills they can take for that. I know you didn't call me down here for sea sickness."

"You're very correct. This is sea sickness, but an advanced case. I have found over twenty other people with serious symptoms like this. However, this man has developed advanced diabetes. His test results are conclusive."

Kem turned toward Captain Blake, and looked him in the eyes. "Excuse me. Did you say diabetes?"

"Yes, Pastor."

"But how would he have passed the medical exam if he had diabetes?"

"I don't think he had diabetes when he boarded the ship."

"We've only been aboard six months! How could he have gotten so bad so quickly?"

"Even in space, diabetes does not develop over this short period of time. You have to have a defective pancreas or a poor diet. This man was 100% healthy. Even then, I would accept one or two cases; but with this many people, a natural cause is highly unlikely. Onboard are several cases of severe obesity, and blood pressure so high, two passengers' kidneys failed entirely. One woman has even gone partially blind."

"What do you think is causing this?" I asked.

"I don't know for sure, but I think the space travel which is accelerating the symptoms." Doctor Richardstein's held a tearful glaze as he spoke, "Your always so caring Jodee, and you have a love for the facts. You love to question things like me. See, I don't deal in miracles or curses; I simply accept the cause and effects of human health. Remember my book was called: *God Wants You to Take Care of Your Body.*"

"Yes doctor, and you remember I loved it. I believe in self responsibility as well," I said.

"That's why it was the Lord's church who sent us on this journey. So, we have enough medicine to treat them, correct?" Kem said.

"Yes, but we need more than just medicine. We have to do something about this fast because we do not have enough insulin, anti-hypertensives, or other medicines to cover everyone on board. And there is nothing I can do for the obesity. Truthfully, I doubt if we'll last more than two months before people start having strokes and heart attacks. The food we have is all preserved."

"What's the problem with that?" Captain Blake asked. Now, even his voice had a little extra strain in it.

"Captain, these diseases might be accelerated; but they are no different than if they were to occur on Earth. It's the sodium, and crystalline carbohydrates: Sugar."

"I knew we'd have trouble when those recluses started raiding the food bins! They've endangered us all! What about the food pills?" Captain Blake said.

"There aren't enough food pills for everyone to have proper nourishment. And these people being effected are not just the lock-ins; they're not only the people who mourn in their cabins. Some of them are crew members and partiers. I've started testing people at random, and everyone seems to be at risk. I hate to tell you this, but it looks like many of us won't live to reach Dogan. Even if by some miracle we do live, we will all be in such bad health that—"

"Please, Doctor, I've heard enough. Thank you." Kem looked at me, and I hugged him. "I'll think of something," he said. "I must have some private time in my cabin. I must have a conversation with God. Only through the Father can we receive a miracle."

Chapter Four   The Rules of Space

Kem had locked himself in the Holy Sanctuary for four days when, in the middle of our rest cycle, the ship rocked and the lights flickered. I fell out of bed and ran into the hallway. Captain Blake's voice was barely audible over the screams and commotion. Our lack of space travel training was showing now more than ever.

"Please, remain calm! It seems a piece of the meteor that was heading toward Earth was pulled down our ship's path. There has been no damage to he hull, so please remain calm, and go back to your quarters! We are assessing the ship's damage, and Chief Engineer Raul will give a complete report in three hours."

I pushed my way through the chaos, and made it to the Holy Sanctuary. His empty food tray lay in front of the door, but Kem didn't answer my knock. I knew he was in consultation with the Lord, and I shouldn't interrupt him; but a meteor fragment had hit our ship and I needed comfort. I pounded in panic, and leaned against the door—determined to wait him out.

After a few hours I came to my senses, and made my way back to our cabin. It must have been my nerves, making me act so irrationally. I knew better than to interrupt a spiritual leader when they are seeking guidance from God. Pastor Abraham had taught us that, in the early days, prophets would go up on mountains to be in isolation, to hear the clear word of God. When Kem was ready, the Lord would return him to us.

Raul's voice suddenly blared through the intercoms, "The official condition of our ship is as follows: We have lost navigational control. While the hull is still intact, it has been weakened considerably; and I do not think it can sustain another hit. Understand the Evangelist is not a war ship, and thus has no guns; so, If it holds up until we reach Dogan, we will be lucky. Please understand, I am but a simple mechanic. My knowledge is of wheels, engines and physics; not the spiritual. My report is only mechanical in nature. Our spiritual leader, Kem, can explain our other possibilities. Pray to the Lord that our ship doesn't encounter any other obstacles. God bless The Evangelist and its crew. Chief Engineer Raul signing off."

After Raul's report, the rest of the night was relatively peaceful. As I sat alone in my room I did a lot of meditating on my own. I thought about my childhood as a Jehovah's Witness. How when I was in college, and my church joined the Church of God and Space, I lost my religion and became an atheist … How Kem's love and gentle words brought me back to the Lord.

Even though I was only away from the Lord for a semester, I was embarrassed that I had lost my faith at all. How could I question the realness of the One God? How could I question the Truth? Kem helped me understand that I was no different from any other believer. But now, without him, I felt myself slipping again.

Why should I run to disturb Kem? He was perhaps the only spiritual leader left. He held an enormous responsibility; one that I could never imagine. Was I really a believer? Did I really trust in the Lord? Did I know with all my heart I was in the hands of God? And that our ship was safe?

I fell asleep with my questions unanswered.

For four weeks, Kem conversed with God. It all ended with an announcement that he was coming out of the Holy Sanctuary. People crowded the hallway to see our leader emerge. We knew he had the answers to all of our questions. We knew God had given him the guidance that would lead to our salvation.

The door slid open, and Kem stood on the threshold. He looked very thin and weak. His hair was matted, and it looked like he had aged years in a matter of weeks. I wasn't sure whether to run to him and embrace him, or to remain in my position as a follower.

"I bear a message from God," Kem said.

"Praise God! *Amen!*" cheered the crowd.

"I would like to share seven new commandments our great Lord has given me for us. These new laws will replace all laws before them.

"One, you shall listen to the authorities, and follow their orders.

"Two, you shall accept the God of Earth as the Creator of man; and the God of Earth as the only God.

"Three, It is God who made man to create science for man's use.

"Four, It is God's will to use science to solve man's imperfections.

"Five, man must not eat animal flesh or plant, unless it is prepared to eat through science.

"Six, man must not steal from or murder other men.

"Seven, it is the Devil who is trying to stop man with disease; and only science will save man from it."

Kem's divine message was just what we needed. The disorderly behavior and food raids quickly subsided after he shared the new laws of God. While the sickness continued, people started to feel better. We had only two months until we would reach Dogan. I was a little surprised how easily the discipline Kem displayed flowed throughout the ship. Only two or three people had to be punished by the captain. Helen Vester refused to take her diabetes medication and was sent to a room near the engine room, which was made to hold those who didn't abide by the rules.

Kem had never been a very physical lover, but since his four-week conversation with God he barely touched me. We tried to make love—or I should say I tried— and he refused my advances. I asked myself why it was so hard for me to accept the conduct of a full believer. I feared my lust and displaced love would be my downfall. If I couldn't learn and assume the behavior of a true believer, I would lose my Kem. I believed I was already pushing him away. I asked Kem to pray for me, so God could help me get back on the path.

Twelve months in space, and we were all stronger believers. Kem's face had put on a little weight, and he almost looked the way he did before he locked himself in the Holy Sanctuary.

The docking bay was full of people as Kem spoke, "Let as send our brothers and sister off into God's universe in peace. David Richmond,

Hayrick Pacculli, Dow Wen, and Helen Vester have made their transitions to heaven. Let us mourn our lost missionaries. We recommit ourselves today to God's new laws in their memory, as we continue on our journey.

"We started this journey with one hundred servants, and we have lost only four. Let us pray for all of our sicknesses to be healed, as only our Father can heal us. Each one of us has suffered poor health, and the pain of seeing our home planet damaged. Even our ship has been damaged, but still we push on. We will finish our task. With the strength of the Lord Almighty, we will make it to Dogan; and it will be the new home of our Lord's children."

With that, he pushed the button to eject the four corpses from the ship.

A week later, a voice came over the intercom, "Attention all missionaries, we are now orbiting the planet Dogan. All wishing to view the new land may do so by coming to any of the observation decks." Captain Blake's words were a harmonious melody, after having to launch so many of our fallen brothers and sisters into space.

I immediately ran to look at the destination. Dogan was a dark green, almost black, with big blue oceans, and multicolored fields: The way Earth was described before the years of war. There seemed to be no cities or even artificial light. As our ship approached, I could see no buildings or any metal structures.

It was day when we landed. Captain Blake gave us a soft landing, so soft you couldn't tell our ship was damaged. I followed Kem to the control room where Captain Blake was making the final tests on the planet's atmosphere.

"How does it look, Captain?"

"Everything is perfect—in fact it's so perfect, some of the levels are off the charts."

"See that, Jodee? The Lord has given us a planet even more perfect than our own," Kem said; then he kissed me on my forehead.

"It appears our arrival has not gone on unnoticed. Look there … A few of the natives are coming out to meet us," Captain Blake observed from a screen. "It seems to be a woman and five little ones."

"Please open the door, and Jodee, please come with me to greet them."

"Pastor, will you need a security escort?"

"No, not at first. Have them stay inside the ship. Only Jodee and I will go first."

The maintenance men who acted as our security followed us to the edge of the door. As Kem and I walked toward the Dogan native woman, I recognized her as the strong woman from the satellite pictures. She was just a little taller than me, and in fantastic shape. All of the children stood behind her. Except for their dark green pigment, they looked just as human as us.

"Greetings. We are from the planet Earth," said Kem.

The woman made a bunch of noises, and funny movements with her mouth. She looked back at the young ones behind her, and continued with the noises and funny gestures.

Kem spread his arms wide, and looked up to the sky. "We bring you greetings from God Almighty."

The woman seemed to understand him. She walked toward Kem, looked him in the face and touched his arm. Then she turned, and looked at me. I froze, and could not move. I felt a overwhelming sense of eager curiosity, and wasn't a bit fearful. She walked toward me. The security gripped their maintenance tools, which also doubled as weapons. Kem waved his hand at them, and they lowered the tools.

The woman caressed my cheek. It reminded me of the way animals sniff each other when they first meet. She took my head in both of her hands, and touched her forehead to my forehead. I felt an electric vibration from my head down to my toes. It felt *refreshing* … She backed away. I shook my head, and everything went foggy.

Chapter Five   Meet the Dogans

The sound of voices roused me. One was Kem's, "Honey, are you okay?"

The other voice was not one I had heard before, "Hello, I am Landsong, of the Jeffe. Welcome."

When I opened my eyes, that voice was coming from the native woman. Her mouth was making the same funny movements, but now I understood her words.

"Hello Landsong, my name is Jodee."

Kem looked at me and said, "Tell her we are messengers from God."

This was another surprise because he never liked me to talk to people before he did. If he was mad or ticked off, he didn't show it. He was all business. I got a little twitch in my knee which I hadn't gotten since I had my first oral exam in freshman year. This time I wasn't just speaking for a grade I was representing the human race.

"We come bearing the good news of the Lord," I said in English. I wondered how she was going to understand me.

"God is welcome here as well. You have nothing to fear, Traveler Jodee. Please allow me to make a thought nexus with the rest of your travelers." She turned to Kem, and extended her hand to him. "Please tell God to place his head here, and I will make the nexus."

"Oh, he isn't God! His name is Kem, and he is our spiritual leader; our link to God."

I motioned for Kem to place his head in her hand. Kem called out all of the missionaries, and crew; and Landsong summoned more Jeffe people. Even the Jeffe children made nexuses. It wasn't long before all of the missionaries and Jeffe had a nexus made, and were able to communicate with the Jeffe.

The Jeffe people had no name for their planet; so we still referred to it as Dogan. Dogan was so beautiful with plants everywhere. It looked very much like prehistoric Earth. It had lakes of royal blue water, and grass fields of healthy green plants. There was multicolored fruit, and bright colored vegetables. The Jeffe themselves looked like plant people. Their skin was smooth. Their hair was curly, and their teeth were white and shinny, like the ivory from elephant tusks. They were all tall and fit. Most of the men had no facial hair. The women were full figured with large breast and round hips. While they all had common features they didn't look exactly alike.

Landsong herself had a warm and loving smile. She seemed to be and adult, but I could not tell her exact age. She had long thick hair shaped into a circle. Her nose was broad, and her cheeks popped out like she had golf balls in them. Her eyes were sweet and relaxing.

"Well, Pastor Kem, I have tested just about every plant in the area; and all of them are edible. In fact, they're healthier than the food on our ship. The antibodies in this one leaf is higher than in some of the medicine we have," Dr. Richardstein said, holding a big, dark orange leaf in his hand.

"Give God the glory. Tell Captain Blake to inform the congregation they can eat the fruit of the land, for it was by God's grace that we are here," Kem said.

Over the next week we ate the food of the Jeffe. It was the tastiest food I had ever eaten in my life. Kem made a point to stand apart from the other missionaries, in hopes of attracting the leader of the Jeffe. The Jeffe sat in circles, and it was hard to tell who the leader was or if they even had one. Blossom Catcher was the Jeffe who did most of the food preparation, Riverdance was the most active of the elders; and Running Sky seemed more like a handy man. Landsong seemed to be in charge of the children, and overall group management.

Blossom Catcher brought Kem and I food. The food had such brilliant colors, and the firmness of the fruit was like nothing I had eaten before. There were large green leaves, small brown peas, and dark orange things that looked like beets; but were soft on the inside. They had nothing to cook food in. The meal was completely raw and smelled delicious. I bit into what looked like a light blue pineapple, and let its juices run down my face.

Landsong was walking around greeting people when she passed us. "Landsong, please sit and join us," Kem said. "I would like to tell you about our Lord and God of the Universe."

"I would love to hear more about God. We do not have the word 'God' in our language. It is one of the many words you have brought to us. The other people who live here like the Wahhim, who live in the mountains, and the Kakkie, who live pass them, do not have a word like your word God. Other people who have come here from the sky have not either," Landsong said. "When we make a nexus, we do not learn meanings for words and concepts that we do not have in our language already. Please tell me about God."

"May I, honey?" I said.

"Yes, go ahead," Kem said.

"God is simple: The Creator of all life. He is our Lord and Savior. It is through the guidance of His divinely inspired prophets, and writers we are taught how to live our lives. Through accepting the guidance of His only Child, we can find salvation, and entrance into heaven."

"A man who can create life?"

"I'm sorry if I confused you, but God is not a man. God is the Creator."

"No, maybe I didn't understand you. Then, what *is* God?"

"What my wife is trying to explain to you is that God is in all of us, and even inside you. God is love, and his son Jesus is the light," Kem said.

"Is this God a person or a virus?"

"Let me ask you: How does the sun rise? Or what makes these delicious plants grow? Or gives a mother the ability to grow a baby in her stomach? Why, it's none other than God!" Kem said.

"Here on Jeffe, we know what created us is the union of all life. We do not have a man who created us. Our sun rises due to the rotation of the planet."

"It is beautiful that you feel that way, but we missionaries believe God is the Creator outside of what science explains. Science is just the creation of God; so even for that, we give God the glory. That union you speak of is God. We are saying the same thing; you just don't know it."

"But you call God a man who lives in the skies."

"God, the Father of all life, is in all of us. Look at these plants, and even the animals around us. God has made us in his own image to care for these other creations. Each one of us could have been born a tree, or maybe even a squirrel, but God made us men."

"Well, our way of thinking is this: God is everything for us. God is not something or anything, but everything. Plants and animals are just another form of our life: They are children and ancestors."

"Pastor, please come to the ship now. I need to show you something," Captain Blake said over the ship's exterior speaker.

"Landsong, I will continue this conversation with you about the glory of God in a bit. I must go to my ship now. We can continue when I return."

I wonder if Kem's comments had turned Landsong off. What if she didn't like the explanations Kem had given her? She certainly explained herself well. I understood what she was saying, better than what Kem said, and I was Believer.

"Jodee, your husband seems to be very closed-minded in his concept of life. Do you understand what I am saying to him?"

Her question caught me with food in my mouth. "Aahhh … what do I think? I was enjoying listening to the conversation your conversation. Kem is our pastor, our spiritual leader. He is the best person to explain God to you."

"So what are you thoughts on what I've said?"

"Well, I'm pretty much a believer in God, like all of us."

"Do you not understand my words? Kem seems to have a problem understanding them."

"I have not studied the Life Manual as extensively as Kem has, but maybe I can help you understand us. Okay, the Jeffe people, where do you believe you came from?"

"The ground, just like everything else," Landsong pointed to the grass beneath us. "Is not everything made of dirt and water?"

"Sure, but, we are not dirt. We have bodies. These bodies are the temples of God. He has made them for us to live in."

"But, where do we go after our life in these bodies ends? Back to dirt, right?"

"Yes, but who made the dirt?" I countered. "We are intelligent life forms. We are not trees."

"That does not matter to us. The Jeffe view all life as the same. All we know, and accept is that we are of the same make-up as everything here. We focus on what connects us, not what makes us different. Jodee, to us a tree is something we need to live. We eat the plants, and the animals to live. We have everything here we need. Just as a hand is different from a foot or an eye. They do different things and look different, but they are part of the same body. Our bodies take in these plants and animals around us, and go to make up our bodies."

I felt a soft hand rest on my shoulder, and turned to see who it was. Kem stood behind me with Captain Blake at his side. They both looked grim.

"I'm sorry ladies, I see you are still having an enlightening conversation about God. I hate to interrupt it, but we have a difficult problem; and we will have to leave this planet very soon. Landsong, I have some very bad news I have to tell you." Kem took a deep breath, and continued, "According to Captain Blake, the meteor that hit the Earth broke into smaller pieces; and now a large piece is headed toward Dogan."

"The meteor is large enough to destroy Dogan completely, because Dogan is much smaller than Earth," said Captain Blake.

"Oh no! I'm *so* sorry! This is *horrible*—I can't believe it! God certainly works in mysterious ways. First he sends us away from Earth on a mission to tell people about him. The Earth is destroyed. Then our people get diseases on the ship. We get here, and they are cured. Now *this!*" I said. "This is such a beautiful planet. Earth was our home, and we are its representatives. We may be all that is left of our people. What now?"

"Calm down, Jodee. It must have been in God's divine order that we came here. Since the food here is so abundant, Captain Blake said we can refill the storage bins; and we have enough space on our ship to carry the most important Jeffe. Captain Blake has spotted two other planets with sustainable atmospheres where we could go, but they will take at least a month to travel to. See Landsong, it was our God who brought us here; and it is through the greatness of our Lord that your people will be saved."

"That is strange, we have not felt anything. If our planet is in danger, I must consult our ancestors," said Landsong.

"Landsong, it's probably too far away for your people to have detected it. I only found it while making a routine scan of our home planet Earth. This meteor is still weeks away, but we only have enough time to make one trip. I took us a year to get here," said Captain Blake.

"Our God has blessed us with science. It is because of this science that we were able to escape the destruction of our planet and travel here. Now we can use the science God has blessed us with to save you all," said Kem.

"If something that dangerous is approaching us, then we may have to hold a collective. We will never abandon our home," said Landsong.

Chapter Six   Ancestors vs God

Kem walked around our temporary settlement, greeting fellow missionaries, making sure everyone was adjusting to Dogan. Running Sky, other Jeffe, and some of our missionaries built houses for us out of the clay; which lined their lake. I'd seen pictures of primitive Earth tribes living in caves and holes in the ground, and I would have never believed that a house made out of dirt and straw could be so cozy.

"Sister Katrina, you look so much better. It seems space didn't do you any good."

"Oh Pastor, I don't think it's space as much as it is this planet. I've been able to exercise in the fresh air, and eat fresh vegetables. Doctor Richardstein even took me off my diabetes pills, and said we could even eat the fruit because our systems were working again."

"Really? Praise God!"

"And praise this planet, and these people! Doctor Richardstein said this planet's food is better than anything our science has produced," said

Katrina. "Maybe those new laws were what God gave us for space, and He will give us something, while we live here on Dogan."

The next day, we accompanied Doctor Richardstein who was invited by Blossom Catcher to watch a Jeffe woman give birth. Landsong was just finishing up some sort of ritualistic activity, which had everyone having their palms pressed together. She said "I'm so glad you are joining. Blossom Catcher thought it would be a good idea for you to see this part of our culture. We are welcoming a new life. We just finished clearing the space."

The house was no different than the clay structures they built for us. It felt warm like a cabin in the mountains back on Earth. A couple was washing coconut shells, and dark leaves which got soft in the water. The dirt floor seemed not to concern them.

The woman giving birth was positioned upright in a large chair with a giant hole in it—sort of like a toilet. No pain showed on her face. She was even smiling and laughing with the people, and seemed to have no problem with us being in the room.

"Pastor, this is phenomenal! These birthing methods are ancient history on Earth, but never having experienced it in person, I find it breathtaking. Blossom Catcher is not just a cook she is a healer of some sort," said Doctor Richardstein.

Blossom catcher leaned under the chair, and the baby popped out in less than an hour. The woman giving birth only strained a little, like she was going to the bathroom, but she never screamed. Another Jeffe woman quickly cut the umbilical cord, and cleaned off the baby: A beautiful, dark green baby boy.

Kem was in a praising God stance with his arms raised up. He said, "God bless this new life. The miracle of childbirth is the same even here, in this world which does not know of His glory."

"Yes, the miracle of life is the same, but their simple birthing method makes it easier. On Earth, we let our love for science handicap us," said Doctor Richardstein. "Yesterday, I convinced Blosson Catcher to let me take neuro-images of the brains of several Jeffe men with the ship's portable MRI. I thought I was misreading the machine, but the Jeffe seem to utilize their entire brain. I even scanned a couple of our crew members to see if the machine was malfunctioning. It wasn't, but even our brain activity has increased since being on Dogan. I think it's because of the nexuses they made with us."

"Well, gather all the information you can, because in less than two weeks this place will be dust fragments; and once again we will be in the hands of God's graces as we travel to another planet. Captain Blake detected another meteor and this one is headed for Dogan. He expects it will destroy Dogan completely. I didn't tell you because I didn't want to take you away from your research. "

"*What?* I can't believe it."

"We have already told Landsong, and I will tell the rest of the missionaries later this evening."

"What will happen to the Jeffe people?"

"We will be able to take a few. We are already in the process of converting some of the storage compartments we used for food, to house as many Jeffe as possible."

Doctor Richardstein's eyes stared off into the sky.

"Doctor, are you listening?"

"Yes, yes. I am. I just can't believe this. Why would God allow this to happen again?"

"Doctor, the Lord works in mysterious ways. Ways we do not always understand. Many times we never understand why our Lord does what he does. We just know that our Lord loves us, and there is no better place to be, but in His good graces."

"What did the Jeffe say about leaving their planet?"

"I can't answer that question. They seem to have no desire to live anywhere else but this planet. They have no concept of God or interest in the heavens. As far as I know, they won't do anything except stay here, and be destroyed with the planet. However, I do believe God sent us here to save these people. There are other groups of people who live on Dogan but God brought us to the Jeffe."

"But this can't be! The Jeffe have a knowledge of the body which is superior to ours. Even this planet, Dogan, is like pure medicine to us. Why would God destroy it? What did Landsong say?"

"She said she was going to consult her ancestors. I don't need to tell you about the purpose of prayer. Without the focus of God, prayer is simple meditation. I'm afraid Landsong cannot mediate herself or the Jeffe out of this situation. No matter how much of their brains they use, only God's grace can save them, as it did us."

"Landsong did say she would hold a collective of some sort," I volunteered. Until now, I had held my peace while they talked; but I felt my talks with Landsong gave me more to contribute to the discussion. I continued, in a more confident tone, "Maybe they do believe in God, but just call him by another name. Pastor Abraham always talked about how difficult it was to bring people together when they called God different names—like the Yoruba people of West Africa. Maybe a collective is how they talk to God, and we just have to spend more time with them," I finished.

"Honey, please leave the interpretation of God to me. This is different from the people of Africa, who were afraid of their conquerors' religion. That woman Landsong was very clear about what her and her people's beliefs were. You heard her yourself. Now you may want to believe something else, but what we heard her say was that they believe they come from dust.

The dust which makes up this planet. That doesn't sound like a different name for God. It doesn't sound like a God at all."

"Kem, I don't mean to argue with you; but I talked to her after you left and she said—"

"It doesn't matter, honey. We are missionaries: Here with a message from God."

"Pastor may I interject?" Doctor Richardstein said. "Talking to Blosson Catcher, I got the same impression as Jodee. Their practices are those of a religious people."

"Doctor, with all due respect, whatever their beliefs are, we have no time left to convince them now. Once Landsong is safe on the ship, and she realizes she can live without Dogan, she and the Jeffe will accept the Lord. On The Evangelist, they will have all the time they need to make a full transition. After they understand the message in the Book of Life they will thank us."

The next day, Kem held a meeting with all of the missionaries and the Jeffe. He and Captain Blake sat at the head table, with the rest of us sat facing them auditorium-style, not in a circle like the Jeffe do.

"Tonight I would like to thank our hosts, the people of the Jeffe tribe, for welcoming us to their planet. It was the vision of our founding father Pastor Abraham Miller, who was so inspired by the images he saw of this distant planet we call Dogan, that he recruited a diverse group of missionaries and sent us off.

"Unbeknownst to him, and everybody else on Earth, we would be more than just missionaries. Shortly after our departure, our planet Earth was severely damaged by a meteor. Our time here on Dogan has been better than expected. So wonderful, in fact, we thought this would be our new home. But by the grace of God, our stay on this beautiful, primitive planet will have to end. The same destructive force which brought an end to our home is headed this way. Captain Blake, head of our ship The Evangelist, is ready to take us, and a few of our Jeffe brothers to another planet; so our races may continue."

Captain Blake stood, and pulled out a piece of paper. "Pastor Kem has selected the Jeffe representatives; which we will take using the same criteria by which we were selected. Our ship is now ready for all of our missionaries to return to their cabins, and prepare for departure."

A few of the missionaries got up and started walking toward the ship, mostly those who had been running around raiding the food storage bins, and having wild orgies. All of Dr. Richardstein's patients remained seated.

Landsong rose, and walked to the front of the room. "We thank you, Pastor Kem and Captain Blake, for the invitation; but we will not be joining you on your trip. We will hold a collective tomorrow to consult our Ancestors, and we will be fine after that."

"With all due respect, Landsong, it is time for me to make myself more clear. A meteor is headed here, and will destroy your planet the way it destroyed ours," Kem implored. "We have to leave *today* in our ship to travel far enough to avoid being destroyed from the debris of the collision. No little prayer meeting with your ancestors will help you now. You must believe us and our God. Our religion is a religion of inclusion, and I think in time you would be able to understand our God; but we do not have that time on this planet. All we want to do is save you from total destruction,"

"Kem, you don't have to be disrespectful! Maybe they know something," I said. I looked at the other missionaries who were just sitting watching Kem insult these people who had help us so much. Even Captain Blake was silent. The Jeffe were sitting there so nice and polite, I wanted to speak up for them. I walked over from where I was sitting among the Jeffe, and stood where everyone could see me. "You're talking to them like it wasn't their lifestyle which helped heal us." Doctor Richardstein walked over to me, and put his arm around my shoulder.

"Jodee, *please.* You are losing your faith again—just like you did in college," said Kem. "Now, you need to get in line, and help divide these Jeffe people; and get the ones I've chosen in the ship so we can leave."

"Losing my faith?" I said.

"Yes Jodee, I knew you were not a true believer; but I didn't know you were such a bad apple. I thought my love would transform you."

"Not a true believer?" I shook loose from the doctor's embrace, and glared at Kem. "Maybe *I'm* the true believer, and your position has clouded your judgment. Maybe God brought us here to this beautiful planet to help us. Look around and see how this planet has healed our sick. It seems like just a blessing to be here. What makes you believe the Jeffe's ancestors can't help them?"

"Because there is only one God, and only God can help the Jeffe. Now stop wasting time; we can have this debate on the ship. Let's go."

"You can have the debate by yourself. Maybe inside your isolation room or somewhere, because I am staying here with Landsong and the Jeffe."

"What?" Kem was incredulous.

"Yes, Pastor," said Dr. Richardstein as he turned to both audiences. "I am too old for another long space journey. I want to live out my last days somewhere where I can be buried. I am also interested in the Jeffe, and I'm willing to give their idea a chance."

"If Dr. Richardstein is staying, then so am I," said Katrina, she got to her feet. Three more missionaries stood up after her. "Who else chooses to stay?"

Ten more missionaries walked away from the group near the ship, followed by more. After all was said and done, almost forty people said they would stay on Dogan with the Jeffe.

"Have you all gone *mad?*" Kem seethed "This heathenistic planet has put the Devil into you! I won't make you leave with us. You have your own free will. Maybe God has brought us here to shake off our weak. God bless you all, and may you find peace in His full grace," Kem pronounced. He walked into the ship, followed by Captain Blake.

Later that night, just before dawn, we all gathered to watch The Evangelist take off. It was a smooth lift-off, but my heart was pumping fast. I hoped my trust in the Jeffe people was well-placed. There would be no turning back for me now. I grabbed Dr. Richardstein's hand, and squeezed it hard. We watched the ship soar in the night sky, until it was over shadowed by the rays of the rising sun, and disappeared from our sight.

Chapter Seven   The Ancestor Collective

Landsong directed us in the preparation of a collective ceremony. We cleared additional space for us alongside their normal area alongside a lake. The Jeffe circled around, and we locked arms; and started humming a soft melody. Even though my eyes were closed, I was somehow able to see. It didn't feel like a dream. It felt real. My vision wasn't limited to just the view from my body. I was able to see and feel from the perspectives of others in the circle, too.

We hummed for what felt like hours. I looked to the sky with the eyes of what felt like everyone in the circle. I could see the meteor. It looked as large as a star … In moments it was as large as a moon. Then it filled the entire sky. I felt a rush and a strong breeze. Between the wind and the sensation running through my body I passed out.

When I woke, it was still daylight; but now the sun was setting. Dr. Richardstein was still asleep. Katrina ran to me from the other side of the circle with a look of amazement on her face, as she pointed with her hand. My eyes followed up her arm to a large burning moon.

"Is that the meteor?" I asked.

"It must be," said the doctor, as he sat up and stared at the sky.

Langsong broke open some of the delicious blue pineapples, and we watched as the meteor shrank down to the size of a large star again.

After the sun had fully set, we could see what looked like The Evangelist. It had to be our ship because only two things were moving in the sky.

"The meteor must have missed us," I said.

"No, it passed *through* us," said Dr. Richardstein.

We watched as the meteor got closer to the ship.

"Oh, dear *God!*" cried Katrina.

"No!" I cried … as the two moving objects exploded.

THE END.

The Programmable Man

A story which hasn't happen yet, but it will.

Lonely Love

Sometime in the not too distant future, a girl named Stacey waits for a booty call. Yes a booty call all because another one of her attempts to find a person to form a life long intimate connection with has dissolved down just serving the basic human needs sex. Even in this world where man has learned how to solve the problems that plagued the planet with its technological achievement it is the basic human problems, which are the last to be addressed. Yes sex, good old fashion recreational intercourse. There's nothing like it and people of this time are just as addicted and controlled by it as they were in the past. It the need for sexual pleasure which makes people settled for relationships, which only fulfill that need and leave other more personal needs unfulfilled. Technology brought man to this ecofriendly world in the clouds. Technology has made it so animals, plants and man can live together on Earth in a harmonious relationship. Through the development of solar engineering the city of Upper New York became the marvel of the world leading the path to alternative living across the planet. Along with strict population control regulations which limit the people who can have children, those who gain permission by having a certain income are still challenged by having to find a mate.

Stacey Maplewood, a single, independent woman is the head pharmacist and the only female in charge of a drug store in the U.N.Y. city is alone in her apartment. The smell of jasmine incense fills her candlelit bedroom as Stacey lies in her bed. Her arm dangles off the side as she holds a glass of wine. On a well-decorated table not far from her bed is another wine glass.

It is empty and next to that is a bottle of 1978 Merlot. On the same table is a plate of scallops wrapped with prosciutto crudo (raw ham) with small cubes of aged cheddar cheese and wheat crackers. The décor is straight out of a Rick James song. Her bedroom is decorated in dark red and white, matching the wine. Inside the wall opposite from her bed, a clock flashes 12:00 AM.

Dressed in a red, silk nightgown with a matching red waist-clenching garter belt, skirt and red, net-laced stockings that come right above her knees, Stacey looks like a French can-can dancer. She doesn't wear any panties. Her hand slides between her spread legs and lightly massages her vaginal hairs to the soft tunes of her classic love music mix with all of the important old school singers and groups. She mixes groups like Journey and Foreigner whose song, Feels Like the First Time, is her favorite. She enjoys singers like the two Barrys: Barry Manilow and Barry White. Of course, she also likes that British singer, Maxwell, whose album runs from beginning to end with no interruption. She drifts into a semiconscious slumber. She listens to the words of the love from these great crooners.

"That's right, love me, baby," she says under her breath. After being single for so long she has become a skilled pro at pleasing herself. In fact, she's gotten so good at it she's scared she's ruined herself. Maxwell's music is her regular stimulant. "Damn, they don't write songs like this anymore." Her hand moves with the melody and her back starts to arch. Her eyes close and her body starts to warm. As the aroma of her natural body fluids start to mix with the jasmine incense, she lets out a soft sigh which echoes in the emptiness of the room. The echo of her sigh reminds her that no matter how good she is, she can only make up half the feeling that a real bedroom partner can give.

I can't believe I have to do this again. Whoever said the hand is mightier than the sword never had a good sword.

Stacey is a child of the early years of music. She refers to the 1980s and 90s as the second golden age and feels nothing has changed since then. Men are still dogs and it's still hard for an independent woman. Man has solved many problems with science, but still doesn't have a clue how to deal with intimate personal relations. Man can be created from a cell of another man in something as small as a Petri dish, but no one can make a man who knows how to treat a woman. Bullshit future. People in the 80s used to dream about the future having flying cars and stuff, but without a man, who gives a fuck about a flying car. Stacey would rather go back to riding horses when a man only traveled around in his village. Shit, if it weren't for self-sex she would have surely slipped into a permanent depression. She was so close to marriage with her ex two years ago she could still feel the engagement ring on her finger. To add insult to injury her exboyfriend married his very next girlfriend. Stacey being a strong women was able to handled that emotion storm because it something like that would have cracked an average chick.

Damn, she thought. Martin the date she waited for was going to be the one who was a break from the norm. He had to. He was fine. He had a beautifully chilled face with natural thick eyebrows. She met him when she filled his prescription for Vicodin. He was recovering from knee surgery after a basketball accident. He even came to her spinning class with her after he started therapy. For the life of her she could not figure out why he wouldn't call her when he was running late. She had been dating him for only two weeks and he had given her just about every excuse for coming late to their dates.

But they had such interesting conversations. He was her African prince. He talked about how his father had three wives and he never wanted to be like him. She trusted him. Maybe he was different than American men. She was still willing to give him a try. Waiting for him always made her mind wander. She would not let her head drift into full-out distrust because once she went there breaking up was the next thing to happen. So, she focused back on her handwork to take herself to a place where her thoughts could not penetrate.

"Excuse me, ma'am." The mechanical voice interrupted her magic. She moved her hand and sat up so fast her wine spilled. She looked at the clock and it was 1:00 AM. She covered herself with her gown. A human-like robot stood outside her bedroom door and continued. "I have finished washing the dinner dishes and bagging the garbage." Spike's metallic finish sparkled like the day she bought him. "May I stand by the door until your date arrives?"

While Spike stood in the threshold of her door she was reminded of the comfort he provide her with his security. Before Stacey lived in Upper City she lived in a government surface residence development. The surface has more crime than the Upper City. Stacey took the risk of living their to save money. Unlike the other people living their she bought a Z200 security robot with her extra cash. Spike was the treat she bought herself after she heard of her ex-boyfriend's wedding. She ordered the male Z200 home protection model. It was the decision that saved her life. The very same night she got her Z200 her house was broken into. Two armed thugs entered her house catching her in her night gown. She felt violated just being seen half naked by strangers. The thieves changed their mind from robbery to rape when they saw her bare skin. But before they could issue their first command her new Z200 stepped in.

"Hey Ms you need to tell your little dog here to back up or we'll put two slugs in him." Said one of the thugs.

"Yeah your little robot here may get all of his circuits blown watching what we're going to be doing to you" said the other thug as he pushed Stacey to the floor.

The very instant Stacey hit the floor the Z200 when into action. The robot disarmed the second thug and threw him over the kitchen table into her refrigerator. The other thug shot five bullets at the Z200 and it didn't slow it. The robot grabbed the gun while shooting the sixth bullet causing the gun to backfire. The fragments of the gun cut the thugs head in half. Stacey was so happy she named her robot Spike after the bulldog on her favorite old-school cartoon Tom and Jerry.. Since that day he aided by preventing three more burgeries before she made enough money to move to Upper City. Now, Spike is an over equipped maintenance robot because Upper City has the best security system on the planet.

Stacey turns off the music. "Thank you, Spike." She takes a deep breath before answering. "Sure, stand by the door and let Martin in when he arrives." She rolls over and finishes her wine. Damn these men.

"As you wish, ma'am." Spike turns and walks down the stairs.

Spike her personal robot makes her feel extra secure by guarding her house at night and charging itself during the day. The Z200 is very life-like. It looks just like a human only metal.

The robots come in male and female versions for the comfort of the owner. In a short time, these robots have become a staple in almost every household. They provide both security and assistance, replacing both domestic help and home security systems. Many people, like Stacey, have gotten so comfortable with the robot's blank eyes that they have allowed them to replace even pets. Science Security the company who developed the personal robot gave the Z200's simulated eyeballs to conceal the red lasers they used to scan optically. However, in low light the red laser can still be seen.

Stacey picks up a small remote and pushes a button labeled 'Digi screen.' The entire wall lights up and shows a woman standing in Times Square on the surface level in front of another woman standing next to a male robot.

"That's right. We've heard from hundreds of satisfied customers. So, why should you be unhappy and lonely? Let the Ultimate Companion fulfill your needs."

That's it. I quit. Martin is just like every other man. I should have never given him my number. Why do I keep believing Jennifer every time she when she tells me oh that guy looks like he's nice? She's not a dating coach she's only my friend who is fitness instructor.

The picture on the wall changes to a man throwing a Frisbee in a park with a dog running to catch it in the air. Then the picture changes to an old man playing chess in the park with a robot man. "There are limits to what your dog can give you."

Stacey turns the channel to a Lifetime movie and slowly falls asleep.

Loveless Love

The next morning, Stacey wakes from a nudge on her hip softly shaking her. Her vision is hazy as she opens her eyes. She closes them as the sun shining through her window causes her head to spin a little. She slowly opens her eyes again allowing them to adjust to the light and sees Martin. As she yawns, she puts her hand over her forehead, soothing her slight hangover.

"Hey, baby, I'm sorry I'm late. My mother called and started talking to me about an argument she had with my sister. They almost got to fighting. If I hadn't gone over there I'm sure they would have." Martin slides onto the bed next to Stacy.

"Why didn't you call?"

"I was on the phone with my mother and sister so long I figured you had fallen asleep. But I must say, you have really decorated your room up nice. I would hate it to go to waste." Martin bends over Stacey, rubbing his lips on her nose.

She turns her head away. "You could have sent me text or something."

"Baby, there was so much high emotion last night I couldn't think clear. I am here now and the same thing is happening. I'm starting to forget all about what happened to my sister and mother. It's all about you now. You look so lovely I just gotta have some. I was looking forward to last night so bad. I can't believe it's over and I'm finally here." He starts kissing her neck and rubbing her body. She looks over to the wall and the time reads 6:35 AM. Martin starts to open her top, revealing her breasts. He kisses each one. Stacey feels his energy, but she still has morning grogginess.

Come on girl you've been waiting for this. Better get yours if you're going to let him get his.

Martin starts rubbing her thighs and starts to pull his pants off. He rubs her good stuff and inserts only his middle finger using his thumb and ring finger to open her walls. Stacey leans her head back and lets out a deep breath. She is starting to feel a sexual buzz. Martin slides her hand to his rock-hard manhood.

I know he's not getting a condom already. I'm not even wet yet. Stacey starts to argue with herself. Girl, maybe it's lubricated and will go in quickly. She takes a last reassuring look at his thick eyebrows and how fine he is. Then she closes her eyes and goes with the flow.

Once he gets his condom on, he puts his tool inside her in quickly.

Thank god its lubricated.

He moves like a jackhammer going to work on a hard sidewalk. His thrusts wore the lubrication off in seconds. His breathing starts to increase and he's barely able to kiss. His arms start to shake and he lowers his body on to hers. Before she loses her breath, he pushes up off of her.

"Hold up. Let's switch positions," he says. "Turn over so I can get some of you doggy style."

Once behind her, Martin starts pumping away, but Stacey starts to lose her sensation. Martin's hands grip her waist tightly. Stacey slides a pillow under her head. It felt like he was masturbating and she was just a mindless sex toy.

"Oh, God, you have the best ass in the galaxy," Martin says as he collapses on Stacey's back.

Damn! Well it's over, thank God. Stacey turns over onto her back and notices the time is 6:38 AM. All of that in three minutes. Might as well have it go fast if I'm not going to get anything out of it.

Martin falls back on the bed. "So, what time you gotta go to work?"

"I'm off today. So, whatcha got in mind?"

"I have to go back to my sister's house. I promised my mother breakfast."

Martin leaves and Stacey lays in her bed thinking about her morning sex disappointment. She feels used, but she only has herself to blame. After eating an egg and cheese breakfast that Spike prepared, she runs her fingers through her hair.

"I promised my mother breakfast. I couldn't call you because I was preoccupied with family drama." Why am I still upset? He's good to his family. So, what's my problem?

Spike interrupts her thoughts. "Ma'am, I lowered the toilet seat and cleaned your room. Shall I prepare a bath for you?" Spike was always there. No matter whether it was a storm or a family issue, Spike never changed. He never got sick or old like a dog or moody like a cat.

Later that day, Stacey meets her friend, Jennifer, for lunch at a small, old-fashion pizza spot in the Mile High Mall over downtown city. Jennifer is her trusted girlfriend and has been divorced for over three years. Jennifer is resilient and never gives up on men, even after she lost her husband on vacation to a Free Sex community in the Middle East. She is now an Exercise Instructor and works at the Movement Center. She left an executive job at City College to work around more men at the Movement Center.

Jennifer talks straight and tells people exactly what they need to hear. "You need to get out a meet more men. All you do is work. The only men you meet are men with health problems. You need to come to a single mingle with me. Hell, I have better men in my aerobics class."

"Please. You act like there is some kind of miracle man I am not meeting. I tell you they are all the same. I give up. I can't take it. I think I'm going to take a break from dating. Shoot, I might even give up sex. Do we really need to have it anyway?"

"I don't think you need to stop dating. And, yes, we need sex. It's healthy. Sex or lovemaking is the most the closest human connection we have and we need it."

"Martin was no different than anybody else. Once I gave him some ass he stopped calling. He used to call me every day. Now I'm lucky if he calls me back. Plus this morning when he finally got to my house, all he wanted was sex. And it was horrible. I felt like I was some sort of blow up doll. I thought African guys were different. But no, he was wham-bam-thank-you-ma'am just like back in college. Men are just out for themselves."

"Been there, done that. Girl, when I was married to Mr. Freaky O'Lot, I did whatever he wanted me to. Dildos, vibrators, other girls. I thought I had to do it as a wife." Jennifer's voice rises. "But I think that's what made him leave me for that Love Colony. I never felt satisfied, forget about an orgasm."

A couple of kids sitting at a nearby table look at Jennifer, She looks back. "Excuse me, didn't your mother tell you not to listen to grown folks' conversation? Bet you wanna know what an orgasm is. You need to ask your mother. Maybe then you'll grow up and give your wives one."

The waitress comes and takes their pizza order. Stacey touches Jennifer's hand to bring her attention back to her. In a low voice she says, "So, do you get them now?"

"What? Dildos?"

"No, orgasms."

"Shoot, I get multiples now."

"What do you use? A vibrator?"

"Hell no, that's so 80s. I don't use no toys. No vibrator or dildo. My shit is straight organic the way God intended. That dildo shit is dangerous. They are good to help you learn your body and where your G spot is. Don't get me wrong, I'm not hating. The dangerous thing is they can be too good. So, be careful, because sex toys are addictive. I know girls falling in love with their dildos. Can you believe it? A piece of plastic. For me it's just a man. No freaky stuff like those Mars videos. You hear them say What happens in Space stays in Space bullshit. I say ain't no man going be with me and just get his. Shoot, I tell them what to do and not to switch positions until I'm ready. Men are clueless. You just have to take control and tell them what you like. There ain't no neon signs leading them to your G spot. When you guide them and they listen, they'll be happy they did. Trust me. Start talking during sex."

"The only way I'm going to get an orgasm is if I give it to myself."

Jennifer laughs. "You're like a drug dealer. I mean you do sell drugs. With all those drugs you got, you ain't got nothing we can give men?"

"Girl, you know if there was one, I'd give it out for free!"

They both laugh as their pizza comes and they start eating.

Love to Love You Baby

That night, Stacey calls Martin twice and by 9 PM he hasn't returned her calls.

"Ma'am, I have finished painting the living room and washing your clothes. Is there anything else you would like me to do?"

"Well, you could clean up the house a little. I saw some stains in the bathroom you could mop up, too." Stacey seemed to be unloading her pain on her home aid, however, Spike did everything she asked. Stacey, a diehard neat freak, walked around inspecting Spike's work. She was always impressed with how he learned to clean. He had learned to be as detailed as she was. He got behind the curtains, under the toilet bowl, and mopped her hardwood stairs with vinegar. She keeps him working until she falls asleep.

The next day when Martin calls, Stacey musters up the strength to avoid answering the phone. She remembers Jennifer's confidence. How Jennifer is damn successful at finding men. She is five years older than Stacey, but has twice as much fun. It wasn't fair. Stacey had to do something about that. There was no reason why Jennifer was going to have all the fun. Stacey knew she was just unlucky with her past few men and all men couldn't be as bad as she thought. So, Stacey calls Jennifer to ask her to

169

take her to find men. She's willing to go anywhere Jennifer goes. Clubs, bars, house parties, wherever.

Later that night, she meets Jennifer at a club on the surface level. Most of the time, Stacey stayed on the upper levels of the city. Jennifer said Upper City was where all of the snooty people were and the surface was where the real people were. New Charlotte was as industrialized as New York and every other major city in the country. Everyone lived and worked above the clouds and even the cars could fly. The surface had been built over and the sunlight never reached down. At night, it was one big social club for regular people.

They are in a bar sitting at a small table for four people. Men are all over the place talking to women. It was like a regular meat market. The men seemed to be holding genuine conversations. The small dance floor had life-size images of music videos on a wall-size Digi screen. Stacey feels good. She feels so good that she believes she might get lucky and meet a nice guy. Jennifer waves the waitress over and orders two drinks. Before the drinks come Jennifer spots a cute guy sitting at the end of the bar by himself.

"Why don't you go over to him and ask him what does he do for a living?" Jennifer says.

"What? Are you crazy? I just can't walk over to some guy and ask him what he does. He would think I was from the government."

"Well, if you were from the government, wouldn't you know his name? Forget it." Jennifer walks over to the guy and says something. When Jennifer walks back to Stacey, she says, "He's a nice guy. Works for the waste management department."

"Hum." Stacey says, rolling her eyes back. She is not impressed.

"He's their accountant."

Jennifer points out another guy by the couches. When Jennifer walks over to the guy another guy walks up to Stacey. A nice looking, tall, well-dressed man with strong shoulders and wearing an expensive designer shirt.

"So, what do we have here? Such hot a bundle of love." Says the guy as he looks her over fully. Not only do his eyes wander down her cleavage, but he leans over to check out her butt. Then he puts his hand on her arm, sliding close to her. "Now, what is young freak like you doing later tonight?"

Stacey was approached by three more guys who had nothing but sex on their minds before she had enough. She could not understand how Jennifer met the guys she did. Stacey watched as her friend sat and laughed with men all night. Not only did she finish her drink and Jennifer's but she had 3 more drinks before she left. Is everybody a pervert out here?

The last guy who approaches her she lets pull her onto the dance floor. When she feels a hand grab her behind while she is dancing she's had enough. What the fuck is this, a high school party? She walks over to Jennifer and tells her, "Okay girl this it. I'm outta here. Someone just touched my ass. Call me tomorrow."

Back home, she lies in bed watching Digi screen. When the Ultimate Companion infomercial comes on, it catches her attention. Once again, the lady standing in Times Square in front of a woman next to a male robot.

"That's right. We've heard from hundreds of satisfied customers. So, why should you be unhappy and lonely? Let the Ultimate Companion fulfill your needs."

The picture on the wall changes to the man throwing a Frisbee in a park with a dog running to catch it in the air. Then the picture changes to an old man playing chess in the park with a robot man. "There are limits to what your dog can give you."

The picture changes to a display room with a table and a robot gel suit draped across it and two computer program boxes. The same lady from Times Square is standing behind the table. "That's right, you get both the Universal Love Maker and Super Personal Advisor programs along with your custom-designed human body suit FREE if you order your Ultimate

Companion now. Don't delay, turn your home assistant into the sex toy it can be. Blow up dolls and battery appliances are for your grandmother's grandmother. Designed by a top Hollywood special-effects make-up artist and made out of the finest silicone rubber, our love suits give customers pleasure beyond your wildest imagination."

Stacey lies back onto her bed and turns off the Digi screen. As she closes her eyes, she thinks about masturbation, vibrators, and sex toys. She slides her hand down to her vagina and starts to massage herself. Unable to relax and take her mind off the men at the club, she turns on her love music mix. After a few minutes of rubbing between her legs to the music, she quits and falls asleep.

Scientific Love

A few days later, Spike answers the door and a delivery robot is there with a large box. Spike brings the package to Stacey. Stacey is eating some light fluffy wheat waffles Spike prepared for her.

"Oh my God, Spike, it's here. I can't believe I am going through with this. I'm crazy."

"Going through with what? I do not detect any erratic behavior from you."

Stacey opens the box and takes out the instruction manual. She sits back on her chair and reads it like she a ten year old kid and it's Christmas day. There are picture illustrations showing how to put on the rubber suit. She installs the Super Personal Advisor into Spike. Now he has all psychological relationship books loaded in. Books like Men are from Mars and Women are from Venus, He's Just Not that into You and Steve Harvey's Think Like a Man, but Act Like a Lady. The program also includes every religious book: The Bible, The Torah, and Quran as well as

The Purpose-Driven Life and Conversations with God. So, intrigued, Stacey asks Spike a few questions and is surprised by his answers.

"Spike, why do men cheat?"

"Steve Harvey says in his book, on page 103, the number one reason is they have the opportunity."

"Okay, Spike, what can we women do about it?"

"Mr. Harvey says the best man a woman can find is a man who has already lost his family. Someone working on his second marriage."

Stacey is so excited. She can't believe how useful the Ultimate Companion will be. She may never go out of the house again. Now, she pulls out the Universal Love Maker program manual and is surprised by the graphic pictures. The pictures seem like porn and she has never been into porn. She closes the book and puts her hand on her head.

What am I doing? I'm not that desperate. This is crazy. She puts the manual down and finishes eating her waffles. She goes to work and all day she remembers her conversation with Jennifer. "Dildos are good to help you learn your body and where your G spot is." She thinks about the rubber suit and how it looks, so life-like. The almond brown color was always like having the perfect tan. The hands looked strong and thick. So much better than the metallic exterior that Spike has now. She thinks of something else Jennifer said. "Dildos can be too good."

Whatever, I got to try this. Shoot I already bought it so I might as well try it out. Once back home after work, she installs the Universal Love Maker program in Spike. She leaves the rubber suit in the box. The Love Maker program includes books on tantra sex, karma sutra, and The 1 Hour Orgasm. It has all of Harlequin novels, every issue of Cosmopolitan and Essence magazines, Casanova romantic movies, and most importantly, every love song ever released.

Stacey spends the evening with Spike. She has him teach her how to Salsa dance. They dance together and she has him perform stand-up routines from her favorite HBO comedians. Spike does HBO poetry so well she fixes her own dinner. Before she realizes it, it is 10 PM and she needs to get ready for bed. Spike fixes her a warm bath and reads a love novel to her. When she goes to bed she has Spike play classic love songs while he lay in the bed with her until she falls asleep.

The next morning, she feels well rested and spirited. As she gets dressed, she sees that she has missed a phone call. It's from Martin. On the message, Martin pleads with her to let him back into her life. He promises to be more mindful of her time. She decides to break it off with him. She calls and tells him she can't handle the stress in her life. Martin argues back so much she gives him the classic explanation to which he cannot argue. "Look, Martin, it's me. I just need space! Please don't call me anymore. I think this is best for both of us."

Stacey does such a good job he wishes her luck.

That day at work, everyone comments on her lively spirit. She credits the breakup for her emotional boost. However, in the back of her head she knows its because she enjoyed dancing with Spike her new imitation man toy.

Show Me How to Love

When Stacey gets home, Spike greets her with chocolate-dipped strawberries. He tells her to lie down because she must be tired. She sits in her big-cushioned chair and Spike brings her a tray with her dinner on it. He pulls up a small chair and takes her shoes off. Using massage lotion, he caresses her feet softly. Stacey eats her food and slowly drifts off to sleep. Moments later, she wakes to a floating sensation and the smell of jasmine. The lights are dimmed and Spike is carrying her to a warm bubble bath. He gently lowers her into the bathtub. Startled and surprised, she jumps, not fully realizing she is totally nude.

"Wow, Spike, I should have gotten you this program earlier."

"Please relax," Spike says. He then commences to wash Stacey completely. He scrubs her feet and removes her calluses. Stacey, starting to get used to the bath, becomes self-conscious about Spike seeing her naked. Embarrassed, she does not let Spike dry her off. He leads her to her bedroom and dims the lights. Stacey changes into her nightgown and asks Spike to get her a glass of wine from downstairs in the kitchen.

"I already have one for you. I would like to give it to you when get in your bed."

"Well, okay, Mr. Romance Program. If I didn't know any better, I'd think you were coming on to me. Matter of fact, if you were a man, you'd be in for a good time."

"I have plans to give you a night of happiness."

It hits her that Spike is just doing what he is programmed to do. She let her emotions get the best of her. Then her imagination takes it from there. She thinks about using Spike like a dildo.

"Nawh."

"Nawh what, Miss Stacey?"

Stacey didn't realize she had spoken her thoughts.

"Oh, nothing."

"Here is the wine for you."

"Thank you." As caution gives way to doubt, doubt leads to curiosity, and that is what pleases the cat, or so they say. "Ah, Spike?"

"Yes, Miss Stacey?"

"Why don't you go downstairs and put on the bodysuit inside the delivery box and come back upstairs." She figures that since she already has the body suit, she needs to see how it works.

When Spike comes back to the bedroom wearing the bodysuit, Stacey has finished her second glass of wine. She has her hands between her legs, which are spread wide.

"Spike, come over here and get in my bed."

When Spike gets in the bed, she wipes his hands off with a clean towel. Then she wipes off his body suit. When she reaches his more than ample-sized rubber phallic she shakes her head.

"Damn, Spike, you're ready already." Holding it between her hands, she tosses it back and forth couple of times. "Okay, let's do this. Give me your hand."

"Yes, Miss Stacey."

"Cut the 'Miss Stacey' stuff, I like it better than 'ma'am', but I'd rather you not say anything in the bed. Just listen to what I ask." She takes Spike's hand and slides it between her legs. After a few minutes of her showing him how to massage her, he is able to massage her on his own. Once her hands are free, she drifts into an endorphin-enhanced trance. She is no longer able to remember that Spike is a robot. As her passion fluids start to run wild, she arches her back and her breathing increases.

"Right there."

After her heartbeat reaches an uncontrollable pace, she climbs on top of Spike and slides his manly-shaped phallic into her. While straddling him, she grinds on him with a fury she has not used in years. Suddenly, Jennifer's voice enters her mind. "You gotta take control and tell them what you like."

"Spike."

"Yes, Stacey."

"Can you move your hips?"

Spike starts to move in a robotic way and it is uncomfortable to Stacey.

"Spike, move like when we were Salsa dancing." Once the robot starts to imitate his Salsa dancing Stacey's pleasure goes through the roof. She even finds that telling Spike to close his eyes prevents his cold, laser-red optical beams from distracting her.

"Oh, God, yes."

"Am I hurting you?" Spike stops moving his hips.

"No, and don't talk until I tell you. Just keep Salsa dancing." Spike keeps the movements and Stacey gets five straight orgasms.

The next morning, Spike is at her bedside with her breakfast and the rubber suit is folded neatly in the chair. He helps her dress and get ready for work. Stacey feels better than she has in months. She calls Jennifer and asks her to meet her in the mall for lunch.

At lunch, she tells Jennifer she ordered the Ultimate Companion. Jennifer is surprised, but curious.

"So, tell me, have you used it yet? I can't believe you got one. I've seen the commercial, but I never thought I would know someone who would buy one."

Scared to sound like a freak, she doesn't tell Jennifer everything she did with Spike. Jennifer is happy for her and tells her maybe this will help her relax so she can find a real man. Stacey pays no attention to Jennifer's comment.

"What time is your next aerobics class? Maybe I'll stop by."

"My next evening class starts in three days. You're going to get down?" Jennifer says surprised.

"Sure. I need to focus more on myself anyway, right?"

Unplanned Love

Over the next few nights, Stacey allows Spike to please her. He now plays music and even does a Chippendale dance routine. Stacey starts to get used to her nightly ecstasy. When she makes it to Jennifer's aerobics class, she is fully content with using Spike to fill her void. In fact, she hasn't thought about having a man since she started using Spike and the love suit.

Jennifer's class is packed with beautiful people, but Stacey is not on the prowl as hard and she used to be. Stacey feels so good about herself she figures she can trade her date hunting time to maintain her sexy body. She always enjoyed the blessing of having a shapely body. She always admired the people who frequented gyms. She looked at a strong, muscular body as the achievement that it was. Everybody used mechanical exercisers to stay fit. It was the diehard purist who still worked out on his or her own. Now, she was in a room full of these purists.

Having them all in a room, she could see what Jennifer had been talking about in building up your body yourself. The people in the gym bodies weren't as symmetrically developed as everybody else in the city was. In the city, all the women have the same size breasts and butts. It was ridiculous. To her, the women in the gym looked beautiful. The men all looked individually sculptured. Some had strong arms, others had thick legs. The people in the gym had more size variation.

When the class starts, Stacey realizes how tight she is. She can barely do the positions. Jennifer is busy leading the class and is not able to see Stacey. That is when he surprised her. He is tall, strong, and has a deep voice.

"Wow, you are really stiff. Is this your first time here?" he said.

Before she even thought about it, she said, "Yeah, I'm friends with the instructor."

His name is Joshua Hooks. He is another aerobic instructor and good friends with Jennifer. He stays next to Stacey the entire class. Stacey can't help to notice Josh has on baggy sweat pants. She figures he is a chubby guy and is there to lose weight. She is sort of glad he is, because she figures any of the "man meat" in this hot body buffet would be trying to pick up women. Josh seems nice and friendly, very different from the men she had been meeting. After class, Josh joins Stacey and Jennifer for drinks at a club. While Jennifer went on her regular manhunt throughout the club, Josh stays and talks with Stacey.

"It's good to see a beautiful woman like you working out. It shows you value your health. Most people wait until age catches up with them before they start working out. What are you, twenty?" said Josh.

She lets Josh compliment her without getting excited like she used too when a singled man noticed something about her. She talked to him like he wasn't an available man. She can't believe how relaxed she is without having the preoccupation of looking for a man anymore. Having nightly orgasms relieves any physical needs she had. She is a different woman. She's friendly and talkative. Now that she isn't looking for a husband, she has time to make male friends.

"You know, Josh, I have to tell you. You are a nice guy, but most of the men I have been meeting have been jerks."

"Yeah, they mess it up for us."

"Well, that's why I am giving up dating. It's too frustrating."

"Giving up dating? That's bad. Wow."

"All the good men like you are gone."

"What do you mean gone?"

"Gone, like married, taken. Don't lie, because if you know Jennifer, I know she has checked you out already. So, I know working around all of these women, you probably have more ass than you can handle."

"I know it sounds like paradise, but exercise centers are bigger meat markets than bars. And while I love Jennifer, she is a great instructor, but she is too fast for me. Look at her now." He turns his head toward the bar where Jennifer is busy talking to two guys. "See, I'm around women all the time now with this new job."

"New job? What do you do?"

"I left a job at Creative Robotics because of ethical differences. My settlement put me in a position where I can follow my passion and help this replacement-driven world."

"I thought you were taking her class to lose weight."

Joshua stands up and walks around to her. Stacey looks around in potential embarrassment. Since he showered he wasn't wearing lose workout clothes and was now wearing tighter fitting casual clothes, Stacey could see he was very fit. There weren't any bulges anywhere. "Exercise is a part of my lifestyle. These gym addicts put so much pressure on themselves to be thin that the stress is unhealthy. Now, does it look like I need to lose weight?"

Stacey's mouth falls open and she shakes her head. Joshua's confidence is a delightful surprise and she finds it attractive. "No, it doesn't." Stacey says with a surprise in her voice.

"I have always valued my physical health. Those Robotechies want to make human to human contact obsolete. Ain't no replacement for a human mother or a human teacher. Robots can't be spontaneous, you know." As the music of the bar changes to a Latin music song, Joshua reaches out and grabs Stacey's hand. "Come dance with me. You know how to dance Salsa?"

On the dance floor, Stacey enjoys Joshua's moves. They are far better than Spike's one-two-three step moves. As Joshua flips her around the dance floor, Stacey imagines Spike being Joshua or Joshua being Spike. It's like mind reading when Joshua whispers in her ear, "Wow, Stacey, you dance good. We need to do this again."

The night seemed to end there. She didn't need to remember anything else. By the time she got home and Spike greeted her with chocolate strawberries and her bath, it was well past midnight. She only took a quick shower and went to bed. In bed, her head filled with thoughts of Joshua. She even denied Spike when he came to give her a nightly dose of pleasure. She even remembered Jennifer saying, "You can have sex with any toy or object, but only two people can make love."

Good Old-Fashioned Love

Over the next few days, Stacey dined out with Joshua and avoided going to his house or hers. She tried to use Spike only once and found her mind on the possibility of Joshua being her lover. She even saw his face on Spike's body when he wore the love suit as he cooked dinner at her house. By Thursday, Stacey couldn't focus on her work. Her thoughts kept switching back from the pharmacy to her first night dancing with Joshua.

"Dr. Maplewood, the referral for this prescription is only for one refill," said Stacey's lab aid. Stacey never made mistakes. She quickly corrected the error. "Thank you, Corena. That's what I love about you. I wouldn't know what I'd do without you."

By lunchtime, she could not resist the urge to call Joshua. What the hell, I'm a big girl. Women have been liberated for over two hundred years now. He's a nice guy, so why should I be scared.

"Hello, Joshua, this is Stacey."

"Well, how are you doing today? It's good to hear from you."

"I'm doing okay. When we first met, you gave me your card and told me the ball was in my court, so to speak. So, I'm calling to make my pitch."

"Okay, I'm at the plate, throw the ball. Where would you like to eat tonight?"

"How about dinner at my place?"

"Sounds like first base to me."

When Stacey got home, she ate a few of the strawberries Spike had made. She only showered, but had no bath again. She had Spike make a romantic meal and put the rubber Love Maker suit away in her bedroom closet. By the time Joshua arrived, she was clean and dressed.

"Miss Stacey, Joshua has arrived," said Spike. Then he showed Joshua to the kitchen and walked back to the front door where he stood in security mood.

After they finished eating and talking about current events, Joshua said, "Well, Stacey, that meal was delicious and you have a very nice place here."

"Well, you can thank your former co-workers, those Robotechies, because I let Spike do everything I can. With him cooking my meals and doing the chores, I can relax. So I guess there are some up sides to robots."

"I didn't say they were all bad. It's just that they can't do everything perfect like the corporate execs tell people."

Stacey turns on her music mix and lowers the lights. She walks Joshua to her living room. She sits him on her cushioned 70s-styled sofa.

"So, Mr. Joshua, you've piqued my interest and I want to find out what makes you tick."

Joshua leans over to her and with his thick eyebrows shimmering in the light, he says, "Really? So let me do my best to show you."

Her nipples harden and pussy moistens. Before the words finish leaving his mouth, he starts kissing her. The kiss is like magic. It surprises Stacey at first, but it is the answer to her needs. She isn't sure if she should respond. So, for the first few moments she stays still, allowing Joshua to kiss and explore her body with his hands. She feels his silk shirt slide against her shoulders as he cups one of her breasts. He kisses down her neck and raises her blouse so he can kiss a path to her other breast.

He lays her down on the sofa. Her hands hold his waist and can't help but to feel his rippled chest and washboard abs. Joshua is willing to lead this love dance. When he leans over to kiss her again, she was able feel his fully toned body. With his ear between her lips she speaks softly. "Where have you been?"

She struggles with herself not to pull through his silk and receive his full human manhood. He kisses and tastes her. She feels the heat of his passion coming from his chest. Without warning, he excuses himself and goes to the bathroom. When he returns he has a washcloth in his hands. He wipes off her stomach, slides down her pants, and wipes her already wet kitty kat. His fondling and lip massage is something she has never experienced and she is a willing subject.

This time, as his lips kiss hers, his fingers enter her wetness. He gently strokes her walls. With his middle finger bent at the first knuckle he is able to touch the soft spot found on the upper inside of her vagina. She could tell from his lack of hesitation he knew what he was looking for when his finger stopped on her sponge like area.   His soft touch made her body twitch. His gentle massage makes her feel as though she has to pee. This is the first time she has had her G spot made love to. It's at that moment she understands what he meant by imaginative and human. As her eyes start to roll back, she prepares for her orgasmic waterfall, but her pleasure is cut short.

Joshua pulls his hand out. Stacey opens her eyes to see Joshua with his finger across his lips and she hears him whisper "Shhh, let me do this for you." Then he lets his tongue lay a path around her nipples down to her wetness. He buries his head in the well-trimmed forest between her legs and without her control it becomes a rainforest.

He looks up at her. "You taste so good." He licks and sucks her clitoris while simultaneously massaging her G spot in a rhythmical dance. His touch is so seductive, both of her orgasmic floodgates burst open with a multiple climatic explosion of pleasure.

When he finally raises his head, Stacey had experienced over five orgasms. That is the last thing she remembers before finding herself on her sofa and it was completely soaked. Joshua is gone and Spike's metallic arm is shaking her awake. She shakes her head and realizes it is the next morning.

Twisted in Love

Stacey can't take her mind of the previous night's passion, at work. She has more energy than when she was in high school. She's too tired to fight off the doubt in her mind that Joshua is like every other man. Her last few experiences has her accept and believe that all men are dogs. Now, Joshua stood in conflict with that belief. Joshua is nice, intelligent, and the most attentive lover she'd ever been with. "This is real, God dammit," she said to herself.

On her break, she decided to call this magic man, rule breaker, shaper of new beliefs, and see if he was up for another night of passion. She wants to believe he is real so bad that she can't wait. If he is just a one hit wonder, then she needs to know. She can accept letting herself slip up once, but she can't handle another drawn-out experience.

"So, Joshua, that was quiet some stunt you pulled last night. Are you a magician or something?"

"No, I'm not a magician. I just think humans are God's creation and women are not only His gift to man, but we are gifts to each other. Please accept my behavior as an act of appreciation. Last night when you fell asleep I felt it was best to let you rest."

"Wow, you are still smooth the next day. I still don't know if you are real. So I would like to get another opportunity to check to see if your appreciation is real or if you were just lucky."

"Well, I have a late session tonight which—"

"What, can't come by?"

"No, I was going to say it lets out at 9 PM and I could be to your house before 10 PM. How does that work for you? And I'll even pick up some Sushi take out on my way there."

Joshua's plans are music to Stacey's ears. She rushes home after to work to get into something sexy. When she enters the door, Spike was there again with strawberries and chocolate. She grabs a strawberry and runs upstairs into her bedroom.

"Will you be taking your bath, Miss Stacey?" said Spike's robotically-toned voice.

"No, I will just be showering."

"Is there something wrong with my services? You have not used me in your bath or bedroom in awhile."

"I have a real man now and I don't need you anymore. Just let me know when Joshua arrives, but don't open the door."

When Spike tells her Joshua is at her door, she jumps up so fast she almost falls down the stairs.

"Are you okay?" Spike said.

"I'm okay, Spike." She opens the door and lets Joshua in. She hands Spike the take out food and pulls Joshua up to her bedroom. When Joshua enters the room he took a deep breath taking in the smell of the jasmine aroma. He looks around at the candle lit room and in a rush, he starts kissing moving her toward her bed. She falls back and has her legs spread wide like she is getting a gynecological exam. She doesn't care how she looks, she eagerly waits for Joshua's magic hands to crawl to her like the night before. And just as he had done before, in moments she is coming in an explosion of ecstasy. With sweat running down the side of her face she wants to take their dance to the next phase. She pushes him up with her feet and says, "You need to stop appreciating me and take off your pants."

He takes her request like he is a human dildo.

When Joshua slides up between her legs and puts on a condom it feels like a roller coaster's first hill. She has no idea what to expect from him. She only knows his oral skills are superior to other guys. Once inside her, his smooth strokes feel so good she thinks she might cry. Then when he speeds up his movements, she closes her eyes and tries to hold back her feelings. She doesn't want him to know how good he feels. His body sways in a circular motion, which drives her crazy. She can't hold out any longer.

"Oh, God, Josh, oh God, oh God. Do that shit. Oh God, oh God, oh God." her screams are so loud they drown out the music. In a burst of wind, he is gone. At first, she thinks it is another one of Josh's pleasure tricks. But when she hears a robotic voice and hears Joshua scream, she opens her eyes and sits up.

"Stop. You are hurting Miss Stacey."

"Ahhhh."

Joshua is thrown in the corner of the room. His head bleeds from the force the impact. Spike heads over to him to finish him off.

Stacey yells. "Spike, what are you doing? Are you out of your cyber mind?"

Spike turns to her. "I am not malfunctioning. I love you."

"You what?"

"According to the relationship manuals in my programming, we were making love." Spike's voice almost sounds full of human emotion.

When Joshua stands up, Spike runs over to him and grabs him by the neck. He throws Joshua through the closet door.

"STOP, Spike, please." Stacey jumps on the enraged robot. With little effort, Spike flings Stacey off of him. She flies over, bounces off her bed and onto the opposite side landing on the floor. As Spike turns to see if she is injured, Joshua comes out of the closet swinging the metal pole used to hang the clothes. Joshua's fingers are holding the pole so tight it looks like he's in an arm wrestling contest. His jaws tighten and his eyes close as he swings the pole at Spike. . Spike falls to the floor from the impact of the blow from the closet pole. While Spike is lying on the floor, Joshua continues to pound the robot with the pole. After a few more blows to the head, the robot energy light flickers and goes out. Stacey lifts herself to her feet and runs over to Joshua, wrapping her arms around him.

"I'm sorry, baby, I don't know why that happened."

Joshua looks into the closet. "I saw your love suit. The thing they don't tell people is that even robots can catch feelings. It's not one of the side effects that would be good for sales."

THE END

A Robot's Nightmare. By Malcolm Carroll

The year was 5000, and humankind had advanced technologically. We'd recently discovered a hostile alien race, while mining on a moon near their home world. Most people thought the aliens provoked us, but actually we were the ones mining a sugar-like mineral that, as we speculated, was important to them. Then, as any race that was threatened would have, they attacked us, and we started an intergalactic war with them. Because of the war, the humans released us robots. Since that time, we had battled our way into their, as far as we knew, home planet.

They were a formidable enemy. The planet they lived on was nature based, meaning very little amounts of metals and minerals were found on the planet. This might make them sound weak, but they used some sort of metal-eating acid that was very effective against us. And there were other animals on the planet that hated us as much as they did.

Their planet, Stratic, was an remote place filled with dense jungles, and dangerous plants; but that didn't stop us from pushing forward.

I was an assault trooper: D-3757. The other troopers called me "Chip." We were a squad of trained robot soldiers in a space ship traveling at around ten light years per second, heading toward their planet. Our mission was to infiltrate their laboratory, steal information, and escape—as our fleet attempted to destroy their world.

Suddenly, as Stratic came into sight, something hit our ship—and we abruptly lost speed. Whatever it was that hit us could best be described as nothing but a space bug.

Spark, our commander, yelled: "What the hell is that thing?"

I looked at the planet, and blacked out. When I awakened, I realized that our ship had crashed.

Instantly, as if nothing happened Spark, started barking orders like, "Salvage what you can from the wreckage!" and "Set up camp!"

When we were done with these tasks and damaged robots were repaired, he allowed us to rest under my makeshift camouflaged tent, where I conversed with Techy, another assault trooper.

After a few minutes Sparks shouted, "ASSAULT TROOPERS WE ARE GOING TO LOOK FOR THE OTHER SQUADS THAT WERE IN OUR FLEET. DO YOU UNDERSTAND?"

"YES SIR," we replied.

While we were getting ready to meet up with other assault squads in the area, we heard a BOOM! and saw a large cloud of smoke. And I saw aliens pouring out of the explosion's dust.

A strong battalion of robots was quickly reduced to only one: Me. The aliens killed everyone in one ambush: In one strike. I could just imagine what the other squads looked like. Parts of half eroded metal blasted everywhere. I was waiting for them to finish me, and for us to lose the mission.

But what happened next was totally unexpected.

The aliens stopped firing, and just looked at me. This standoff lasted for about five minutes. Then I saw them carrying something big that looked like a plant. Soon, I realized that what they were carrying was a disrupter: A life form that releases an electromagnetic pulse that knocks out all robots in a one mile radius. The aliens activated it, and I went black again …

The next thing I knew, I was in a room made of wood, their primary building material. I was strapped up to a pole, but not by ropes … it was some sticky substance that was tough. Suddenly, a small group of aliens appeared, carrying what looked like plugs. They asked me a question. I could not believe it, but it seemed they had learned English …still their use of our language seemed rusty. They asked me for the blueprints of my robots troop; I quickly declined. Then they put three of the plugs on me, and hot burning electricity shot through my body. When they took them off, my body circuits cooled; and they asked me the question again.

I replied with a firm, "NO."

This time they put five plugs on me, and they kept them on for an even longer amount of time. When they finished, I felt as if I was fried to bits. The next one is sure to finish me, I thought.

In the next moment, a Juggernaut smashed through the wall, and a score of assault troopers followed. The aliens fled into a corner of the room. Because of my low ranking, I'd never seen a Juggernaut before. It looked like a hulking silver-coated assault trooper, with hardly any facial features, and gargantuan arms. Instead of a gun, it had big fists for brutally pounding its enemies.

No wonder they're only used for special missions.

Its huge hand launched me onto its back. Then I remembered I had to finish my mission. As if it was reading my mind, the Juggernaut made a huge U-turn, headed toward where the data facility was, and retrieved the data. We escaped right before the rest of our fleet came, and destroyed the planet.

After four hours of space travel, traveling at ten lights years per second, I walked out of the space port and into a thirty-five story building to report the mission to the leaders of the military.

"Well … the entire fleet you sent was destroyed, except for me. But I retrieved the data."

"Good job, Private D-3757! Glad we have soldiers like you! Take the data you have to Doctor Yoshima, and his crew. Then come back to receive your new ranking … Commander." Yoshima was the technician who built robots like me.

I delivered the data to Yoshima, and walked back to the leaders of my planet. When they gave me my markings, they told me that whenever they need me I should answer their need.

And I accepted.

THE END

Interview of a Monster.

Prequel to The Death Pledge

When I first got the assignment to cover the story of Jefferson Washington, the barnyard boxing sensation known as the King of Africa, I was taken aback. Me, Hirum Langston, award- winning writer assigned to cover a story about a brutal, illegal sport. Bare-knuckle fighting or boxing without any gloves or whatever you want to call it's pit fighting. I would have much rather been investigating one of Gravel T. Woods' new inventions or spending some time with Fredrick Douglass talking about ways to end slavery. However, Reginald Small is a man with great purpose, so even though this is something I do not understand, I will approach it with the utmost respect. I have only been to the South one time in my life and the experience there was life- changing. Reporters for the north, especially of the abolitionist school of thought like me, were never invited to news worthy occurrences on the Plantations of the South. I guess they are scared we will find out about some hideous slavery activity. That makes this opportunity all the more sweeter.

Arrangements hadave been made for me to stay at a rooming house or, as they say, a bed and breakfast. I have heard stories about this fighter, the King of Africa, that make him seem like a terror. All of these stories are relayed orally, of course. Barnyard boxing and any form of boxing is against the law in all of the Northern States. Human fighting is barbaric and inhumane. Even when these fights were held up North before the laws were passed, they were held in secrecy. The South maybe filled with cornhusking hillbillies, but even they aren't primitive enough to celebrate this savagery. On second thought, with all of the reported incidents of slave labor and its hideous atrocities, fist fighting is a step up.

Saturday, October 7, 1851

The ride to the bed and breakfast was treacherous to say the least. I have never rode for so long on an unpaved road. The carriage reached South Ridge, Virginia, well past midnight – about two a.m. Coming downstairs, I tried to settle my shaky nerves by thinking about what good stuff these country folk have for breakfast.

"Say, is this your first fight?" a man said to me. I was holding a spoon serving myself a helping of grits.

"Ah, I ah. I'm not a fighter," I said. Not knowing what to say. I didn't really want to tell people who I was. "I'm just here with a friend."

"Well, I hear that the wager man is running late," the man said in a lower voice than he had the first time. "On the count of people placing so many bets."

"Is that so? Well, I don't expect to be betting any money on this fight."

"Well if you do wanna make yourself some take home money. I'm taking bets on Haymaker Hazlitt. He's going to show that jungle ape the proper order of the food chainevolution."

I walked away from the man who'se excitement over the fight caused spit to fly out of his mouth while he was talking. So as not to have his oral fluids fly onto my plate I walked around him to find a seat at the end of the table. While I didn't mind a breakfast buffet, it does demand a certain etiquette that I just don't think these Southern fight fans are capable of.

The fights was set to start a bit little after noon time, leaving enough time for the main fight time to finish before sunset. The rooming house was filled with nothing but travelers like myself. Everyone was here to see the African King fight. The dining room table quickly filled up with an assortment of characters. Men came from as far Ssouth as Atlanta and Savannah. I met a group of men from Newark. They owned a shipping company and rode their company's coach down to South Ridge. There grass outside the house was filled with coaches and horses from the porch all the way out to the road.

The breakfast was good. Nothing like fresh eggs and cheese. I talked to the men about as many subjects as I could but the subject of the fights always took over. I must admit people are certainly excited about these barnyard fights. "I heard that African King fella punched a white man in front of the mayor and ain't nothing happen to him," one man said.

"I heard he punched a horse for looking at him the wrong way," another man said.

"Knocked the horse out cold with one blow."

I heard so many stories, which I think weare a bit exaggerated, just at the breakfast table t. hat I started to get a little excited myself. I excused myself and when went back to my room to take a nap.

"Come on out! Tthey just bringing the African King out," a voice screamed. It startled me. I looked at my watch and it was 11:30 a.m. I guess that carriage ride took a little more out of me than I expected. Anyway, time to go to work and get this story. So I ran a rag over my face and skipped down the stairs.

"Easy, young fella. They got him covered up. His trainer Jim don't want him to be teased by any of the boys here," an old man said. He was sitting in a rocking chair drinking a glass of lemonade on the porch looking at all the chaos from a safe distance. "They're going to be bringing out some pork sandwiches in a few. You need to make sure you get yours first cause they are sure to run out today.

Ill pork. "Ah is that all they'll have is pork?" I said.

"Hell no. She been frying chicken and making tater pies all week."

Thank God. I could eat some chicken, but I had a bad experience with a piece of pork when I was a child. "Okay, thank you Sir."

From a few feet off the porch, I was able to see the big wagon carrying the African King roll in. It looked like a big box covered with a show curtain. I Like the ones they use on stages at the theater.

I noticed the fighting area was filling up quickly, and I also saw they had started selling the sandwiches. I rushed over and got a box of chicken and three fluffy biscuits. I took an end seat on a mid- level bleacher. The announcer was already talking to the crowd by the time I got situated.

"Today we got a treat for you fight lovers. I ain't talking about no cock fights or no dogs fights. I'm talking about two big ole giants fighting. Men so big there ain't no place for them in the world but in this here ring. First we got two scrappy young fellas that promise to give you something that you ain't expecting. They both say they've got killer in their blood, so it sure to be a pleaser. Then we got what you all came here for. We got a fighter who'd make the gladiators in Rome run home and get their mammas. He's all the way from England. It took him two weeks to get here, and I bet he ain't happy about that. Haymaker Hazlitt," the fat announcer said. The crowd screamed and cheered so much you would have thought he had already won the fight. "He told me yesterday that he heard Virginia had a colored problem and he wanted help us solve it. Hahaha."

Then the crowd got quiet. Real quiet.

"Now you know we've got this fighter trained by Old Jim. This fighter is half animal and half monster. He started in the fields of North Carolina. You know picking cotton and sugar cane. Now he's been chopping down every man we've put in front of him. All the way from Africa, we've got the African King!" This caused the crowd to boo and scream curses.

The first fight was a spectacle to say the least. Both men about the same size traded punches and slaps at each other for over 5 rounds. They knocked each other to the ground. Each time they got up before the bell rang and got back up with new energy. By the ten10th round, I could barely predict who would win. They fighters both looked to be within an inch of their lives, yet they still fought. Every time they fell to the ground,

I couldn't help but think "Wwhy get up?". One time I yelled, "Sstay down, dummy!." That made all of the men sitting around me turn and look at me. I wouldn't say that again. But why? Why do they get up? This was the stupidest way to display courage. Then by the tenth round, out of the blue and totally unexpectedly, one of the fighters threw a right- handed punch at the other fighter's head and misjudged the other fighter's distance. The other fighter, seizing an opportunity he had been waiting for, followed with a devastating upper cut which connected with the jaw of his adversary. The blow knocked the fighter off his feet and into the first row of bleachers.

When they finally got a word out of the laid- out fighter, all he said was "Wwhere am I?."

They quickly cleared the ring and the announcer pronounced the fighter the winner. He then called for two volunteers and stood them on both sides of the ring.

"Now you fellas will get the first shots at the African King," the announcer said. He stepped aside and in walked Old man Jim, a. An old man with wrinkled skins and a big round belly. He was followed by what seemed to be just what they said: a monster. The African King. Dressed in overalls and wearing a straw hat, he looked normal, except he was twice the size of a normal man. He had large muscles –. nNot the ones with definedition. His muscles were, just large. His chest was big like a wheel barrel. He looked around at all of the people and offered what almost seemed like a smile. The two men in the ring were each given a piece of wood. Following the instruction of Old man Jim, they swung the slabs over the head and back of the African King. While each piece of wood broke over the African King's body, he barely flinched. Holy cow, he wais strong. I'dve only seen men this strong at the circus.

"You see. He's got no feeling," someone screamed from the audience.

"No soul," the announcer said. "And now I bring you this animal trainer all the way from England, Haymaker Hazlitt."

The African King backed away from Haymaker as soon as Old man Jim climbed out of the ring. Haymaker – a tall man, equal to the height of the African King – just starred at the big Black fighter. When the bell rang, Hazlitt was all over the African King, throwing lefts and right punches. The African King barely moved as he raised his arms to block the punches. The crowd cheered. It didn't seem like a fight at all. By the second round, Haymaker had thrown almost all of the punches while the African King just took a beating. Midway into through the second round, Haymaker landed a punch which that caused the African King to stumble. Haymaker, sensing an early victory, roared out a barrage of more punches. The African King fell to the ground. Well, not all the way. He came down on one knee. But you would have thought he fell out flat on his back, like the early fighters did, by the noise of the crowd. I started to think that this was no fight; it was a rigged public beating. This couldn't be the guy people traveled so far to see.

The African King blocked Haymaker's punches from that position until the bell rang. After that he got up and walked over to Old man Jim. Jim splashed him with a cup of water as he sat down. He offered the African King a jar of some sort. It had green liquid in it. The King took a big gulp and Old man Jim said something I couldn't make out. When the bell rang, the African King jumped up and dropped his arms to his sides and squatted down. Haymaker paid him no mind and rushed in as usual. This time the African King caught Hazlitt with an open- hand slap. Haymaker stumbled back a step. He shook his head and charged again this time he was slapped twice. He tried to punch the King, but his punches were blocked. The King jumped around on the sides of Haziltt, slapping him in the side of his head and body. Hazlitt turned as fast as he could, but that only added to

197

the blows' accuracy. Frustrated, Hazlitt rushed toward the African King. The African King side stepped and punched Hazlitt in the cheek. Hazlitt, now mad and turning red, said "Come on you beast. Sstop running and fight me."

The African King stopped moving and just stood there with his arms to his side. Hazlitt hauled back and aimed a blow at his opponent. The African King lowered his body to the ground and let the punch sail over his head. The move caught Hazlitt so off guard that he lost his footing. The African King jumped up in the air like a frog and came crashing down on Hazlitt's head. Hazlitt fell straight down. His face connected with the ground so hard, he thought it was a brick. The ring man quickly rang the bell. Hazlitt pushed himself back up to his feet and wobbled back to his chair. The once- noisy crowd was quiet. I dared not say a word.

When the bell rang starting the next round, both fighters looked refreshed. The African King looked like it was the beginning of the fight, and Hazlitt looked like he was surrounded by a group of bandits. He didn't seem to have his earlier poise. He held an arm out to keep the African King away from him. He walked around the ring like he was looking for an opening. The African King just stayed in his position with his arms dangling and in a squatted position. The crowd started cheering "kill him, kill 'em."

Hazlitt, feeling the love from the crowd, it seemed like he'd been waiting for to charge the African King. He blocked the first slap and almost tackled the King, a. A move which I thought wasn't allowed. I thought the rules were for fist fighting only. Anyway, Hazlitt, having the African King pinned against the rope, rammed his knee into the ribs of the African King. He pushed the King back with both hands around his neck choking him. The referee just stood there watching. The African King fell down to his knee and Hazlitt rammed his knee into the King's head. The crowd cheered. Some men stood up. Hazlitt punched the King, knocking him over onto the ground.

Now with the African King finally laying on the floor, Hazlitt turned to the cheering audience and raised his arms. When he turned back toward the African King, the King was almost back on to his feet. Hazlitt rushed him with his stereotypical confidence and swung and the King. This time the King was already on one knee and the blows were easier to block. He blocked them both and followed with an upper cut to Hazlitt's chin. The blow stood Hazlitt up straight. The African King punched Hazlitt in the stomach, causing Hazlitt to bend over. As Hazlitt crouched to hold his stomach, the African King cupped both his hand together and swung them into Hazlitt's face. Hazlitt stood erect and motionless. Blood drippeding out of his mouth and his eyes were shut. You I couldn't tell if he was going to fall forward or backward. All you I could tell was he was unconscious. His head was tilted to the sky and his arms danggling on his sides Hazlitt's body told the crowd who the winner was.

This was by far the most thrilling event I have ever witnessed. As barbaric as it was, these fighters are a cut above the rest of us. I can't wait to talk to Jefferson Washington, the African King tomorrow.

Chapter two

Meeting the Monster

The night after the fight was like the day after a hurricane or some other natural disaster hit. Word got around the Haymaker Hazlitt was injured so bad that he didn't survive. All of the men who traveled great distances to watch the fight were heartbroken. Some of them left in the middle of the night. The breakfast, which was previously full of lively discussion, was now empty and void of verbal emotion. The fight coordinators refused to crown the African King a champion. They considered him more than a side show but not a champion. Whether he had a crown or not, the African King was the fighter to beat. He had beaten everyone. Not just the fighter from Europe; he had beaten everyone there. The color house servants who filled the buffet were nervous. I saw one man refuse a tray of orange juice by knocking it over on the male servant who was carrying it and he saidsaying "I said I don't want no juice, nigger."

I didn't intervene in the happenings. I stayed invisible. Being unnoticed made for better reporting and deeper observations. Plus what could I say?. Many Northerners who came to the South to release their racist urges, which they couldn't do in the North. They were able to do things that they would be arrested for in the North. People said "Wwhen in Rome do as the Romans do." I could not participate in what was against my morals, so I did nothing. All I could think about was that this was the day I would get the chance to speak to the African King, and nothing would side track me.

Old man Jim had a servant come to me while I was finishing up the last of my homefried potatoes.

Shacking, the thin colored male said "You be mister Langston?" I nodded. "Well em. Old Master Jim be ah waiting in the barn. He said you should come out there and talk to him now."

I had my note pad with me and I finished my food up quickly. I followed the servant out to the barn. Inside sat Old man Jim. He was a fat man. He looked stuffed. His skin was tight like a pig. He wasn't a jolly man with jiggle fat. He looked lazy and pompous, like he hads servants do everything for him.

"Have a seat Mr. Langston," he said. I obliged and saet on the barrel he had sat for me to sit on.

"You can call me Hirum," I said.

"Now I don't know what makes you want to talk to Jefferson. He don't know what he's doing. He's just a dumb fighter. All he knows is fighting. You in the place where he comes from now. ____"

"What, Africa?"

"Africa, now dat's a dangerous place, full of wild animals and dangerous diseases. No place for a civilized man like you or me. We couldn't survive out the in the African jungle."

I broke eye contact with him and looked around to see if the African King was able to hear him talking. The barn was pretty empty. There were two stalls in the rear. One held horses and another was covered with the same drapery as the carriage the African King rode in.

"Was Jefferson born in Virginia or Africa?"

"It don't matter where he was born. He is a savage African. A savage to the core. As any other of them wild Africans animals are. Does it matter where a lion was born? No. A lion very well have babies in stove. Ddoes it make them biscuits? No."

"So what makes him fight better than all of the other Africans here?"

"See, I'm like an animal tamer. See, all I did is get biggest one I could find. See, just because they are natural fighters, doesn't mean they can fight well. You can't teach 'em but you can train 'em."

"Okay," I said.

"See if all them Africans could fight, we wouldn't have so many of them here. I'm no different than a plantation owner."

"So how do you teach . Ah– I mean train your fighters?"

"A good overseer knows how to keep them broken and weak. Separating they packs. You know, mother from child and father and stuff. But I'm different. I want them to be strong. I take a slave, a simple animal, and feed the animal in him. I don't breake 'em like they do with the whip. I make 'em fight. I make 'em learn that fighting will get him food. I make 'em go into a rage. A raging animal. Then I hurt the animal. Make 'em feel pain. Pain from me. So he'll listen to me because he'll fear me. I continue to hurt him until he doesn't like me. I take him away from everyone, so all he knows is me. I make him scared of people. Then that fear becomes a desire to hurt. And that's how you make a beast. A demon. A monster!"

As he was talking, I saw an old lady walk out from behind the curtain.

"A monster. Wow. I'd say you were successful. Well, that's great. Now I figure I'm ready to talk to your fighter. This demon you've made."

"Okay, but you can't be in there by yourself. I will have Mama Ester be in there with you. She keeps him calm with that African religion. He don't fear no Christian God , only that ancestor stuff."

Mama Ester? That must have been the old lady I saw walk out of the pein. I followed him over to pein and, just as he approached the curtain, he paused. and Wwithout warning, the old lady ran in front of him. She was holding a bucket of water.

"Please, Mr. Jim, Jefferson is resting. You want him to fight that Indian in two days, he gotta make time for rest. He ain't feeling too well after you told him the man he fought last night is dead," the old lady said.

Old man Jim pushed the lady out of the way and walked in. "Come on. He won't mind she is just over protective of him." He motioned me to follow him into the pein. "Now Ester, wake him up. This man came a long way to talk to him."

I looked around and I saw no parts of the African King. There were blankets and pots for cooking but no fighter. I saw an assortment of African carvings. I recognized one as is the same as the monument that's being made in DC for the first President George Washington. Then I saw something move underneath a pile of hay. It was him, Jefferson. He sat up, and, while only leaning up half way, he was almost as tall as me.

"Yesser Misser Jim. Ies not sleep. Jus nappin," the large fighter said.

"Good. Now put some clothes on and talk to this man," Old man Jim said. Jim walked out of the barn. He was followed by Mama Ester.

"Please give him time to rest. He has to rest. His body needs rest to heal. You love to fight him and want him to win, but you don't let him heal. He needs to heal if you want him to go on. He is not animal," Mama Ester said from outside of the door. She spoke with an accent I didn't recognize.

"Ester, I have just about as much of you protecting him. He's a fighter. The savage is loose in him. Now do as I say. You're going get in my way one too many times. You're lucky he can't be controlled without you, or else you'd be no good to me."

The old woman was draped in multi- colored cloths. Not pants or dress, t. The cloths were wrapped around her entire body from her head. Her arms stuck out from some where I could not tell.

"Perhaps I could talk to you a bit," I said. "This would give Jefferson time to relax. I see you are responsible for Jefferson's health. So let me ask you a few questions first."

"Okay sweetie. That would be nice."

We talked for a few minutes about the inhumanity of having people fight. She is was a very nice person and very forthcoming. She even got me to share my feelings about slavery, which that I hadn't expected to. A knock came to the barn door. It was a soft knock. Not the type of knock Old man Jim would give.

Two young girls stood outside the door when Lady Ester opened it. One girl was white and seemed to be the leader. The other girl was a colored girl. She wasn't light enough to be a house servant. She clearly worked in the fields.

"Yes can I help you girls?" said Mama Ester.

"We want to see that big black fighter," the white girl said.

"You are too young to see him. Plus he is not a breeder. Now leave us alone," Mama Ester said.

"We are not too young. My father said since I weigh 150 pounds I am grown woman. And I'm ready for a big man like the African King," the white girl said.

"And they's ready to start breeding me and iyes wants my baby to by someone famous," the colored child said.

"I said he's no mandingo. Now gets," Mama Ester said as she slammed the door. She grabbed my arm and walked me back to where we were sitting.

"Wow is that strange?"

"No. Old Jim is not a nice man. He keep Jefferson away from women before he fights him. He say give him focus. All it does is drive him crazy. He brings different women in here for him to release himself with. Dees women are not clean. They passt dirtiyness onto Jefferson. I've had to cure his loins more than once."

"So, there's no Queen for the Africa King?"

"No, no child, he have no wife, no woman, no one special in his life. A man needs a woman to make him a man. I'm an old woman, like his mother. I cannot give him what he needs." Mama Ester said as she drinks a cup of something green. "If I wasn't here to protect him, sex would destroy him. Old Jim would see to it."

"What is that you are drinking?"

"This is a mixture a simple herbs and vegetables. All they feed us is waste. Pig guts and such. These things are not good for anybody."

"That makes sense. Can I try a little?" She poured some for me in a large wooden cup. The drink was warm to my mouth. It tingled on my tongue. "It feels alive. Do these carvings represent anything to Jefferson?" I pointed to the one which looked like Washington's monument.

"They all represent different things. We are not slaves, we are from Africa. I was born there. These are things my parents used to teach me about life. Now I use them to teach Jefferson." She picked up the long pointed carving. "This is a symbol of resurrection. It is a_____"–"

"An Obel something?"

"An Obelisk. This shows Jefferson how death is not permanent. It is merely a transformation to another life. It points up to the sky. To the sun that gives the energy for all life."

"Yes I remember, an Obelisk." Benjamin Banneker, the D.C. architect, was very knowledgeable about Africa. D.C. was filled with African symbols.

Our conversation was interrupted by Jefferson himself. The big man stood over me and I swear my eyes watered. I did, in fact, manage to fall off the barrel I was sitting on.

"Is ya'll still talking bout me?" Jefferson, AKA The African King, said. He reached down and pulled me up. "I don't mean to scare you. You needen be worried. I knows it ain't fightin time."

"I am Hirum Langston. I am a reporter for the New York Liberator. Can I ask you some questions for our readers up north?"

"Yessir. You're one of them papers that write good news about Negroes. So, you're like Freddrick Douglass?"

"Well not exactly like Mr. Douglass, but you're a man of many accomplishments. My first question is, how do you feel about being made to fight?"

"Mama Ester always tells me that I'm not an animal like mister Jim wants me to be. He wants me to be a monster but I don't want to. I don't wanna hurt no body. They say that man comes all the way from across the waters just to fight me. Now he dead. I don't want him to die. I know that hurt his family. I would to tell them I'm sorry for what they make me do. This world is not nice. Making people work in fields all day and beating them just because they are Black. Mr. Hirum maybe if you can tell me why everybody hate people from Africa then I'd be able to tell how it feel to fight. I ain't never had nobody treat me right. Like a man pose to be treated. I ain't never knew my mother or my father like you. Mama Ester is all I got. I fight so's I can eats and live without getting whipped in the field. Yeah I fight cuz I got to. I figures that maybe if I beat them all, they will start treating us color folk better down here."

"What do you think about when you're getting ready for a fight?"

His eyes opened wide and he looked dead in my face. "Mister Hirum, there are so many things I think about when I get ready. As many times I fight I still get scared. These are big men. Some bigger than me. They all try to kill me. When I get hurt, all the people cheer. I don't know why. So I get mad. I gets all my madness together and use it to defend myself. They try to kill me so's that's why I try to kill them. I try to kill them for all the bad people. All of the people who hurt people like me. I know my thoughts ain't right, but my thoughts keep me from getting killed. When I'm dead, I know the ancestors will understand. They'll take me to a better place. People don't understand how beautiful the world is. Mama Ester says I've been blessed with natural fighting ability. If I could fight all the bad people I would. That's why when I punch people I try break my hand through their skull so I can reach their brain and pull it out. I want show that their brains ain't no different den mines is."

I cannot explain how surprised I was to hear such a deep and inspiring message from a man who is described as a demon and a monster. This trip and interview do nothing but reinforce questions I've always asked about the Southern society. I often wonder who ares the subhumans? The one who is made a slave, or the one who makes another a slave?. Old man Jim calls Jefferson a monster, and I'm sure it's the other way around.

Chapter 3

Making the Monster

I went to sleep that night with the many thoughts my interviewers left me with. Mama Ester seemed to be Jefferson's saving grace, and the depth of Jefferson's awareness was quite surprising. I know Reginald didn't expect me to find out what I did. This fighting is very savage, but somehow amidst that barberaarity and all of the hoopla, there seems to be a professionalism. To Jefferson the African King, it is both an occupation and a social responsibility. It's funny how I'm talking about a person who just killed somebody and I was described it as a social responsibility. Only in the structure of slavery could something like this described in such a way. I do not plan to start writing this report until I am back in the North where I can be out of these trees, as they say. Then maybe I can gain a greater perspective from being able to see the entire forest.

My thoughts were interrupted, as was my peaceful post- interview meditation. Screams and cries were coming from outside. I looked out of my room window and it was so dark outside, all I could see was the dancing reflections of light on the ground and trees. It sounded like a crowd of people. I put my shoes on and wrapped my robe around my shoulders. I rushed down the stairs and out of the house. There was a crowd gathered by the barn holding the African King.

I heard Mama Ester's voice say "Please leave him. He was doing what he is made to do."

I ran closer but the crowd was so thick I could not make it through to see what was going on.

"Out of the way you witch," screamed a man with a Northern accent. Then I heard a loud smack.

"Oh," Mama Ester said as I heard a thump on the ground.

"The big nigger is in there."

"Get the nigger who killed the white man."

I pushed and pushed but all I could see were the backs of heads. The crowd started to shake the door. Then I heard a loud shot gun blast.

"Get back. There be no more killing today," Old man Joe said. He was holding an shot gun standing by the front door of the barn when I finally made it through the crowd. Mama Ester lay on the ground before him. Her clothes were torn off of her body. She looked dead and lifeless. Oh my God, did they kill Ester?. Jim pointed the shot gun around at the crowd and they slowly backed up. "You've done enough trouble for one night."

As Jim stood there over Mama Ester's body he said, "Ggrab her and slide her back into the barn. I wanna put her body in a way so that Jefferson doesn't see it. I need him to be right enough to fight a crazy Indian tomorrow."

My mouth hung open as I tried process what just happened. I looked down at Mama Ester and back at the retreating crowd. Old man Jim grabbed my arm a shook me.

"You heare with me?" He looked at me and I shook my head.

"Yeah."

"Well grab her arms for me."

We slid her body into the barn trying to be quiet. As I let her body go and stood up I bumped into Jefferson. He didn't even notice me. He dropped down to his knees and embraced Mama Ester.

"Why?"

"Dammit," Jim said and he ran off to a chest by the side of the barn. He opened it and took out a jar and a ragp. He poured the liquid on the rag and cupped it in his hand.

Tears were pouring out of Jefferson eyes and he was starting to hyperventilate. He held Mama Ester's body cradling like a baby.

"It ain't right. She ain't hurt nobody," the big giant of a man said. He rocked side to side increasing with every motion. "Why, why." He pushed Mama's body on the side and started to stand. "Ain't nobody going even do anything to dem. They just going to let dem get away. I gotta_____."

Catching him in mid stand, Old man Jim jumped on the fighters back and covered him mouth with the towel. The big fighter stood up but quickly fell to the ground unconscious.

"Now help me roll him back over to the cage."

Although Jefferson weighed well over 25 stone,s the two of us were able to the carry and hoist him one leg at a time into the cage.

"That will hold him. He'd be alright by morning," Old man Jim said.

"What are you going to do with Mama Ester?" I asked.

"I'll give her to some of these fieldhands. They gotta have a negro burial ground around here somewhere." He put one of his hands on my shoulder. "Damn shame though. She was a nice old lady. You don't find many slaves like that, I tell ya."

He walked back to the main house with me and called over one of the servants. He said something to him and pointed over to the barn. The black servant nodded and ran away from him. Old man Jim looked toward me and waved.

"Thank you, have a good night sleep."

I tried to get the mostwhat sleep as I could, but it wasn't easy. I kept thinking about Mama Ester. I swear I felt the same pain that Jefferson felt. I ate my meals and stayed mostly in my room. I few times I looked out at Jefferson sitting in the cage. Old man Jim sat in front of it on a barrel with his shot gun in his lap.

After lunch I walked with one of the servants as they brought a meal out to Jefferson. He was still sitting in the corner motionless. The box of food slid toward him and bumped up against him. Jefferson didn't even acknowledge the food.

"Hey I'm sorry about Mamma Ester. I hear they gave her a proper burial. But like you said, this is a bad world, with bad people. She don't have to be bothered with it no more," I said.

"Yes, Hirum," Jefferson mumbled. "I know that she is in a better place now. It still don't take away the pain. My logic can't explain that part but I cannot figure out what to do with the pain. Feel like I got hole in my own heart. Just feels empty. Like nothing in there."

"Maybe if you eat something. Why don't you have some of the food? Huh"

"Food is life, and I don't know if I want to live anymore. My chest hurt some bad."

"Well eat and lieay back down."

"Can't rest too much. Ggotta fight today."

I looked over my shoulders and saw that they had fixed the ring and was ready for the next fight.

"Okay do your best to relax."

"Mister I don't know if I can. They made me a fighter and all I know how to do is fight. Maybe if I show them that nobody should fight me they will stop fighting me."

"I don't know," I said knowing good and well that they would fight him until he was dead. Just like any other slave. He doesn't get paid for these fights because they're illegal.

Later that afternoon there was even more crowded than the crowd for the previous fight. The African King was scheduled to fight Chief Savage, an Indian fighter. When they brought Chief Savage out to the ring, I thought of Jefferson's idea to fight so well he wouldn't have to fight anymore.

"Chief Savage the nigger killer," the announcer said. "Today he's going to scalp The Africa King." The crowd cheered.

Chief Savage wore a traditional bird feather headdress and leather straps. He even had two small tomahawks in his waist. He looked so stereotypic wearing bright body war paint –. tToo bright for a real camouflaged tribal soldier. Everybody knew that Native Americans didn't scalp anybody. In fact it was the army who paid for Indian scalps, but I guess you could tell these hillbilly rednecks Columbus discovered America and they'd believe it.

Jefferson looked dazed as he walked into the ring. His arms hung loosely from the sides and his bottom lip poked out. He was wet like he'd been sweating, and saliva dripped out of his mouth. I wondered if Old man Jim had to drug him again.

Before the bell rang, Chief Savage had already punched Jefferson. The Chief yelled and screamed as he jumped around swinging wildly. Chief's punches were untrained and while they were powerful blows, they missed theire marks. Chief Savage did not have the precision of a true Native Warrior.

Blow after blow failed to connect with the African King. After the bell brought the first rooundll to an end, Chief Savage was breathing heavy and gulped his water. As his trainer spoke to him, he threw the cup of water at him.

As the second round started, Chief Savage's punched became more accurate. He finally hit the African King's face. Still the blow failed to effect emotion in the King.

"You are not a dangerous fighter. Weak slave. I didn't come to dance with you," Chief Savage said.

"You are not a real Cherokee. Why do you mock them?," the African King said, then he delivered his first blow. The African King raised his arm so fast his uppercut made contact with the Chief's jaw. The Chief was raised off of his feet and out of his headdress. With his headdress off, his blond hair dropped to his shoulders.

"I have never heard of a white Indian," the African King said as he stood over the Chief. "Leave this fight before I am forced to hurt you severely. I am not able to restrain myself."

"This is not a fight,er and I am not a boxer. I am an assassin.," Tthe Chief jumped to his feet and pulled out his small tomahawks. "You will no better defend yourself than you were able to protect you old mother."

As the Chief charged, the African King stood still. The Chief swung his blades, cutting the chest of the King. The cutting blows knocked the King back on to the edge of the ring and finally to the ground. The Chief held a tomahawk in the air ready to deliver a fatal blow. "Now join your African witch lady."

The African King kicked the Chief in the groin. He stood up, threw his arms to his sides and raised his head. Tears started to form in his eyes. "You killed Mama!"

The African Kings lowered his head and, with deep red eyes, he charged the fake Indian. He swung with an intensity and speed that the Chief was not able to defend. His punches reached the Chief before the Chief was able to block them. He punched the Chief, backing him up and swinging him around. The Chief was weary, and his body turned with every blow.

The Chief turned to face the King and raised both tomahawks. "Die, nigger!"

As the Chief swung his weapons, the African King grabbed his arms. The large former black slave held the imposter by his wrists. Their faces came within inches of each other. The African King lifted his head to the sky and let out a loud scream. Then a deep crackling sound was heard as both of the Chief's arms were pulled away from his body.

As the Chief's body fell to armlessly to the ground, the African King stood holding the arms high. "Mean world you cannot kill me."

The bell rang over and over hysterically creating more excitement. People ran everywhere. I saw Old man Jim run the African King through the chaos.

Chapter 4

Death of a Monster

Once Old man Jim felt he had hidden Jefferson, he came back to the fighting area. By the time he came back, the crowd had just about dissipated. A few individuals were still talking about the fight, but most had left.

I must have been in shock. because I had thought I had seen it all the after the fight with Haymaker, but the Chief Savage fight has left me speechless. The exhilaration I felt after watching my first fight is nowwas a distant memory. I just sat watching people from the steps of the rooming house.

"Where did everybody go?" Old man Jim said.

"I think most people just left and the others are inside eating." He looked tired and he had dirt all over his clothes. He sat down next to me and wiped his face. "What happened to Jefferson?"

"I think he lost his mind. Maybe the death of Mamma Ester really got to him. He is nothing but an animal. All he needs is some rest. I don't think I will have him fight any time soon."

"Any time soon? What about not anymore?"

"See what you don't understand, my reporter fella, is that he's an animal and he don't need what we need. We can think. He is all emotion."

"I think there may be some animal in him, and I think these fights just feed the beast. I think you are playing with fire. I think you've made a monster now. I don't think he was one before. The man I interviewed a day ago was different. I think if you keep him in this fighting environment, he will explode beyond your ability to control him."

Just then a house servant came screaming past us. "The girls, the girls!" The man ran across the porch and around the side of the house. That area was where the servants sat and entered and exited the house.

"Now what?" Jim said.

"Where did you hide Jefferson?"

We both stood up and walked toward the front door. We were bumped and almost knocked over by a rush of men.

"Get your rifle. Come on," a man said.

"What's going on?" I said.

"We got us a nigger to lynch!"

A lynching. I wondered who it could be. I turned around to see what Jim thought and he was gone. Out of sheer curiosity, I followed the crowd. I'dve never been to a lynching. I never knew they could be so public. They said this in front of the colored staff.

They ran into the woods across the field. It seemed like a crowd of over a hundred. They held torches, and everyone had a gun or some sort of weapon in their hands.

"That's the man who raped those girls," a colored man said as he walked past.

"Get away from my fighter," Old man Jim said stepping from the center of the mob.

A couple of the men who were running the fight grabbed him. They threw Jim up against a tree and a servant tied him to it with a rope.

"Its way past that now, Jim. You slave is out of control. These girls were innocent," the man said as he looked over his shoulder to two girls. They were the same two girls who had tried to see Jefferson the night before. Now they looked like little girls. They huddled together under a blanket.

I wanted to say something, but before I could find the direction in my body to approach them. They crowd cheered as Jefferson's was hoisted up. He was beaten and had bloody bruises all over his body. He looked like he had been dragged through black mud. They hadve a thick rope tied around his neck and that was draped over a branch.

Jefferson only moved a little as the group of men pulled the rope back. People threw rocks and things at him. This was no ordinary lynching. Because it was both a black girl and a white girl who was were raped, there were white folks and slaves in the mob.

"I didn't do nothing of the suchesh," Jefferson said. "But you don't care. This world is bad. All of you are bad. You don't want to make this world right. You just go along with everything. Even my African brothers and sisters, you are the worst. You gonna join in on this. You gonna do this to me? I was fighting for you."

"Shut up you monster," a woman said. "Just die!"

Jefferson opened his mouth "Take this body from–____"

At the same time his mouth moved, a man dropped his torch to the ground and a flamed ran from it. The flame ran all the way to Jefferson and engulfed his body in a blaze. Jefferson screamed and his body began to

221

shake. His heavy body bounced up and down so much the branch holding it made cracking sounds. Then Jefferson snapped loose and fell to the ground.

"Arrh!" he said as he charged the crowd.

Jefferson ran still in a blaze leaving a trail of fire with each step. He ran toward the girls, and but before he could get to them, a black servant jumped in front of him and shot him in the head with a rifle. Jefferson was so strong he still managed to grab the man by the neck. Then another man shot Jefferson from the side. Jefferson's body fell to the side in what seemed like slow motion.

It was almost midnight when they finished burying Jefferson. They had to bury him in the slave cemetery. The local minister said a prayer. He was followed by another black man who brought out Mamma Ester's carving. The carving that which looked like the Washington Monument memorial.

"This Obelisk turned the right way symbolizes the resurrection of spirits, but since we do not want this spirit from every returning we shall turn it upside down." The man turned the pointy side down and slammed it in the grave.

My carriage ride home was full of more reflection than I had ever had in my entire life. I wondered if any one would believe that Bare Knuckle boxing was once legal and safe There were colored fighters like Tom

Molineaux who fought and traveled abroad to fight. Now this mockery of a structure is more of a problem than an outlet for sport and athletes.

I don't know if I'm even going to write a story about The African King. It's not a story of pride anymore. Now it is nothing more than a tragedy. Maybe if I called it The King of Monsters or The Monster that Monsters Made or The Monster of Monsters. I honestly don't know. This is really a question for me as a journalist.

Yours truly

Hirum Langston.

Tired of dying

"This is some straight bullish. God is tripping for real. I give up. I am tired. What are we suppose to do now? Why should we go on? Give me one good reason Stan?" Milton stood up and walked toward the window. The view was all smoke and ash. He turned to his childhood friend who had partnered with him on every adventure since kindergarten. "And don't give me any of that start the human race from the beginning crap because its not going to work. The girl that was with us is gone. Brenda is dead. She just walked out to get eaten. She is gone and so is everybody else. They are all dead. And the ones that aren't dead are walking around eating them. This is a Zombie World and everything is dead or dying."

The heavy set kid stood up and walked over to the kitchen area of the apartment they had been living in. His shirt and body was dirty and smelly. His eyes were swollen and red. His lips were drier that the Grand Canyon in the summer. "Calm down," he said. He opened the refrigerator door and took out and scratched up bottle of Bacardi. He opened it and swallowed it straight.

"Calm down? Calm down time is over. I was calm before. Sure I can think of a way to run and hide from these creatures but why?"

"We just need to calm down. This can't be the end."

"You obviously think so too. Cause your drinking the rum you said you would save until we find more people. So, don't give me that. It's a Zombie World Stan!"

"Yes I know."

"No you don't get it. They are everywhere. The whole got damn world. All we've been doing is running around. And we ain't going nowhere," Milton said.

Cutting through their conversation is the sound of the security alarm and a red police light begins to flash. Milton and Stan both jump up run down to the first floor to a command center styled room. The room has TV monitors with visuals of each corner of the compounds perimeter. Stan looks at each screen until he sees images of zombies running down a driveway.

"There they are," Stan said as he pointed to the monitor. "Brenda must have attracted the bastards. Let's get the guns, they're only a few. I call the sniper."

"Nawh, fuck the sniper. Let's give them some heat," Milton says and turns to Stan and smiles.

"That's what's up."

The two race each other through their compound and Milton makes it to the base of a ladder first. Stan turns away and climbs up another ladder on the opposite side of the main entrance. The two guys put on motorcycle helmets. They turn to each other and before they grab their guns they issue each other a thumbs down signal. Stan grabs the large two handled gun and squeezes the trigger causing a burst flaming liquid to spray out. Two of the zombies hit by his fiery streams quickly turn them to fire.

"Yeah baby die bitches," Stan yells. "What you thought yall could run up in here and eat somebody. Not on my watch. You must be outta your mind."

Milton carefully aims his gun which is almost twice the size of the gun Stan is holding at the zombie closest to the gate. The zombie is a large man who is wearing denim jeans and a orange reflector vest like a construction worker. The zombie is pulling at the barbed wire covering the wall in a crazed effort to climb. Milton flicks a switch and tightened both of his grips and squeezes the trigger. A even more powerful stream of liquid fire sprays out of his flame thrower. The powerful burst blows the hefty zombie of the gate and onto the ground. Milton follows the man with the steam and until the zombie burst into fire and explodes. That's for Brenda. He thinks.   He then aims the gun at two more zombies and blows the head of one while the other falls to pavement as the powerful flaming streams blow off its flesh.

As the two use the flame hoses to continue to cut down the raged undead Milton's movements become robotic and efficient. After all of the corpses lay burnt and smoldering he climbs down and takes off his helmet. Stan walks over with a bigass coolaid smile on his face.

"Not that's what I'm talking about. Ain't nothing like burning up some Z boys to make you feel better. Feel me?" Stan puts his arm around Milton as they walk back into the building.

They walk up to the roof of the seven story building where some skinned smoked chickens are hanging upside down. Milton breaks a leg off and walks to the edge. While looking out at what remains of the small town they've survived in he focuses on the green grass areas surrounding it. The noon day sun is hanging high in the sky.

"You can barely see Memphis from here," Milton says.

"Yeah but its still infested and I'm glad I'm not there. Every time I kill a Z boy I think about how we all escaped. It was like thirteen of us."

"Thirteen now just two," Milton said as he looks down at a bunch of marks on the side of the wall. Two rows of small groups of scratches are crossed out. "Two years." He turns to a windmill pole and looks up at the blades cutting through the soft breeze. "Man you know them zombies would never get in here. This place is a fortress. And not for nothing but we can stay here years. But why?"

"You still tripping! When I saw you hitting those Z boys like a white policemen in 60's spraying civil rights marchers I thought you forgot about Brenda."

Milton takes a large bite of his smoked chicken. With food in his mouth he says "It's bigger than Brenda. And on that note Brenda was the last woman and how are we going to start the human race over without a female?"

Stan smiles and grabs a whole chicken. He looks around over the other side of the building and says "Oh boy I know it's the end of the world when you a whining over some sloppy looking woman. It's not like Brenda had a big ole butt like the girl in LL Cool J's song. Plus she lost her mind anyway. She went crazy."

"Crazy or she accepted reality."

"Maybe she didn't want to sleep with you. Hahah!" Stan continues to laugh.

"Maybe God wants us to die? Hahah!" Stan bites the last bite of meat of the chicken bone and points it at Stan. Making Stan gag on his food. "Now wants so funny about that?"

"It's not funny and I'm not laughing at that. I am just happy to hear you talk about the lord again. I thought you stopped believing in God. Look Milton we've been fighting these undead for a long time and you never mention God."

"I don't know whether its God or fate or whatever. I'm just thinking. The only reason why we have been fighting is because we're scared to die."

"It's just instinct to ____"

"To what survive? We've been doing a lot more than surviving Stan. So we're way past instinct. Brenda crossed over. She don't have to kill every day." Milton gets up and opens a storage case revealing a neatly packed rocket launcher and over ten rockets. He carefully pulls it out and hoists onto his shoulder. While he looks through the scope he says "No more death."

 "So what are you trying to say?" Stan asks.

Milton takes the big gun off his shoulder and drops his head looking at Stan "I'm saying are you scared of death?"

"Nawh son. I just want live." Stan yells.

"Fuck this life!" Milton yells louder.

Stan gets up and walks around in a slow circle. He pulls out the bottle of rum from his side pocket and takes another one of his big gulps. "Okay. Okay. I'm with you. I'm down. I for damn sure don't want to be in the muthafucca by myself. So whatcha wanna do? How you wanna go out?"

Milton smiles and leads Stan back into the building. The two of them spend the rest of the day collecting all of their weapons. They also collect all of the speakers from each of the apartments. They bring everything down to front gate. They clear away the crispy fried bodies from the night before. They form everything into a circular bunker. With the sun setting behind them they look at each other.

"Damn I didn't even know we had all this shit," Milton said.

"I know."

They go inside the building where they piled all of the food on the table. After they finish eating all the food they go to their control room and Milton stands next to a switch marked lights. Stan has his hand over a large dial.

Together they say "one, two, three."

They turn the dial and flick the switch causing all of the perimeter lights to come on and loud music to blast.

"Kick in the door waving the four-four," Stan sings.

"Yeah Biggie. That's it," Milton says. "Tell God I said hi."

"Come on lets go." Stan motions to Milton and they run back up to the roof. They each take turns firing rockets at various buildings in the town. The barrage of explosions turn the town into a hellish fire.

"I bet they can see this fire from Memphis," Milton said.

Stan points to movement in the grass past the town. "Here they come," Stan said.

"Let's go. You ready?" Milton said.

"Like you got to ask."

Down in their bunker with the music blasting they mount their guns and start shooting zombies as they charge their fort. Ugly zombies which have real rotten bodies from years of humanless flesh to eat. Some of them already missing body parts others missing clothes but all charging and moaning. One by one the guns of Milton and Stan bring them down.

The first wave they knock out in less than an hour. Milton drinks more of his rum. When more zombies start to come Milton walks over to a turret cannon he mounted on the side of the bunker and starts chopping down zombies until the zombies have to climb over their own to get to them. The noise of the gun bring more and more zombies. The zombies start to climb over the wall and Stan has to turn to shoot them from every angle of the bunker. The waves of zombies start to get so close Stan can almost touch them.

Milton and Stan each stretch their hands out to ease the cramping. They change gun after and Milton looks at their gun pile and they are down to two submachine guns. He motions to Stan to take out his grenade. Stan pulls his out. A zombie so close hits his hand knocking out the grenade. Fortunately the pin is still in. Milton picks it up and tosses it back to Stan.

When Stan turns back to shoot more zombies a bright light shines down on them and zombies start to fall faster than they were taking them out. Milton looks up as a rope ladder drops down between him and Stan.

Brenda's voice screams out from a speaker while hanging out of a helicopter "Hurry up and climb up the ladder. I don't know how long we can hold them off."

THE END

ASS KICKIN TIME

Chapter One

"So, shorty which one took your lunch money?" I asked the little ten-year old boy who stood strong and confident by my side. He took one last look over his shoulder at his two friends and smiled. He raised his hand and pointed to a kid sitting on a BMX bike.

Without hesitation I walked over to the hefty little bully. He was about my size so that meant he was older than me. I was big for my age and to this date I haven't met anybody my age who was my size. This kid was pudgy and was definitely too big to be picking on these little boys.

"Hey my man. What's the deal with taking little man's money?" I said to the little bully.

"I don't know what you're talking about. And why are you asking? I ain't never seen this kid before." Now the bully step's off his bike like he's a tough guy.

I think he's guilty. Yeah he took the money.

MAPPP!

My blow catches the bully right where his neck meets his jaw. A perfect hit and it knocks him on his ass. As the bully falls back over on his bike I looked at his two friends "They call me Bryan the Bully Beater." I proceed to step over the surprised kid. When he looked at me I grabbed him by the collar of his shirt and held my hand out then slowly balled it into a fist. Then when he tried to say something I punched his ass again. "I know you took the money. Now I'm going to be taking it back just like the Repoman takes cars.

The bully was so scared he didn't fight back when I took his wallet out of his pants. That was the normal flow of things for me. Kids called me a playground hero but to me it was just an excuse to fight. See everybody is smaller than somebody at some time in their life it's not like big people are born at seven feet. You may think I'm lucky now but I wasn't. Yes it's true, I was born over twelve inches long. That's a big baby. I grew up fast. In kindergarten I was as big as a third grader. By the time I was in the third grade I was almost five feet tall, the size of a short man. Since I weighed about 150 pounds I looked like a teenager. That seems like a blessing but they say the best blessings still have to be discovered. Being a big kid got me in big kid mess. I was regularly beat up. I was attacked so much that my uncle made my mother enroll me in Judo classes. That was the best gift anybody ever gave me.

In six months I received my brown belt and was already sparing with Black belts. The kids I fought in class were real teenagers. My teacher said that all of the ass whippings I had received had given me a natural response to defend myself, which is hard to teach. He also said that I was tough and had taken a real punches before so sparing was like practice to me. It was in my martial arts school (my second home), which gave me my sense of purpose.

Learning to fight changed my life. It made me realize my size blessing. I was large for a reason. It brought joy to my heart sticking up for the little guy.

Those were best times of my life. I was able to fight and inflict pain and still feel like I was going to heaven when my time on earth was complete.

TIME TO CHANGE

Being Bryan the Bully Beater was a short lasting career. My playground activities got me noticed by a lot of people. First it was the kids. They would thank me a buy me sodas and chips with their money. That was cool. Who could get mad at free snacks. Their parents came next. They thank me and one mother followed me to my house and told me mother. That was just the icing on the cake though. The part I liked was when some would text me. Man nothing felt better than beating some body up who deserved it. I could kick them in the chest or flip them over as hard as I could and not worry about a referee calling it a foul. Street fighting was the best thing God created. The screams of the kids you punched were different then the opponents in the sparing matches. Some times it was so much fun beating up bullies that I would continue to beat them even after they gave back what they had taken. What can I say I was addicted to the rush of doing something good.

Whoever said that good deeds don't go unnoticed was a correct. I thought being a Bully Beater was the best thing I could do. It was something I enjoyed and it felt good but my career as a hero for the weak was short lived. One day while talking to some kids, one of them pulled out a women's handbag. I couldn't believe that these kids whom I had been defending were picking up some of the greedy behaviors other kids had. I immediately explain why we needed to find out who lost the bag and return it to them.

Taking the bag back changed my life. Here I was the playground protector, Mr. Physical, user of fear and intimidation returning a purse. It felt nice but corny. I did good every day but it felt more manly. So I rang the bell and this little old lady answered the door. Her name was Ada Soko. Ada is what she asked me to called her. She invited me into her house. Not ever having returned something to someone like this before I didn't know what to expect.

Ms. Ada walked me over to her window and showed me how she watched me reclaim kids lunch money.

"So, you like doing nice things for people?" she asked.

"Yes. I don't think it's fair that older kids who are bigger than other kids use that advantage to hurt other people." I was proud of myself plus it was the explanation I had given to kids and parents all the time. People are so mean in the world somebody doing what I did was a rare commodity.

"So, the world isn't fair? Is that what you believe."

"Yes. And all I do it try to even it out a bit."

"Don't you think the world has always been unfair in this way? And if so what difference do you think your actions are going to have over the course of time?"

Man this lady was making me think. She was getting deep, it took me back to the core reasons why I got into fighting in the first place. I was bullied and then became a Bully beater but in reality I was just trying to help people. Is there another thing I should be doing? Is what I'm doing wrong? Should I just sit back and let people hurt other people?

"What are you talking about Ms. Ada I'm confused."

"Good. That means your mind is working. I just wanted you to think about the world and time." She handed me a newspaper. The headline said something about a mother and child killed in a fire caused by a faulty gas furnace.

"Do you think it is fair that that lady and her child were killed?" she asked me.

"No. But what can we do? You can't fight Fate. Right?"

She walked me over to a wooden African stool with a feather and clock carved into it. She sat me down and then squeezed next to me. Before I could say anything the whole room went black. I mean real black. Blacker then Pitch black that movie with the big flying lizards type black. It was so black I couldn't see the blood in my eyelids. You know how when you get punched and you see stars. Well, I couldn't even see my own stars. That's how black it was.

When the room became light again she stood up. She walked me out of her apartment. She lived on the second floor of a small brownstone building.

We walked down the street and for some strange reason it seemed like a whole week had passed. I mean I didn't study what clothes people were wearing on anything but it felt different like I had been there before. She led me over to a building across town. It was a small four-story building, which probably had about four apartments. It was the middle of the day so everybody must have been at work.

Ms. Ada rang the bell and a lady answered over the intercom.

"Yes" said the female voice over the staticky intercom.

"Hello Ms. I am from the Health Department and need you to sign for this delivery. Can you please come down." When Ms. Ada said that she turned to me and put her finger over her lips.

The lady came down to answer the door with her baby in her hand. She looked at Ms. Ada and me.

"Are you the lady from the Health department?" She asked. As she opened the door a rush of a gasous smell came out and I had to cover my nose.

Ms. Ada said "yes. Let's step down here away from the building and under the shade of this tree."

As the four of us walked over to the tree which maybe three car lengths from the door of the building a loud bomb came from below the building. When the lady looked back Ms. Ada kept walking. I turned a looked at the building and watched it explode into flames. Ms. Ada grabbed my arm and walked me all the way back to her building. She sat me back down on the stool and sat beside me again. Then the room when black again. When the room came back into view she handed me the newspaper again. This time the headline read Woman and child survive building explosion.

That first trip back in time changed my life forever.

TIME TO SAVE LIVES

It seems like only yesterday that I became a Time Lark but it was more like five years ago. What Ms. Ada had given me was life changing. It gave me a greater purpose. I was so happy I would smile when I saved lives. Even though I was prohibited from touching people, whispering in their ears or persuading them in another way was easy enough for me. I soon learned that being physical was too much work. Why get myself bruised up when I could travel back in time with this old African stool. I was kind of like a un-superhero because I had no superpowers. I helped people dodge the fate of someone else. See when I just help innocent kids by beating up their bullies I was a perfect candidate for a Time Lark. Now, as a Time Lark I get to help prevent people from becoming innocent victims.

I looked for people to save the same way Ms. Ada had taught me. All I had to do was to look in a newspaper and find somebody who was killed before what seemed like their time. See we all have a time to die and while you can't escape the hands of death you can accidentally fall into them. That is were The Goddess of Fate allows us Time Larks to come in. While messenger The Grim Reaper collects the spirits of the dead she doesn't mind if we lighten his load by a few souls. See we can't save everybody so we each use our own factors in determining who we try to save.

239

Sometimes the people don't heed our call and find death anyway. Either way I like to believe we make a difference by giving some people and extra chance. We are like the little parasites, which follow whale sharks around. While the Grim Reaper can take our souls at any time he has never had to use his scythe on a Time Lark. Ms. Ada believed death was so natural that the Grim Reaper's scythe was just symbol of him being a harvester of souls and not a weapon of death. Whatever the Reaper's scythe was it did not concern me. I was happy enough lurking behind people and being that voice in their ear helping them avoid death. The day was a good day but all my days are good now. I'm eighteen and my body has just about finished growing. My technique of saving lives had to be different than Ms. Ada's was. She was an old lady only five feet six inches tall and I'm well over six feet five inches tall. She felt I was ready to go on solo missions over a year ago. The only concern she had was if I was to over stay my time trip. See Time Larks were only allowed 24 hours to save people. Actually no Lark had ever tried to stay any longer. That's why it was important to know exactly when the incident was going to occur.

The mission I was on today was a postal shooting. Some guy had been mad about being fired and planning to go crazy in the post office. He would kill about four of his former employees and one innocent guy I read about. The paper said this guy Raymond Chaney was taking care of his grandmother all by himself. I decided to help save this guy because I figured his grandmother would suffer without anybody taking care of her.

My plan was simple just keep him from going in the post office for a little while. Just long enough for the shooting to happen. I walked up to him as soon as I saw his van pull up. Dagg he was needy. He had an old beat up white van with so many rust spots it looked like it had the chicken pox. He was wearing old faded clothes and was on the heavy side. No make that fat. Anyway, I don't discriminate. Who cares if his arms are covered with tattoos? He's a momma's boy or a grandmamma's boy. I was saving his life so he could continue to take care of hers. If he ate himself into obesity and died from diabetes it wouldn't be today.

"Excuse me Sir I'm asking people to sign a petition on increasing the punishment for child trafficking." This was a trick distraction I used a lot. It was a guaranteed attention grabber. Most of the time as soon as I would finish the first page of my questionnaire the incident would happen and I would already saved the person's life.

"Not interested" said the Raymond. Then he pushed past me.

This was only a minor setback. The good thing was he did respond and I had about ten yards before he reached the post office door. Maybe, if I tried to be a little more aggressive. Everybody cared about protecting children.

"So, you don't mind if there is an underground network stealing our precious children? Please mister I only need a simple signature from you and my organization will do the rest." I ran in front of him again. That seemed to trigger him and just like a charm he stopped and started lecturing me about the government.

"The government needs to do something about the clothes these kids are wearing. These girls walk around dressed like they are grown women. They are asking for trouble."

I really didn't care what he was saying. I just wanted him to stop.

"Yeah. I like the pull your pants up law. Saggy pants aren't cool at any age."

By the time he finished telling me what he wanted the government to do we heard the shots inside the post office and less than a minute later the police pulled up. That was when I made my smooth get away. When I looked back Raymond was already giving his statement to the police. I'm sure he regarded me as soon kind of angel.

When I arrived back home and walked out of my room my sister was staring in my face. Things were a lot easier when she was younger. Now, she was twelve and had a lot of questions about why I would disappear in my room with the door locked for so long. One time I forgot to lock the door locked and she came in while I was gone. When I got back from my mission she said somebody had stolen my African stool.

My mother was easy. I just showed her the African stool and explained some of the symbols to her then she was all in. She liked the fact that I wasn't fighting as much anymore. Even after I started time traveling with Ms. Ada I still found time to beat up a few more bullies on the side. It's all how you manage time. However I sort of had to stop repoing lunch money when I grew over six feet.

"Hey Bryan where you been? And why you keep disappearing?" Rebecca said while standing in my face. She was such a loud little girl. But she was my sister. She was tall like me. She was five feet seven inches and in the ninth grade. She didn't just have boys coming up to her but guys my age were checking her out. Through my years of being Bryan the bully beater I had made our neighborhood a safe zone for my sprouting young sister.

"Mind your business Becca. Why don't you go out a play with the other little kids instead of snooping around in my room. Gosh."

"Gosh!" she repeated.

That was the last I saw of her.

TIMES HAVE CHANGED

According to the police Rebecca was raped before she was killed. Her body was found in a public garbage dumpster behind a grocery store the next morning. My mother fainted when she got the phone call from the police. We were both going crazy wondering why she didn't come home. My mind raced. I could not imagine anything like this happening someone in my family. Of course it was totally possible but no where in my wildest thoughts could I think of something like this. I was busy looking out for some older boy stealing kisses from her but not a rapist.

Even though my thoughts raced I stayed cool for my mother. I had no fear I was a Time Lark. I knew exactly what to do.

I was just glad they found her soon. I knew she had to have been kidnapped or something because there was no way she had run away. We had searched her room thoroughly and everything was there. Nobody runs away without taking something with them. If she had run away it would have been my fault. There was no way she would have gotten mad at me enough to run away. Hell, no way. So, even if she had gone missing too long I would have gone back in time to yesterday just to help her avoid capture. Now, with the police's confirmation I was set. I just needed to calm my mother enough to get to my stool.

I was on my stool and back in time in a few minutes. My years of saving people had made suggesting a change in behavior to Rebecca easy. I would only have one shot because Time Lark could only go back to the same moment in time once or else they would risk running into themselves and that would kill the Lark. So, I went back to after we had our argument.

"Hey, Rebecca"

"I thought you went downstairs. What?"

"Hey I heard there were some strangers in the area snatching kids up so if you see anybody weird tell me and I'll come beat them down." She loved to watch me fight. So, even if she didn't see some strangers I'm sure she would find somebody doing something. She cried wolf more times than I could remember.

"Oh so you think you are the only one who can beat up bullies? I've been practicing my fighting you know."

"Becca please I'm serious. If you see somebody looking around then let me know cause I want to kick some butt."

"You don't fight anymore. You're a retired Bully Beater."

"I know it's been a long time. That's why I want to find somebody to fight today. So just do what I say. I will be in the playground looking for the kid snatchers myself so if I don't spot them you may."

"Okay Bryan."

Boy she was tough. What does she know about fighting! She only came to Judo classes with me to watch me fight. I don't think she even remembers the escape moves I taught her. I remember the first match she fought. She was only eight years old and she only won because she fought a boy her age. She towered over the little fella. Growing fast benefited her more than it did me.

She was on the playground all oblivious like she was looking for somebody. I kept my eye on her the whole time. She walked everywhere. She walked around the side of the building and I ran after her. By the time I got there she was yelling at a man. That's him I thought. I ran over to the guy and pushed him away from Rebecca.

"Bryan what are you doing? Why are you following me? Come on. This is just a boy from school." She said.

"I'm sore" she was so excited she didn't let me finish.

"You ain't sorry you want to follow me around. I bet there ain't no crazy person. You just wanted to scare me from talking to any boys."

Well there's goes my hook. Now I just have to follow her without her cooperation. I should have known she liked boys too. The last thing I wanted to do was to make her think I didn't trust her and I was some over protective brother. I had to make this right.

I looked at the guy again and he was younger than what I thought when I ran up. Boy I was an over protective older brother. Who knew what feelings you have inside your body. I have to learn how to manage my emotions like I learned how to manage time.

"Hey my man. I'm sorry. That's my little sister and I just lost control for a minute. I hope I didn't hurt but you can be friends with Rebecca." He seemed like he heard what I was saying but he just didn't believe me. Well, Rebecca was pretty enough if this guy was too scared to like her then another kid will. There was nothing else I could do. I couldn't think of anything else I could say when I heard the tires squeal. I turned my head and Rebecca was not standing next to me anymore. Oh dammit. Could I have lost my sister again? I took off toward the sound of the noise. When I turned the corner Rebecca was lying on the ground crying. Thank God. She was surrounded by a group of people.

Through watery eyes she said "You were right. I'm sorry Bryan." She held out her hand to me. Her fist was baled up and the when she opened it up she had a hand full of hair. "He tried to pull me into the van. He just asked me which way the grocery store was. I didn't even think about what you said until he grabbed me. Then I kicked him and pushed back from him and that's when I tripped on the curb."

"You ain't hurt right?" I picked her up and gave her a tight hug. She didn't know how happy I was.

TIME TO GO TO JAIL

The courtroom was packed. News papers were there and television reporters standing outside. It was the trail of the year. Who would have guessed Raymond Chaney the guy I saved from the post office shooting was a pedophile. The forensics department was able to use the hair to identify the person. Rebecca was hailed as a hero. Raymond had been arrested for exposing himself to a girl when he was in high school. He was given probation and two years counseling. His hair was found in the clothes of a woman who was raped and killed. Because he was a juvenile his DNA was not checked. But since my sister was thirteen the detective department investigated more and searched the area for child crimes and Raymond was called in for questioning. My sister then identified him in a line up. After she identified him they searched his house and found bodies of eight other women. Raymond had an old well in his backyard and had been throwing the bodies in it. Many of the bodies had decomposed so much they had to use dental reports to identify them. Raymond had been killing women for a long time. No one knows how long. The prosecutor estimates Raymond started is rampage after his mother took ill ten years ago.

All I could think about was if I wouldn't have saved him from the post office shooting he would have never been able to snatch my up my sister. Then I wouldn't have sent her out looking for kidnappers and the police would have never found the other girl's bodies. I looked over at the families of the other victims and I could feel their pain.

The judge banged his gavel "All rise for the reading of the verdict."

My sister, mother and I all stood ready to hear the death sentence." The photographers started snapping pictures of us as we stood. But when the judge only gave him life in a mental institute we all said "what?"

We were should the judge had made a mistake but we were wrong. Turned out the Raymond had been diagnose when a mental problem and he should been monitored. My mother said "the city is just trying to cover for themselves."

My sister was too young to get mad she was just happy he was caught. I on the other hand I was not satisfied. A mental institute! What was that all about? For all of the women he killed. Life in a mental institute did is fair. This fool should be killed.

When we got home I went straight to Miss Ada's house. I explained to her me feelings and why I felt I had to do something. She told me there wasn't anything I could do. Once I changed history I could not got back to the same time and affect the same incident. Even if I could go back in time to before the post office shooting and take back my good deed I would not be able to save the other girls he killed.

What could I do? I sat around Miss Ada's house for three hours before I asked her "What if I when back and saved every girl Raymond had killed?"

She said "he would more than likely find other girls to kill." She was right. Dammit.

"Miss Ada what if I went back to before he killed the first girl and killed him?" It was a brilliant idea. I was proud of myself.

"Miss Ada deflated my bubble by telling me "The Goddess of Fate strictly prohibits Time Larks from killing people. Taking Souls is the sole responsibility of the Grimm Reaper." I mouthed the exact words along with her as she spoke them. There was nothing I could do. It was the same energy in me that made me become a bully beater that made it hard for me to sit back and let some guy harm eight girls. As a Time Lark I changed things. Nothing has happened yet. So even thought these crimes have already happen I can go back to before they happen and make sure they don't happen. I can save them. I have to save them. I will save them. It is my job to save. I'm not just a Time Lark. That doesn't define me. I'm Bryan the Bully Beater the Time Lark.

"I'll see you later Miss Ada." I said as I walked out of her house. I didn't know if I'd ever see hear again.

"Bryan please baby, don't do anything stupid. You have your whole life to saves lives." Were the last words I heard from Miss Ada.

From the police report I was able to find Raymond's address and the date he was released from the institution. No need to say anything to my mother or my sister I would be back in no time and the world would be minus one more bad guy. Then when I sat down on my stool and got ready to go break the rules of Time Larks from behind my door I heard.

"Bryan what are you doing in there?"

There goes my sister again. "I'm working on something. I'll be out in a minute."

"I'm coming in. I want to thank you for making me a hero. It was you who told me I would catch a killer."

"Becca don't come in here. Just give me a minute. Okay."

"Okay."

TIME TO KILL

Raymond was the same as he was the day I saved his life at the post office. The only thing was he looked a little younger. But he was just as fat. When he answered the door I felt just like I did when I took on a kid who had bullied me. It was my first bully beating. All I did was remembered how mean the kid was to me and then I pretended I was him. With Raymond I pretended I was the combination of all of the bullies I had fought.

"Hello, can I help you?" he asked as he stood with the door cracked open.

I stepped in closer and punched Raymond in the face. He fell back and grabbed his nose. Yeah baby I must have broken it.

"You may have fooled the doctors and the judge but I know your not cured." I stepped in his house and closed the door behind me. Then I grabbed his fat sloppy ass and punched him again.

"I ain't hurt anybody!" he screamed.

I kicked him in the chest and he flew back and landed on his dinning room table. The table broke in half and he fell on the ground. "You will. Creeps like you get off on power and hurting people. You have a problem that can only be cured one way." I turned to look around. "Is your grandmother here?"

When I turned back Raymond was swinging one of the wooden table legs at me.

"My grandma's gone she won't be back until the weekend. By then I will show you how I treat girls."

He must have thought this was a joke and I was some amateur. The good thing was he just confirmed my belief. That made my blood boil. I ducked under the table leg and gave Raymond and upper cut so hard he stumbled back into his kitchen. I followed him with another kick to his ribs. Then I continued to punch him in his face. He laid on his kitchen floor with blood coming out of him mouth and noise. He was finished all of his fight was gone.

He spit out a mouthful of blood and said "You're just like me. You're killer too. Don't think you any better than me."

I walked over and unlocked his back door. Brushes and trees surrounded his backyard. There was a old wooden child's clubhouse near the far corner the well had to be under it.

"I saved your life once and that was a mistake. I'm just correcting that mistake." I took the table leg from out of his hand and slammed it through his chest. His head fell to the side. I had done my job. Now eight lives had been saved.

Just like I thought the well was under the clubhouse. Raymond's dead body was pretty heavy but I tossed it in the well like an old bag of trash.

I got back to my stool I was feeling like a champ ready to go back to my base time. I had a lot to tell Becca and I figured I'd go see Miss Ada as well. As the world went black it didn't seem to come to light again. I started to panic. Then I returned to the world returned again. I was back in my room but something seemed off.

A deep menacing voice came from behind me. "You have been ordered to death."

I looked around and saw a tall figure standing in a black rope with a hood over its head. The Grimm Reaper! The scythe in is hand was taller than him.

"I was only correcting a mistake I had made. The man I killed was a killer." I backed away from him.

"Your life has been recalled by Fate." Then he swung the scythe it ripped threw my bed in one swing. I jumped over it and punched into the hood. My fist met with hard bone like a skull. The Grimm Reaper tossed me across the room. I heard my sister outside the door turning the doorknob.

"Bryan what are you doing in there?" she screamed.

The Grimm Reaper advanced and swung the scythe again and this time it cut me in my chest. The cut was bad. I was done. I was wrong to mess with time and fate.

I stood up and tried to get to the door. "I'm sorry Becca." Were my last words as the blade from the scythe caught me just between my jawbone and collarbone. My head flipped in the air and landed next to my stool.

TIME TO REVIEW

Miss Ada's name was at the bottom of the stool and my sister returned it to her. Ada told Rebecca everything she had told me. I hope she doesn't follow in my footsteps. If I could talk to her I would tell to leave time alone.

The Girl from Negro Mountain.

Chapter One

It was way too late for them to be driving through the mountains but they had under estimated how long it would to get to Negro Mountain and back to Baltimore. The sky was pitch black you couldn't see no stars at all even if you had 20/10 vision or if you had your eyeballs shaved down like the Riddick from the movie Pitch Black. The road looked like it was being swallowed by the darkness, like a black hole in outer space. The van headlights were no good they barely made the edges of the road visible. Then to add to that it was a fifteen passenger van. The big old van was too bulky for narrow road Jovan had to ride the brakes hard on every curve just to stay on the road. It was more than enough space to carry two councilors and one seven year old child.

Jovan had to summon all of his driving skills and concentration to make it out of the mountains without becoming human road kill and raccoon food. Jovan knew that what would happen if he crashed. They would lay on the road pinned under the heavy van and then some night creature would smell them. When the creatures come they wouldn't be able to fight them off. Raccoons, possums, bats, snakes and even the little creepy crawlies. Jovan's thoughts ran wild in the darkness. Containing it wasn't easy for him because every time he looked into the woods it was so thick and dark he saw things shapes of things that couldn't be real. He saw a pack of giant gorillas. Then a tyrannosaurus rex. He shook his head. He knew they were just figments of his imagination but whether they were real or no they were distractions and any little distraction could cause him to miss a turn and run off the road.

Jovan made a quick turn almost missing a curve in the road. His copilot Stephanie jumped up straight as she awake.

"Jovan you okay," Stephanie said. "You need me to drive?"

"Stephanie you driving ain't going to make this place any less spooky," Jovan said. "I just want to get back to our house of horrors and off this mountain of hell."

"Yeah that story was kind of spooky," Stephanie agreed. "I listened to a little bit of the interview with the mother. I know she's a crackhead and all but, there's no way somebody could make all of that stuff up."

"Giant mosquitoes and an attacking hair weave." Jovan laughed so hard he made himself coughed. "That is crazy."

Stephanie said through her own laughter "They did find that guy's body in woods. They said it looked like it had been eaten by the woods. Like the trees came alive. Like the trees held him while the bugs ate him."

"Well," Jovan said. "As crazy as the lady's story was the little girl made it through it all. That would be a lot easier to believe if the people who were all killed weren't all drug dealers."

"The police said it was a drug hit by one of Baltimore's gang's," Stephanie said. She was the logical one of the two case managers. She glanced back at Destiny who was sleeping in one of the back rows of the long van. She could see the top of the little girl's head without having to lean over the seat.

"She's sleep," Stephanie said as she pulled out her cellphone. "Damn still no bars. How can people live out here, it's like the dark ages."

"See that's the problem I have with the system," Jovan said. "Why take a child from this calmness to a group home in the city? Our tough kids will eat this little girl up. They call it toughing her up but I don't think it does that."

"Well, father was a drug dealer so none of the facilities in this area would take her from here to Baltimore. One hundred miles and not one place." Stephanie took a breath and relaxed her building stress level. "Well, maybe its better. She's a little mixed race girl and these redneck country hillbilly's probably wouldn't know how to handle her anyway."

Jovan couldn't believe Stephanie's thinking. "What? Anywhere would be better than The Carroll House. How could it be better? Who are we going to put her in the room with? Not Angie, she's too big for her and plus she should be listed a sexual predator. Lucky thing she's only twelve. She would eat this little girl up."

"Yeah," Stephanie agreed. "She would have this little girl wearing her tattoo on her in no time. Okay let me think. They got to put her somewhere. What about in with Brianna and Julissa?"

"First of all Julissa is a psychopath. She shouldn't be in a room with anybody. She cuts herself and fights everybody. Maybe that's why they put her in with Brianna the drug addict. You know they be in there getting high. I haven't caught them yet but Brianna thinks she's smarter than us. That little is to too grown."

"It ain't her fault her brother used her as a prostitute for his friends," Jovan said.

"That's wild," Stephanie "Maybe that's why she is with a thug like Julissa. Remember that time she fought that boy?"

"Who do you think was working that night," Jovan nodded his head. "And she didn't fight Kyle, she whooped his ass."

Destiny kept her eyes closed as she listened and absorbed everything the two case workers said. She couldn't dream much because she had too much to think about. She had watched her father burn to death and her mother inflate and almost explode. The spirit of Nomis had answered her prayers and protected her from her uncle and her father. Now she was leaving the security of the mountain and she would by herself once again. All she had to remember Nomis, the good mountain spirit was a little stone in her pocket.

"Kyle is stupid," Stephanie said. "I feel so sorry for him, he's been in the system since he was born. You know his mother was a crackhead prostitute and she died of AIDS two weeks after he was born."

"He ain't special. All of the kids are got issues. They either been raped, beat up or both. This little girl's issues ain't nothing on our heavy hitters. I give it a week before somebody tries something on her. We'll find out how tough she is in no time," said Jovan as he continued to drive the van through his imaginary tunnel of hell.

Their arrival into Baltimore was like traveling from a horror of nightmares and ghosts into a world of real monsters. Carroll House was located on South Gay street in downtown Baltimore right around the corner of Baltimore's famed Baltimore Street also known as The Block. The Block was home to all that was bad in night life. The 400 block of East Baltimore street has been the city's sleaze central since the 1920s where famous Burlesque dancers like Blaze Starr dazzled audiences. Now the area is home to Larry Flynt's Hustler club and other strip clubs and countless sex shops. The streets of East Baltimore are the marketplace of prostitutes and drug dealers. This was no place for a foster home but nobody cared because the rent was cheap.

As Jovan pulled up to the front steps of the Carroll House, home of the cities cared for children, the neighborhood was in full bloom. Half naked prostitutes walked past the Foster care facility as Stephanie opened her door. Before she stepped out she looked back and saw Destiny's head slaying quietly on the seat. Good she thought maybe she wait until the some of the scantily clad prostitutes cleared the street to take the little girl from the mountains into her new building.

"She's still sleep," Stephanie said to Jovan as she walked around to the back of the van. She grabbed one of Destiny's bags and followed him to the front of the building. "I figured it would nice if you carried her in so the first time she would be seeing The Block wouldn't be it was full of night people. She is already going to see enough baby monsters inside she doesn't need to see the grown up ones outside."

As the two Carroll House workers walked back to the van to get the little girl from the mountains she was nowhere to be found.

The streets smelled of pure night life as only the street lights, car headlights and neon signs illuminated the area. It smelled like the breath of a drunken man after he just finished eating a used baby diaper and bathing in a bathtub full of hotdog waste. The funk of bodies used for sex bathed in aroma of the food rotten in the trash cans that lined the side streets of Baltimore Street. Destiny tried to take short breathes after breathing through her mouth gave her the ratchet taste of the street which was far worse than the smell.

Destiny pace slowed as the lost sight of the big passenger van and her transporters. She looked for some place where she could gather herself. There was no way she would go back to the place called Carroll House. Drug using children and others who fight who would want to stay there. It sound just like how her grandmother warned her. It was just the place where children went when their parents failed them.

Destiny had failed parents but she wouldn't fail herself. She could find a path on her own. She knew everyone wasn't a monster like her father. She could tell the nice from the nasty. She would find someone who was nice and live with them, someone like her grandmother.

Destiny walked past store front with thin women's underwear, rubble objects which looked like some sort of tube and balloon female women toys with round mouths. She wondered who would play with such dolls. She walked past women in short mini skits and long boots all the way up to their knees. She watched as men drove by in cars slowed down and yelled vulgar things out to them. The women smile and didn't look offended. They would walk over to the cars and lean in. One woman got into a car with one of the men and drove down the street.

Destiny continued past the women with the inappropriate clothes. As she walked a boy not much older than her, a teenager no doubt spoke lowly to a group of men walking in the opposite direction.

"I got than rock. That good stuff," the boy cried.

Destiny careful not to let him see her listening to him wondered what the teenage boy was talking about. She watched as the boy approached the men. He flashed them something in his hand. One of the men handed him some money and took what the boy had in his hand.

"Crack," Destiny accidentally said above her breath. Just as she tried to avoid her words were overheard by the boy. The boy turned toward Destiny.

"What the fuc you talking about," the boy said as he walked toward her. Destiny stood frozen as the boy addressed her. He was taller and bigger than her. His breath was fowl smelling just like and unflushed toilet that had sat for a week. The boy spoke angrily as he grabbed Destiny by her shoulder. "Yo you got some nice lips. You're by yourself." He pushed Destiny back against the wall.

"Where's your boyfriend?" the boy gripped Destiny as he spoke. He reached his arm around her grabbing the little girl's butt. "Scream and I kill you."

The boy turned pulled his future victim along with him. Destiny gasped as she held back a cry of fear. If only she would have kept her mouth shut. Now her destiny was unknown. It didn't seem like she was going to like it. A crack dealer, so young. He was just like her father. Maybe she was in a bad city, a city with no good people.

As the boy dragged his prey along fear could not be restrained from Destiny's face. "Only nasty freaky little girls come around here. So let me give you what you're looking for."

Destiny wanted to cry out for Nomis the spirit of the mountain but she knew she was miles from his protection. She thought of the caseworkers now but even they were out of earshot.

Before the boy could finish his announcement his face was met by the palm of a man. The force knocked the boy to the ground. The man motioned his other hand in his pocket. "Make another move toward this lovely little girl and I'll put a cap in your ass so big you could throw a basketball through it."

The boy got up and ran away. The man was pudgy. He wore an overcoat. He had a nice trustworthy smile. Destiny returned his glace with a smile of her own.

"Something tells me you don't belong here," the man said as he bent down on one knee.

Destiny looked into the man's black eyes and warm face and said "I am on my own. They were taking me to a house for kids with bad parents. But the kids are bad to and I want to find some good people to live with."

The man smiled a wide tooth grin. "Well you are one lucky girl." The man put his arm around Destiny's shoulder and said "I may not have the best food or the cleanest place but I think you'll like it."

"Okay," Destiny said as she followed the friendly man who had just saved her. The man reached down and held Destiny's hand. She though wow, just like her grandmother did. She had found a place to stay and she would be able to finish school and do her studying without have to being offered drugs in some house of bad kids.

"I don't know how you can take the smell of these blocks," the man said to Destiny. He pulled out a handkerchief from inside his jacket and a flask from another pocket. He poured a little of what was in the flask onto the handkerchief. He continued to walk as he returned the flask to its pocket. "My senses are not as resistant as yours." They walked past more porn shops, whores and druggies. The man talked as though he and Destiny were invisible. "In the early years of Italy before they had sewers people would hold scented fabrics to their noses. I too like to take a whiff of a beautiful fragrance before I start my journey through these retched streets."

The man offered the handkerchief to Destiny's nose. Destiny looked up into the man's warm and caring eyes and said "okay." Destiny took a deep inhale and her eyes closed. Her thoughts drifted into a dark blackness.

She felt a little sting on her fingers. She held her eyes closed enjoying the emptiness of the darkness. She moved her hand a little. She couldn't smell anything. She felt another sting on her fingers this time the feeling was increased to a pinch. It need increased to a bite and pulled her from tranquility. When she opened her eyes she was scared to see a rat chewing on her finger. She quickly snatched it away. As she withdrew her hand her eyes took in the view of the room she was in.

Destiny was in some sort of cage. The walls of the room were stained with blood. The floors were littered with the remnants of food. Half eaten bones mixed with food wrappers on the floor. Roaches and rats rummaged through the filth.

Moon light shined down into the dim light room. A chair and blankets could barely be seen. Destiny could only hear the faint sound of her breathing echoing off the walls.

"Hello," said Destiny as she sat up. She slid over to the edge of the cage and gripped the bars with her hands. "Is there anybody there?" Still all she heard was breathing. She held back the temptation to scream louder for fear of alerting the man who had locked her in the cage.

As she pulled her hand back from holding the bar she noticed her hand had dirt on it. But on further inspection what she thought was dirt was blood. Then she looked around the small cage and blood was everywhere. She looked closer and saw scrapings in the concrete wall. They looked like they were made from human fingernails.

Her mind raced with horrible thoughts of tortured little girls. Her grandmother had warned not to talk to strange men. She said that pedophiles could be anyone. That they didn't have a specific look like in the movies. Her grandmother told her stories of these sickened men. They would rape young girls and keep them in the basements of their houses for years and years.

Destiny's own breathing began to become more difficult the more she thought of her grandmother's warnings. Her eyes began to swell with water and she could not hold back the tears. She had been wrong. The world was no place for a little girl. She was not ready she could not survive. She needed her grandmother now more than ever. Being spanked by her father was nothing compared to what was going to happen to her now.

"Nomis," Destiny said as she pulled out her stones from her pocket. "Oh spirit protector why did they take me from you? I wish you were here with me now." Destiny's words continued until they turned to moans.

Her crying was interrupted when the door opened and the formally nice man stepped through carrying a plate of food. He seemed to be larger now than when she met him on the street. His massive body blocked out of the light as he stepped toward Destiny's cage.

"You are crying," the man said. "Don't cry. I brought you something to eat."

"You are a crazy person and you are going to hurt me in my stomach. You are mean. You put me in here to keep me here for years. So you can rape me and beat me," Destiny sobbed all of her words. "That is why I'm crying, you pedophile."

The man approached Destiny's cage and pulled out the keys. "My you have a powerful imagination. However, you have it all wrong. Pedophiles are not bad."

"They are bad. They force sex on children," Destiny shouted.

The man unlocked her cage and opened the door slowly. "Pedophilia is a way of life. We believe that children show know the joy of love making."

He proceeded to lead Destiny out of the cage. He put his arm around her softly as she walked out. She stood only to his waist so, he bent down onto one knee.

Destiny's stifling started to subside. She thought about how people don't always tell children the things and how they don't let child do things that adult do. She knew she could understand things her mother didn't. She knew she was smarter than her father. The only thing was this man wasn't talking about making decisions or intelligence.

"It's not love making, its rape," Destiny shouted. "How are going to teach me about love when you have me locked in a cage?"

"My child love is the window to all forms of learning. People in this world aren't taught how to love. You see the fifth walking on the streets. It saddens me when I think about it, such ignorance. Selling and buying sex is the byproduct of no guidance. That's what happens when you make it up and try to figure out love making on your own. The world is full of the blind leading the blind."

He reaches out and caresses Destiny's cheek and then he wipes the tears from her face.

Destiny thinks about how her parents fought with each other. How they didn't show their love, their yelling and cursing. That's couldn't be love. Maybe that's why they couldn't love her. Pedophilia is the belief in love for all ages? She remembers her mother saying crack was like sex. It was so good she would robbed and steal for it. Crack was bad but sex wasn't and it was just as good.

The man took Destiny's hands as he stood up. "Once you experience real love you will understand what adults don't want you to know. Let me show you."

While standing, he put one of his hands behind Destiny's head and reached for his pants with his other hand. As Destiny noticed a bulge rising in the man's pants she was instantly reminded of the bulge in her uncle's pants she would see after he bounced her on his lap. It was her uncle's penis and he wanted to stick it in her. He was bad and so is this man.

Destiny looked around with only her eyes and she saw more blood on the walls and trash on the floor. The cages weren't for love students they were for prisoners. If kids didn't want to learn sex from him he would force them. He would rape them.

As the man pulled his hand from out of his pants his bugle was pushing through the zipper of his pants. With the bulge only inches from her face Destiny pulled her head back and slammed it forward with all her might.

The man screamed in pain and shoved Destiny back across the room. "You crazy bitch," the man yelled as he grabbed his penis with both of his hands.

Destiny gathered herself not hurt much from the fall. Her adrenaline was on fire. She searched the floor for something to defend herself with.

"I wanted to show you the easy way," the man said with his hand inside his pant massaging his penis. "I guess now I will have to show you another way."

Destiny shivered with fear and frustration. She knew what would happen to her. The man was large, much bigger than her father. There was no escaping the room either. She reached into her pocket and grabbed her stone. "Dear grandmother you failed me. There are too many monsters in the world and Nomis cannot protect me. You brought me here. You let this happen to me. You and Nomis. I hate you. I hate you." Destiny's voice bounced around the room creating maddening sounds. She took the stone out and hurled it across the room and the lights flickered.

The louder Destiny screamed her anger more the few lights in the room flickered. The floor began to fill with roaches and rats. The man kicked a few of them from his path as he took steps toward Destiny. Then a rat jumped on his leg and bit him. He reached down and brushed the rat off his leg. Another rat jumped on his back. He fell to the ground trying to brush the other rat off. Once on the ground roaches and other large insects swarmed him. In a matter of seconds the man was covered in rats and bugs.

Destiny stood in the mist of the may lay and watched as the man's body was consumed by the bugs of the city. After the mad gave his last cry of pain and all of the flesh had been eaten from his bones Destiny searched the floor for the mountain stone. She put it into pocket and found her way out of the man's house.

She was only down the street from where she remembered meeting the man. She quickly ran back to the Carroll House. The police were outside talking to the two case workers. She walked up behind them and snuck back into the big van. She dusted herself off and left her hair messy.

When she stepped out of the van both of the counselors noticed her at the same time.

Stephanie ran to her. "Where were you?" she said as she hugged Destiny. "We've been looking for you."

"Don't tell me you have been sleeping in the van this whole time." Jovan said. "But I looked in the van." Jovan turned to the police officer. "Honestly."

Stephanie walked over with Destiny in her arms "It doesn't matter. She is here with us now and we will protect this little girl from Negro Mountain."

Destiny smiled with a tight grip on the stone in her pocket and feeling the real source of her protection.

THE END.

Sci-Fi Streetz

Meet the author.

Jeff Carroll is a writer and a filmmaker. He is pioneering what he calls Hip Hop horror, Sci/fi and fantasy. His stories always have lots of action and a social edge. He has written and produced 2 films, Holla If I Kill You and Gold Digger Killer which won BEST Picture at the International Hip Hop film festival. He has published 3 books the novelization to Gold Digger Killer, Thug angel Rebirth of a Gargoyle and It Happened on Negro Mountain. His short stories have appeared in both The Black Science Fiction Society's anthology and their magazine. He writes out of South Florida where he lives with his wife and youngest son. Connect with him at his blog http://hhcnf.blogspot.com/ and on Facebook, Instagram and Twitter.

Jeff Carroll is also the author of the non-fiction book The Hip Hop Dating Guide. When he is not writing Sci-fi stories he enjoys speaking on Healthy Dating to college and high school students everywhere and goes by Yo Jeff.

Enjoy Other Books by Author Jeff Carroll

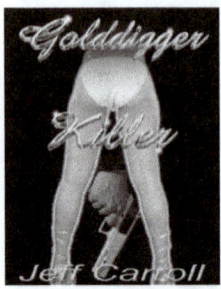

Gold Digger Killer. Rape victim Imani seeks to rid the world of Misogyny and becomes the gold digger killer in this chilling tale. Set in the glamorous world of Hip Hop.

Thug Angel; Rebirth of a Gargoyle tells the story of Maurice Keita a thousand year old gargoyle who is peacefully raising his daughter but when werewolves attempt to stake claim to his turf they find out he is a gargoyle and the wrong immortal to mess with.

It Happened on Negro Mountain. While being relocated to Negro Mountain Six year old Destiny is terrorized by her gangster father and her recovering crackhead mother can't protect her. Once her prayers begin to be answered by the spirit of the mountain Destiny becomes the girl you don't want to pray for you.